THE WEIRD TALES OF
DOROTHY K.
HAYNES

THE WEIRD TALES OF
DOROTHY K. HAYNES

Edited by
CRAIG LAMONT

With a foreword by
JOHNNY MAINS

This collection first published in 2024 by
The British Library
96 Euston Road
London NW1 2DB

Introduction © 2024 Craig Lamont
Foreword © 2024 Johnny Mains
Volume and selection © 2024 The British Library Board
Stories © The Estate of Dorothy K. Haynes

Cataloguing in Publication Data
A catalogue record for this publication is available from the British Library

ISBN 978 0 7123 5576 6
e-ISBN 978 0 7123 6803 2

Frontispiece illustration by Sandra Gómez.
Photograph on page 10 reproduced from "A Daemon and a Pen", an article
by Alexander Reid, courtesy of the estate of Dorothy K. Haynes. Illustrations
by Mervyn Peake on pages 31, 202 and 282–3 reproduced courtesy of
the Mervyn Peake estate. Illustration by Leonard Rosoman on page 288
reproduced from *Choice*, ed. William Sansom (Progress Publishing, 1946).

Cover design by Mauricio Villamayor with illustration by Sandra Gómez
Text design and typesetting by Tetragon, London
Printed in England by CPI Group (UK) Ltd, Croydon, CR0 4YY

CONTENTS

FOREWORD   7

INTRODUCTION   11

STORY SOURCES AND SELECT BIBLIOGRAPHY   18

A NOTE FROM THE PUBLISHER   21

No Such Person   23
The "Bean-Nighe"   28
Matthew Lurk, Tractorman   39
The Wobbly Castle   50
The Man in the Wall   59
Oblige Me with a Loaf   67
The Head   75
Scots Wha Ha'e   81
Gas   89
Barleyriggs   98
Help the Railway Mission   109
Black Chain   119
The Boorees   129
Don't Look in My Window   138
Dorothy Dean   147
Day of Wrath   161
The Moonbow   166
Vocation   173
The Memory   182
Up, Like a Good Girl!   189

Changeling 201

Those Lights and Violins 213

Suspended Sentence 231

The Curator 238

Thou Shalt Not Suffer a Witch... 255

A Horizon of Obelisks 273

APPENDIX I:

 THE LETTER FROM MERVYN PEAKE 280

APPENDIX II:

 THE TEXT OF "SUSPENDED SENTENCE" 284

FOREWORD

Lamenting is the horror fan's melancholic foe when it comes to talking about the authors they love and the stories they've read by them. The amount of times I've heard "I wish I could read the stories of [insert author here] for the first time again. I'm so jealous of anyone who does." It's a phrase I said not too long ago when talking about Robert Aickman. In a room of about forty people, it floored me to discover that only two people had experienced his fiction. There are not many other authors who I wish I could read the fiction of again for the first time; M. R. James is certainly at the top of the list and, breathing down his neck: Dorothy K. Haynes.

My first experience of Dorothy K. Haynes was "Up, Like a Good Girl", a grim and ghastly slice of orphanage horror that's as bleak as they come. I remember finishing the story, wondering what on earth I had read. It made me feel *dreadful*, so of course I read it again! My second Dorothy K. Haynes' story was "The Borrees", bat-demon chimney-horror at its finest. These were found in the anthologies *Gaslight Tales of Terror*, edited by author R. Chetwynd Hayes, and *The 14th Fontana Book of Great Horror Stories*, edited by Mary Danby (herself a writer and a direct relative of Charles Dickens). These books I discovered in the cobwebbed corners of dark and gloomy second-hand book shops in the eighties. It was a brilliant time to have your eyes gouged out by dusty volumes that had waited patiently for unsuspecting teenagers, such as myself, to be caught up in so much *delicious* horror.

7

Dorothy quickly became a favourite author and decades later, to pay her back for many hours of entertainment, I reprinted two of her stories in *Celtic Weird* and *Scotland the Strange*. This year I also proposed a volume of her stories to the British Library with me as its editor. The answer was an immediate yes and the BL got in touch with Dorothy's Estate to talk terms. It turned out that there was a gentleman called Craig Lamont who was knee-deep in Dorothy's archival dust and the Estate were keen to have him involved. My editor asked if I would like to co-edit the book with him. I gently declined, purely on the basis that Craig is *living and breathing* the archive in a way that I'm not. He is absolutely the best person for the job and has a nuanced understanding of Dorothy's work that goes way beyond my simple adoration. I readily stepped aside.

I'm over the moon with the book that Craig's put together, collecting some of the lesser-known stories from Dorothy's *oeuvre*, putting his countless hours in the archive to skilful use by presenting some unpublished stories. You have no idea how amazing it was to get the email containing scans of original stories that I had never read before. Some that had her handwriting on them! I devoured them all in a single night and "Don't Look in my Window" is a terrifying classic in the making. I don't know how I would have managed reading that story as a teenager. It's making me tremble thinking about it now... and I find myself lamenting all over again.

JOHNNY MAINS
Devon, 2024

JOHNNY MAINS is a British Fantasy Award-winning editor and author who specialises in recovering "lost" supernatural works from the archives. He was the Project Editor of the 50th anniversary re-issue of the inaugural *The Pan Book of Horror Stories*, an institution that contained several of Dorothy's tales. Mains has edited *Celtic Weird*, *Scotland the Strange* and *Halloweird* for British Library Publishing.

Dorothy K. Haynes, c. 1950s

INTRODUCTION

Dorothy Kate Haynes (1918–87) was born in the historic town of Lanark, where she resided for the majority of her life. When she was ten years old her mother died and she was sent north with her twin brother Leonard to Aberlour Orphanage, in Moray. As I have explained in the 2024 re-issue of Haynes's memoir *Haste Ye Back* (1973), those few years in the Orphanage fuelled her imagination with dark, foreboding shadows. Haynes recalls the melancholic, often horrific songs the girls would sing, and the Orphanage founder's testimony, from 1883, of seeing the ghost of a child's mother in the dormitory. For all that she casts the Orphanage in a positive, life-affirming glow, there is no doubting the importance of that place in her development as a writer of weird, macabre tales.

Woven into Haynes's masterful web of prose we find a cast of everyday adults and curious children alongside ghosts, cadavers, creatures, and witches. There are past lives bleeding through, time-slips, and bouts of delirium. These stories take place on the road, in graveyards, haunted houses, abandoned hotels, museums, orphanages, and historic towns just like Lanark of old. If you recognise Haynes at all it is likely you know her most enduring work, *Thou Shalt Not Suffer a Witch*, a short story collection first printed in 1949 with illustrations by Mervyn Peake. In 1981 her second collection *Peacocks and Pagodas* was published, containing a raft of new stories. The most recent collection, also named *Thou Shalt Not Suffer a Witch*, was published posthumously in 1996. Between 1949 and 1981, Haynes published a variety of writing in *Scots Magazine*, *People's*

Journal, Scottish Home and Country, and *Good Housekeeping*. These were domestic tales, some in the "Carry-on" style, and journalistic pieces on local and national history. Haynes's writing was also regularly broadcast on BBC radio programmes. But the real treasures of her dark prose can be found in the horror and ghost anthologies edited by Mary Danby, Ronald Chetwynd-Hayes, and others throughout the 1960s, 70s, and 80s. In these numbered anthologies published by Pan and Fontana, Haynes is printed alongside Sir Walter Scott, Stephen King, Agatha Christie, and Edgar Allan Poe. Writing about Haynes's talents, Alexander Reid once said:

> Every now and then... she becomes possessed by a daemon who transforms almost every line she writes to poetry, and who has a knowledge of the darker side of the universe which had she lived in the middle ages would have put Miss Haynes, as his collaborator, in serious danger of the stake.[*]

Playful though it is, Reid's summation of Haynes is an apt one. Writing in and out of the contemporary timeline, Haynes has a predilection for persecution and doom, supplying a masterful dose of dread for us to sympathise with her helpless characters.

In the book you are now holding you will find 26 stories, only 10 of which were printed in the main collections dated 1949, 1981 and 1996. As for the other 16, the majority have been selected from those rare, out-of-print anthologies in which Haynes is but one of many published authors. Five stories ("The Man in the Wall";

---

[*] From the Haynes archive, an article titled "A Daemon and a Pen". Source unverified.

"Don't Look in My Window"; "Day of Wrath"; "The Moonbow"; and "Suspended Sentence") are published here for the first time. Until now they lay dormant in the Haynes archive, held lovingly by Dorothy's son, Leonard Gray, in Lanark. Amongst the hundreds of typescript and scrapbook pages kept by Leonard, these rarities have been overlooked, perhaps forgotten by the author herself during her most prolific period of writing. It is a real joy to let them loose on the pages that follow.

We open with "No Such Person", an unsettling story about a woman in a graveyard being harassed by an angry angel who seems to be a gatekeeper to the afterlife. This story was first printed in a collection titled *Choice* edited by William Sansom in 1946, pre-dating Haynes's novels and debut book of stories. As one of her earliest productions it seems right to begin here. We move next to "The 'Bean-Nighe'", an eerie washerwoman folk figure who you would rather not have the misfortune of meeting. Later, in "Changeling", Haynes puts her own twist on another dark fairy tale, when a witch takes little Moreen from her home to the land of the little people. In "Matthew Lurk, Tractorman" we find an unfortunate spirit lingering on in the land of the living, making a nuisance of his wife's new husband. We find a similar spirit in another story, in which Crosbie "The Curator" encounters the ghost of a young girl who met her end in the tourist destination known as The Monument. After this we take a bounce on "The Wobbly Castle" with little Barbara, who is surprised to see a "sad lady, dressed in black" confined to one of the bouncy castle towers. For the rest of the children, it seems, there are only painted inflatable turrets, nothing more. But Barbara is sure and tries desperately to convince her aunt. After this we meet "The Man in the Wall", one of the unpublished gems which follows on nicely from the lady in the castle. At school, Jessie tells her friends there is a small old man who lives in her house behind the wall. Her friends press her for details, and as the stories become less believable a more realistic horror is revealed. Key to so many of Haynes's stories are the narratives of children. In these cases we find the spectre of Aberlour haunting her once more. The cruel determination of the childish imagination meeting the hardened resistance of the logical adult brain often leads to tears, or madness, as it does in "The Boorees". But Haynes can also stretch her horror to snapping point, as is literally the case with "Don't Look in My Window".

Elsewhere, Haynes makes use of the diary-entry narrative for her hauntings in "Barleyriggs" and "Those Lights and Violins". Keeping a track of time is important especially when its fabric can be so thin, as we find in "Oblige Me with a Loaf" and "Help the Railway Mission". Behind the rosy nostalgia for antique cars and products connecting these stories, Haynes works her magic with time. In the case of the loaf—and the shopkeepers—we are presented with mould, decay, and revulsion. Time remains inexplicable in "The Memory". Drawing from her own experience in Aberlour, Haynes tells the story of an orphanage girl, Bessie, who can remember witnessing a man being hanged. The worried matron reassures Bessie that this was impossible, that she was only a baby when she was admitted. But Bessie does not want to forget it, she is "afraid of the blankness, afraid of the great spaces of oblivion" on either side of the memory. The next story, "Up, Like a Good Girl!" is perhaps one of the darkest of Haynes's orphanage tales. Evidently "short on entertainment" the girls obsess over the legend of the death of an orphanage girl before them. By the end of the story death creeps into the girls' dormitory, no longer contained to orphanage lore.

I have included here another of Haynes's unpublished stories. "Suspended Sentence" is a classic time-slip tale. The narrator can remember the old, paved streets before the motorway was built, and confirms her flashbacks with a newspaper article where she—or the previous version of herself—was tried for assault and destined for the gallows. This ties nicely with the other important rope in the story: the one used by the girls who are skipping and singing a jump-rope rhyme. As it all comes into focus for our narrator, she realises "time has slipped, and I'm swinging loose".* Haynes's time-slip stories bring to mind supposedly true cases, such as the Kersey Timeslip Incident of 1957, where three boys seemed to stumble backwards through time in the small English village of Kersey. They also recall other stories in the short story tradition such as Arthur Conan Doyle's "Through the Veil" (1911), in which a battle scene from Britain's ancient history becomes all too real following a couple's visit to a crumbling Roman fort.

In many cases Haynes's characters are driven to madness. For "Dorothy Dean" the imp on her shoulder is but one of many horrors made real by her unrelenting imagination. In "Gas" the author plays a trick with a looped narrative to have us question whether the dental patient is still dreaming under the influences of anaesthetic. The monk in "Black Chain" invites a watery grave for himself through jealousy and poor timing. In "Scots Wha Ha'e" we find the ghosts of William Wallace and his wife Marion Braidfute haunting

---

* As is evident in Haynes's typescripts for this story, she once had "Swinging Loose" as a provisional title.

some unfortunate English tourists. Medieval customs of punishment are invoked in the award-winning story "The Head", first published in 1945. The thief in this story is chained up in an old Lanark-like town, with only a head—hacked off and displayed on a pike—for company. "English", the jailer proclaims of the head, "we'll see how he likes the view of Scotland..." In two stories the dead are brought forth by way of a séance. In "The Moonbow", previously unpublished, the narrator discovers a visual phenomenon which likely caused the death of her friends Julie and Edward Tressel. In "Vocation" the threats of damnation from beyond the grave lead the narrator into a convent, living a life defined by the "boredom of eternal obedience".

This brings us neatly to another important topic for Haynes: religion. The author's Episcopalian upbringing in Aberlour without doubt fired her imagination with glowing symbols and rites. As we see in the description of the suffering saints, frozen in their torment in "Dorothy Dean", and the hellfire of "Vocation", Haynes was not shy to tackle the subject. In another previously unpublished gem, "Day of Wrath", we find perhaps her boldest effort. Taking its title from a phrase found in the Old and New Testaments, this orphanage story features a girl dutifully polishing a small crucifix. Feeling pity and disquiet in the company of this small brass Christ, she removes the screws holding the object together "in a real crucifixion". What happens next will likely cause surprise. In "Thou Shalt Not Suffer a Witch...", Exodus 22:18 inspires the wicked title. This graphic tale of persecution and murderous madness remains the most widely admired and best-known work by Haynes.

Invoking editorial privilege I have saved my favourite story until the end. Linking back to "No Such Person" to close the circle, we begin again in a graveyard. A dead man has been woken by the gravediggers before his time, and he spends a strange day reliving a scene from his past. Before long the truth of his fate seeps coldly into his bones. It is one of the most heart-rending and pointed works of prose I have read, and it was the first story of Haynes I encountered. Back at the graveyard, the dead man waits for the sound of the trumpets, and for eternity to "begin—or end".

CRAIG LAMONT, 2024

Craig Lamont is Lecturer in Scottish Studies at the University of Glasgow. He has previously edited on scholarly editions of Allan Ramsay, Robert Burns, and John Galt. His chief interests in Scottish literature and history are memory, print culture, and the short story form. He recently edited a new issue of Haste Ye Back *(Jarrolds, 1973; Association for Scottish Literature, 2024), a memoir by Dorothy K. Haynes, and he continues to work on her archive.*

STORY SOURCES AND SELECT BIBLIOGRAPHY

COLLECTIONS OF STORIES BY DOROTHY K. HAYNES

Thou Shalt Not Suffer a Witch and Other Stories (Methuen and Co., 1949).

Peacocks and Pagodas and the Best of Dorothy K. Haynes, introduced by Trevor Royle (The Scottish Fiction Reprint Library, Paul Harris Publishing, 1981).

Thou Shalt Not Suffer a Witch, introduced by Angela Cran and James Robertson (B&W Publishing, 1996).

COLLECTED IN *THOU SHALT NOT SUFFER A WITCH* (1949)

"The 'Bean-Nighe'", first published in *The Windmill*, vol. 1, issue 2, ed. Reginald Moore and Edward Lane (William Heinemann, 1945).

"The Head", first published in *Writing Today*, issue 2, ed. Denys Val Baker (Staples Press, 1945).

"Gas", first published in *Modern Reading*, issue 6, ed. Reginald Moore (Wells Gardner, Darton & Co, 1943).

"Thou Shalt Not Suffer a Witch...", first published in *At Close of Eve*, ed. Jeremy Scott (pseudonym for Kay Dick) (Jarrolds, 1947).

"The Memory", first published in this collection (1949).

"Changeling", first published in *Modern Reading*, issue 8, ed. Reginald Moore (Wells Gardner, Darton & Co, 1943), and collected in *The Mandrake Root*, ed. Jeremy Scott (Jarrolds, 1946).

COLLECTED IN *PEACOCKS AND PAGODAS* (1981)

"Dorothy Dean", first published in *Frighteners*, ed. Mary Danby (Fontana Books, 1974).

"A Horizon of Obelisks", first published in *Pick of Today's Short Stories*, no. 10, ed. John Pudney (Putnam, 1959).

COLLECTED IN *THOU SHALT NOT SUFFER A WITCH* (1996)

"Vocation", first published in *The Penguin Book of Scottish Stories*, ed. J. F. Hendry (Penguin, 1970).

"Up, Like a Good Girl!", first published in *Gaslight Tales of Terror*, ed. R. Chetwynd-Hayes (Fontana Books, 1976).

UNCOLLECTED STORIES

"No Such Person", first published in *Choice: Some New Stories and Prose*, ed. William Sansom (Progress Publishing, 1946).

"Matthew Lurk, Tractorman", first published in *The Twelfth Ghost Book* (Barrie & Jenkins, 1976).

"The Wobbly Castle", first published in *New Writing Scotland*, issue 4 (Association of Scottish Literary Studies, 1986).

"Oblige Me with a Loaf", first published in *The 16th Fontana Book of Great Horror Stories*, ed. Mary Danby (Fontana Books, 1983).

"Scots Wha Ha'e", first published in *The 11th Fontana Book of Great Ghost Stories*, ed. R. Chetwynd-Hayes (Fontana Books, 1975).

"Barleyriggs", first published in *The 12th Fontana Book of Great Ghost Stories*, ed. R. Chetwynd-Hayes (Fontana Books, 1976).

"Help the Railway Mission", first published in *The 17th Fontana Book of Great Ghost Stories*, ed. R. Chetwynd-Hayes (Fontana Books, 1971).

"Black Chain", first published in *Argosy*, May 1967.

"The Boorees", first published in *The 14th Fontana Book of Great Horror Stories*, ed. Mary Danby (Fontana Books, 1981).

"Those Lights and Violins", first published in *65 Great Tales of the Supernatural*, ed. Mary Danby (Sundial Publications, 1979).

"The Curator", first published in *Prevailing Spirits: A Book of Scottish Ghost Stories*, ed. Giles Gordon (Panther, 1976).

UNPUBLISHED STORIES

"The Man in the Wall", date of writing unknown.

"Don't Look in My Window", date of writing unknown, though after 1951 (given mention of A Levels).

"Day of Wrath", date of writing unknown.

"The Moonbow", date of writing unknown.

"Suspended Sentence", broadcast at 10:45 on Radio 4, Thursday 18 October, 1974.

A NOTE FROM THE PUBLISHER

The original short stories reprinted in the British Library Tales of the Weird series were written and published in a period ranging across the nineteenth and twentieth centuries. There are many elements of these stories which continue to entertain modern readers; however, in some cases there are also uses of language, instances of stereotyping and some attitudes expressed by narrators or characters which may not be endorsed by the publishing standards of today. We acknowledge therefore that some elements in the stories selected for reprinting may continue to make uncomfortable reading for some of our audience. With this series British Library Publishing aims to offer a new readership a chance to read some of the rare material of the British Library's collections in an affordable paperback format, to enjoy their merits and to look back into the worlds of the past two centuries as portrayed by their writers. It is not possible to separate these stories from the history of their writing and therefore the following stories are presented as they were originally published with minor edits only, made for consistency of style and sense. We welcome feedback from our readers, which can be sent to the following address:

British Library Publishing
The British Library
96 Euston Road
London, NW1 2DB
United Kingdom

NO SUCH PERSON

It was hot in the graveyard when the angel came at her, screaming and hammering like an angry bird. It was a wild angel, with feathers broken and limp, the wing flesh pink and angry where the sun had burned the baldness.

The woman put her hands over her head, wrists crossed, fingers hooked and trembling. "No—no!" she whickered. "Leave me alone, leave me!"

After her scream, there was no other sound than the batter and whine of wings. The sky was dark blue, ready to split with the heat, and the gravestones burned under their lichen. When the angel fluttered back a space, the woman dropped her hands, and screwed her eyes against the glare. The ruined church let hot light through its arches, and the dandelions in the grass burned like flat yellow suns. What time was it? No time at all, said the dandelion clocks, full and grey blooming. The angel stood apart in a clear space, where a grave lay like a green mat spread over the roughness. His face stared dead as stone. Only the wings looked alive, sore and tender between the broken spines of the feathers.

"What is it?" said the woman, bundling her apron in dry scurfed fingers. "Attacked like this in a holy place! I'd like to know what I've done to be attacked by such as you? Is it the Judgement?" She listened for the sound of the Trump, blowing from the roofless shell of the church, from the sky, from the graves, anywhere, but heat held even the birds silent. "Is it the Judgement?" she said again.

"The Judgement?" The angel leaned on an obelisk, and all the skulls stared from mossed eye-sockets to see an angel weep. He put his hand to a stone urn, and the stone cloth draping it softened to his touch, so that he wiped his eyes, and draped the urn again. The soft folds stiffened once more to stone. "Oh God!" he said. "The days creep, and the nights creep, and it's all so slow... you think of what's to come, the glory, maybe, or the fire, and the fire would be welcome, so long as it comes quickly..."

The woman saw how the waiting was weary for him, the longing for the last day, when the Lord would whirl the holy and the hopeless through blue barren space. Body and soul... "What would you say happens to souls, now?" she said curiously, with the timidity of the newly dead. "Do they rest while they're waiting?" She looked around, as if to see them standing like mutes at their own headstones, but there was no stir in the quiet walled place, no stir but the flit of bees and dragonflies.

"They all rest," said the angel jealously, "packed flat in the coffins, on the corpse chest. But not you!" The wings flapped and battered, and the woman screamed again, and ran zig-zag through the grasses. "Leave me alone, don't you dare—it's wicked to go for an old woman as never harmed nobody!" It was her turn to weep now, with fear and self-pity. She was a poor creature to draw down holy wrath.

She looked at herself, the apron in harsh hessian, the grey men's socks stuffed into old shoes, and the black dress slavered and soiled in front. She forgot how she had come to the graveyard, standing in her working clothes with nothing to do. It had always been like this, continual living in the present, with no memory, and no will of her own. Always, she was dependent on other people, speaking the words framed for her, moulding her character to another's whim. Now, the driving will seemed to have been withdrawn, and she was tired. She began to tremble, and a faint sickness dampened her skin. Her mouth was dry, rough as a green gooseberry.

"I thought you'd let me in," she said meekly. "I never meant no harm. If there's any offence, it was no intentions of mine."

"I can't take you," said the angel. "I can't account for you. Don't keep asking me."

"But you can! I'm here, an old woman. You can see with your own eyes. Surely you can see me!"

"But you're not real; you never were, you exasperating old fool! Look at you, slattern, dirty, silly—there's no room for you that's no person." The angel laughed with sharp teeth, very small and vicious. "You'd no life; you can't remember any. Tell what you remember."

She clapped her hands to the ache in her head, trying to shut out the prying voice.

"What do you remember?"

"Coffins... and candles by the bed... not mine, though; other folks'. I've sat by them many a time. There was another woman there, a fat one, just me and this friend. We used to talk about deaths, the two of us."

"What after that?"

"I don't know. My memory's none too good. She was fat; I think she was good to me, that woman was, always praising me, to my face and behind my back... she's the only one clear to me now."

The angel waved lean fingers impatiently, and moved his wings, the sore tips blistering and peeling. "Well, you can't come in. Don't you see, you can't? I have to account for souls and bodies, and what do you think you are? What do you call yourself?"

"I don't know, I'm sure," she said, all bewildered. "Could I go back, then?"

"NO!" he screamed, exasperated. "You know you can't! Oh, mad, crazed fool, keeping me here to scorch in the sun and argue! What would you go back for? There's no place for you there!"

"But there's none for me here, either! If I went back, my friend would speak for me. She was good to me, my friend was. She'd tell you."

"Where would you go, then? Would you find her?"

"I don't know." The weary, persistent conversation went round and round, and the sun drew sparks out of the hot granite. This must be eternity, she thought, time going on and on...

The angel quietened, and retreated a little, as four shabby men came over the turf, limping and staggering beneath a plain, heavy coffin. There were no mourners, and the clergyman looking in a hurry, mopping his brow, and muttering over the burial as though his tea was poured out, and waiting at home. Dust to dust... a red dust seemed to rise as they lowered the coffin. This was what death should be, with the soul tucked up neat and cosy, to rest unchallenged through the rolling years. Here, there was no interference; the angel kept back, shabby and gaunt. The old woman crept over to watch the grave being filled. Where was *her* grave? No-one bothered with her; no-one looked at the shadowless figure, or spoke to her, or abated their work because of her curiosity.

When they were finished, hurrying away to happier work, the grave looked like a hummocky bed, with the turves replaced anyhow, rumpled and dry. The woman looked at the one cheap wreath, fingering the card among the already withering petals. "To Sairey Gamp," it said. "With tender loving kindness. B. Prig."

There was a sudden brilliant flash of memory, a second's comprehension. The old woman stumbled through the tall grasses, the seeds and fluff sticking to her skirt. She tripped over sunken stones, calling aloud to the angry angel.

He was in the shade of the church, leaning tired against the ruined wall. Here the air was cooler, the dazzle of the sun shut out by stone and hanging ivy. The old woman swayed with breathlessness, and steadied herself on a bunch of leering nettles. She did not feel the pain. "I know!" she said. "I know now. I remember! I'm Mrs Harris."

It seemed a long time till the angel answered, and then she stood, trying to take in his decision waiting while the sting of the nettles began to sear through her like a sword. Even when he repeated it, she still did not believe what he said.

"Mrs Harris?" he laughed, stirring his wings scornfully, "Mrs Harris? There's no such person!"

THE "BEAN-NIGHE"

here were only three colours left in the world, the purple of the night clouds, the yellow streaks in the western sky, and the colour of the river, dark green, like a channel filled with broken bottles. The water came smooth round the bend, a motionless black ink-line, then chopped into little green waves as the river broadened.

The girl dragged her feet a little, raking the white frill of pebbles by the river bank. She was thinking of the croft, just beyond the last hump of the moor. She had three miles to walk to her work in the morning, and three to walk back at night. They kept her so late at Knockhallow, cleaning and carrying and cleaning again, that it was nearly always dark before she got home. In the winter, when the snow was too deep to be crossed, she only came home once a fortnight. Sleeping at Knockhallow, with the winds roaring round the turrets and draughts creeping round corners, she shivered for the friendly warmth of her own bed, with her sister sharing the same plaid and pillow, and the fire left on all night, glowing red on the rough walls. In the summer, when Jeannie kicked and scratched, and Ian was coughing through the wall, trying to smother the noise in the blankets, she gasped for the loneliness which at least allowed her room to breathe. She lived in a perpetual dream of being otherwise, but did not realise it, because she did not know what she wanted. At the end of her day's work, all her thought was to be home again, free to sit or sleep, with nothing to do.

The heather had faded to grey, the trees beyond the river were like black paper-shapes gummed against the sky, and bats were nothing but flickers in the air. In the gloaming, sounds carried a long, long way, distinct as a bell in an empty room. The girl stopped to listen to the loneliness. A bird shrieked in the trees and flew away, trailing a sob behind it; something darted from the heather, rattled a stone, and fled, and from somewhere by the waterside came the splash-clap noise of a woman washing clothes. It rose above the glug and gurgle of the current, stopped for a while, and began again. It would be her mother, washing out something for Ian. When he coughed a lot, and spat red mouthfuls into the jar by his bed, his clothes were often soaked with sweat, and his mother, having no water in the house, would take them down to the river, rinse them, and leave them outside to dry.

The splash-clap grew louder, then stopped as Mary drew near enough to see. "Mother!" she called. "Will I help you, mother?" The woman did not answer. She was bent double, dabbling with her hands, a dim white smudge in the greyness. Her white gown was down to her ankles, and the garment she was washing clouded the water like milk. It looked as if she had risen suddenly, urgently from her bed, and hastened to the river while still asleep, treading trance-like on heather and thistle. She rubbed and rinsed at some stain, soused and splashed the water, then stood up, lifting streaming white linen at arms' length, wringing it, flapping it, and soaking it again. Suddenly, disturbed, she looked over her shoulder, and Mary saw that it was not her mother at all. This woman was short, with a withered, mean face, and small, horrible feet grappling the ground, bare, webbed like a duck's.

The girl stepped back, too frightened to speak. One more

29

backward step, and she was running and stumbling over the stones, looking over her shoulder to see whether the ugly woman was following. Her legs were wet, spattered with drops as if the washer had whirled the wet garment to strike her. She could see nothing now but a white shadow, standing quite still, staring after her.

Inside the kitchen, her mother was warming milk at the fire. Big and comforting, with her hair halfway down her back, she put a cup and plate on the table, and lifted a finger to her lips. "Jeannie's just sleeping," she said. "Dinna wake her."

"Mother, mother—"

"Wheesht, can't ye? What is't? Is there trouble up at Knockhallow for ye?"

"No, no, mother. Mother, there's a woman down there, washing—I don't like the look of her. You should have seen the way she glowered at me, and the ugly face of her—"

"Mary! Did she speak to ye? Did she speak?"

"No, but she would have come at me, if I'd waited."

"Did you speak—ask her anything?"

"I only said 'Mother.' I thought it was you; washing like you sometimes do, for Ian. Then she turned—"

"What was she washing, Mary, for the love of God? Did you see?"

"Something white—I don't know. I didn't like it. Mother, what's wrong? What have I done, mother?"

"God help us, child, you'll wake your brother. *He* doesn't need to know yet. Mary, yon was the bean-nighe, that washes the shrouds of the dying. Bless your nimble feet that she didn't catch you, Mary, or she'd have lamed you for life. There was old Donal Fergus that she caught on the hip with the wet shroud, and he never walked again."

Mary saw that it was not her mother at all

"But whose shroud?"

"Somebody soon to die. Oh, Holy Mary, and *he* took a bad turn this day, after his breakfast. Three cups of blood, and him still weak from the last bleeding he took—"

"Ian?"

"Aye. She'd have told you that, if you'd crept up and held her. She has to answer, if you catch her first—but the risk's not worth it. It's Ian she's washing for."

"But she has no right! She's got no right to come and tell people things like that. What right has *she*—with his shroud, getting it ready before he needs it—"

"Hush, dearie, quiet. It gives us time to prepare. It's a sorry job for her, too, to wash the dismal things, all night long, always desolate. Even God must be sorry for the poor creature sometimes."

In the morning, she did not go to work. The horror of the bean-nighe was upon her, and she was afraid to leave the house. Let the cook at Knockhallow storm in her kitchen, let the housemaid do the menial tasks herself; she would stay away till the death was past, and her brother's body carried over the threshold.

"What's wrong with Mary?" asked Ian, pale among the pillows, beautiful as no man ought to be.

"Oh, she had a sick turn during the night," said the mother. "I'm keeping her off work for a day or two."

"Poor mother!" He twisted his lips, trying not to cough. "Always somebody ill in the house. Never mind, I'm better this morning. It won't be long till I can fish again."

The woman turned away, before he saw her tears. He was always so sure he would be well again, always talking of the river, where the salmon printed silver circles in the air as they leaped under the sun.

As the day grew hotter, he was carried out to sit at the door, and Mary sat beside him, silent, till he wondered why she would not speak to him. She felt she could not leave him for a moment, must make the most of her time with him, but she was in agony lest she should say one rash word. The river was a navy blue line in the distance, the moor heaved slanting shoulders of brown and yellow, and the sun burned like a spot of bright solder. Their mother worked, and Jeannie worked. Only the girl and her brother were idle; they sat limp in the quivering air, he tired with the heat, she tired with terror.

Remembering her father's death, she tried to think what it would be like to lose Ian. There would be the sombre waiting at the bedside, and the flatness of the moment when it was all over. There would be black clothes to buy, a coffin and a funeral to pay for. (It cost a lot to drive horses over the moor to the graveyard.) There would be festivity of a sort, eating and drinking, a gathering together of neighbours far distant, and after that, a little more room in the house. No more nights disturbed with his coughing, no more sickening glimpses of blood in the jar by his bedside. She thought of these things as she sat beside him, and she could hardly believe them, because things like that belonged to dreams and stories. Nevertheless, she never doubted her mother. If it was possible for her to see the web-footed washer (and there was no doubt that she had seen her), it was possible for the omen to come true. It did not occur to her, then, that she could be washing the shroud for anyone else but Ian. It could not be for Jeannie, who was a healthy elf, able for a woman's work; not for her mother, who was only brought to bed when her children were born; not for herself because such things could not apply to one so ordinary. No, it was Ian who was going to die, and though it would be cruel to tell him so, it would be a mortal sin to let him die unprepared.

But two days passed, and Ian did not die. The mornings broke blue and hazy, and the sun shifted, till its heat bored into the head like pain. The heath rustled underfoot, the flowers whitened and dried, and the rocks burned. Only the thistles seemed to thrive, their green-silver spikes tense with strength, their plumes burning like blue gas jets.

The second night passed, and on the third day, Ian was better than he had been for many months. It might be true that he would one day die of his sickness, but when? Would it be within the year, or the month, or the week? Since all must die, the bean-nighe tells only of the death which is soon to strike. Perhaps it was not *his* shroud. Then whose?

The work of the croft was left undone. Who could tend land and cattle when there was so soon to be a death in the house? Jeannie did not know what worried her elders, but she would not work when everybody else idled. True, the house had been cleaned ready for the funeral, but it had been done quickly, and now there was not enough work inside for three pairs of hands. Ian did not notice. Sunk in his book, drowned in deep ponds of print, he lay at the door and heeded nothing. Time went by like a slow, hot cloud, and life stood still, waiting for death to come and free them from their waiting.

On the third night, a faint breeze of doubt troubled the watchers. Nothing had happened. Perhaps, nothing would happen. Ian was cheerful, his cough nothing more troublesome than an odd huskiness in the throat. Mary began to worry about her work. She did not care for scrubbing stone floors, and running here and there with never a minute to herself, but the drudgery of a big household was better than the idleness of suspense. Up at Knockhallow, there was laughter in the kitchen, and comradeship below stairs. She spoke to her mother about it.

"Mother, hadn't I better be going back to work? Perhaps they'll not take me back at all, if I stay away too long."

"Go back to work, and your brother like to die at any minute? Shame, Mary! The least you can do—"

"But, mother, he's not dying yet. Is he not better in himself? Wouldn't you say so, now?"

"Oh, merciful Lord, I don't know what I'd say! If it wasn't that you swear you saw the washerwoman—"

"Mother, would it be among us the death had to be? Are you sure it would be among one of us?"

"It would. Who else is there? Can you see any other house across the moor? Is there any other family near us? It was one of us that saw the bean-nighe. And isn't it likely to be Ian would go next, him that has the same trouble as his father? Would you say it was one of the healthy ones that would be taken?"

"No. Only, Ian is better, and we might have to wait and wait— I'd rather it would come at once, mother. I don't like to wait on, not knowing."

The woman went to the door, and looked at the river. It was sunken and dry, hardly visible in its channel. She looked at her daughter, and her eyes were half frightened at the suggestion she made.

"Mary, there's only one way to know. You'll have to ask her."

"Ask her? Oh—no! I wouldn't go by her again—she's frightsome, mother!"

"You'll have to. If you don't find out, we'll never know till it's too late. Any one of us might be taken, and Ian left. We might be taken sudden, and no time to prepare. If it should be Ian, we can tell him—I don't think he'll be feared to die—"

"But if it's not Ian? Suppose she says it's you? How will I tell you? Or if it's me? What would I do?"

"What's before us will not go past us. We're as well to know it all, when we know half. Listen, and I'll tell you how to manage. You'll have to mind yourself. Creep soft, as quiet as you can, so's she won't hear you, or know you're there, then catch hold of her tight, so she can't get away—"

"Can't you do it, instead of me? You don't know how she glowered at me. I couldn't face yon again—"

"It's best for you to go, seeing you saw her last time. If you grasp her tight, she can't harm you. It's like a nettle."

"Wouldn't you come with me?"

"Someone has to mind Ian. Go, now, like a good girl, Mary. When it's dark, that's when she comes—"

There were only three colours left in the world, the purple of the night clouds, the grey of the heather, and the long black line of the river. She had waited a long while in the house, sitting at the fire till both Jeannie and Ian were asleep. Now, it was so dark that the afterglow had drained out of the sky, and the trees across the river were as vague as tumbledown steeples.

Long before she reached the place, she heard the splash-clap of the washer. Tonight, no bird called, no bat was a-flutter, no small-legged thing scuttered among the roots and stones. The sound was much louder. Her throat burned with a sour fluid of fear, her face went cold, yet she could not turn back. She stood and stared at the river, straining to see with her eyes what she was already seeing in her mind.

The strange washer was there. Seen like this, anonymous in her white garment, she was pathetic rather than horrible. Bent over the water, the white shroud slapping as she beat it on the stones, she was only a tired, sad body washing in the dark. There was a world of heartbreak in the way she lifted the linen, the water dripping from it in silver fringes. Was she there every night, or did she move from river to mere and swamp, wherever her ghastly work awaited her?

Mary wanted to weep at the misery of the thought, but fear, and the questions she had to ask, made her wary. She took off her shoes, and crept barefoot towards the river. The bean-nighe went on washing, deaf, deafened by the sludge and splash of her work. The girl's lip was between her teeth, her breathing fast and heavy, her heart beating like a muffled bell. One hand was stretched out to touch the trailing white hem, when a stone slipped under her foot. She stumbled, her hands blind in front of her. The being turned, her small face screwed and angry. There was a whirl of wet cloth, the stinging smack, smack of wet cloth on bare legs, and Mary was lying alone, with the dark river beside her, and not another soul in sight.

After the bean-nighe had gone, the sounds of the night began again. The air was full of the flutter of wings, the trees rustled, and owls answered each other across the river. It was the first drop of rain that roused the girl. Her head shielded by her arms, her shoulders raised, cowering from ill usage, she pulled herself together and tried to rise. Her legs seemed to be made of lead. The stinging had left her flesh, and all she could feel was a dull numbness, an aching suggestion of pain to come. Whimpering, goaded by fear to a desperate strength, she knotted her muscles and forced and strained to move herself. Her legs lay useless, like two heavy sandbags anchoring her to the riverbank for ever more. The rain came quicker now and quicker, hissing into the river. The night was very black. She raised herself on her arms and dragged herself slowly, slowly, but the rain seemed to force her down and weary her. Suddenly, in despair, she gave up and screamed for her mother.

The footsteps came rushing over the brow of the little hill. Her mother had left Ian, the house, everything, when she heard the wild howl of her. "Walk, Mary, lass!" she kept pleading. "Try, for the love of God!" But Mary could not walk. The woman carried her in her arms to the croft, sure footed with love, keening all the way. It was only when they were safe in the kitchen, with the moor and the river shut out, that they remembered that a deeper tragedy was still in store for them; and they did not know on whom it would fall.

MATTHEW LURK,
TRACTORMAN

t was a fine spring morning when Matthew Lurk's tractor overturned. He sat hunched between the big wheels, his donkey jacket smeared with clay, and his cap, too small for him, welded on to his thick red neck. A tune went round and round in his head, not quite strong enough to tease his vocal chords into song; and suddenly a large and ridiculous pig shot across his path. The tractor swerved, overbalanced on a rut, and Matthew, much shaken, eased himself from under the ribbed tyres, and looked at the great red hulk still trembling, like an animal not quite dead. Blue smoke seeped out, distorting the daylight, and there was a heady smell of petrol. "Fumes going for me," mumbled Matthew, and edged back unsteadily. "I've had a bit of a shake, right enough," and he went off dizzily, dragging his rubber boots and blinking against the bright sun.

His wife was not in when he got to the cottage. The fire whispered, stew murmured on the hob, but on the sink was a bowl of potatoes, half unpeeled, the knife lying in the water. "Stupid," he said, and went to lift the knife; he was a careful man with tools; but he did not seem to be able to grasp it, so he went to the fire, and stretched out on the chair, sprawled half over the hearthrug; and he would have slept heavily if it had not been for his wife, sick-faced, coming back with a gaggle of women all bent on putting the kettle on, and having a long wallow in whatever grief had upset Dolly.

Someone had been hurt, and taken to hospital. Whoever it was had been pronounced dead on arrival. Dolly stared and stared, and sobbed without tears, and Matthew stirred himself and leaned forward and said, "What is it, then? What happened? Who was killed?"

There was no answer. His head sang, and his body was light with weakness. "Well, who was it?" he shouted. "I've had an accident too, if you weren't so bloody wrapped up in other folks' business."

They didn't seem to hear him. All their concern was for Dolly, her arms on the bare table, and little shivers going through her like they had gone through the overturned tractor. Suddenly, he was sorry for her. She had always been soft hearted about other folks' troubles. He stood up to go over to her—what would the rest of them think, him sitting there unheeding?—when Mrs Tripe, the grieve's wife, put an arm round her shoulders.

"Come on, love. Over to the fire. Come on over an' get warm."

She half screamed, struggling backwards. "*No!*" she squealed. "Not on his chair! I couldn't—"

"But it won't hurt him, love. He won't want it now..."

"It wouldn't be right," sobbed Dolly.

He didn't like the way they were ignoring him, expecting him to give up his chair when he had just escaped a serious injury. He thought of the great red machine, pathetic on its side, and remembered how he had emerged thinly from the wheels. Perhaps he had been luckier than he thought. Of course, there would be Hell to pay if the tractor needed repair. Never mind what might have happened to him.

And then the minister came in, awkward at having to offer comfort on a bright spring morning. Matthew had never had a great deal of time for the Rev Timothy Fergus, and now, even allowing for the delicacy of his mission, he felt that he could have acquitted himself better. He mumbled and wavered, and made vague allusions to things like God's will; but eventually the message got through, and when he had gone, Matthew, who had never done well at school, but who could figure things out accurately enough if he took his time, and met no complications, knew with a definite and shocking certainty that he had died at twenty minutes to eleven, and that it was his ghost, unformed and invisible, that had trod shakily from his squashed body, and made for the place that he knew.

"But it's daft!" he screamed, in a voice as silent as steam. "I'm here!" Nobody listened. He went over to his wife, when she was left alone, and put his hands on her, but it had no effect at all. He could have struck her for her lack of perception. His hand stroked her hair, and then he permitted himself a sudden tweak. She never winced. Exasperated, he stamped out of the house—surely she saw him, heard the thump and squeak of his Wellingtons, and the brush of his jacket against the chair?—and went out to where the tractor had been righted and removed, and the smear of the earth covered with fresh soil.

There was no one there. Everyone had gone for dinner. He stood about for a while, feeling the cold spring wind go through him, and then, restless, he made off again to the little cottage hospital.

"Who do I ask?" he wondered, before he puzzled out that it would be the mortuary where it—he—lay. He wanted terribly to see, but at the same time he felt rather diffident about it. He had never liked putting people to a lot of trouble. He did no more than peep through the window, and that was enough. The body was there, sheeted, scary-like, the sort of sight that set kids screaming; and there was a coffin, cheapish looking... Tomorrow, or the next day, the lid would be screwed down, and they would bury it, and then—"God!" he whispered, his voice no louder than thought, "What an escape I've had!"

He was halfway home before the implications of it all wormed their way through to him. What had he escaped *to*? And if this was death, where were all the dead? There must be so many more of them. No one could see *him*. He couldn't even see himself, except in his mind, and the thought of his mind rocked his precarious balance. He moved by thought, but it was not easy, not so easy as walking. He saw normally, but only what was there, the visible.

"I'm here," he thought. "The others must be somewhere too." But he could neither see nor sense them.

As yet, the future was bounded by definite dates. After the funeral, he thought. The funeral would resolve things. Once the body, that stiff sheeted thing that was the cause of the trouble, was out of the way, he would get back to some kind of routine.

He clung to this through the uselessness of invisibility. People didn't even brush him aside. He got himself along to the graveyard, and bowed his head over the coffin with a feeling of grief and regret. It would have been nice to speak to someone, to go home with them to the funeral tea... nobody stopped him going, but he was all alone, ignored, when he should have been the guest of honour.

They spoke about him. The Rev Fergus said comforting things to Dolly—silly things, about his pain being over, and being happy in Heaven; and though it went against the grain to contradict the cloth, he felt that the man was opening his mouth and talking rubbish. There was no pain; never had been, except once when he had had appendicitis; and as for Heaven—well, he had never believed what the hymns said. It was too much of a fairy story. He had thought of death as being shut up underground, and, not liking the idea, had pushed it away from him. "When it happens, I won't know." And now he knew.

If he had had a choice, it would have been to stay here always, in this cottage, with Dolly. Now this, it seemed, was what was to happen, and he should have been glad; but it was disappointing, empty, heartbreaking. He hung about, watching her, and she didn't know. He sat and nodded and moped, and yearned towards life, as it had been, dirt and sweat to wash from his hands, hunger, and the need to be sustained. There was nothing, not even sleep. Not even darkness. Night went by in a kind of luminous greyness, and, vaguely, he began to worry about a word he had never comprehended before—Eternity.

Each day was so long! It was like standing outside a lighted window, tapping at the glass, and knowing that nobody heard; and soon the light would go out, and there would be nobody there, till morning came, and Dolly wakened, and the world wakened, everybody but him, because there was nothing to waken *from*…

He had always been scathing about ghosts, sheeted things carrying their heads and trailing chains and moaning. "'Taint any such things. *I* never seen one; you tell me anybody seen a ghost…!" And of course nobody had. They were all in stories. Because how could anyone *know*, not seeing, what ghosts were? He didn't know himself. He was Matthew Lurk, in his own mind, and the dizzy journey to Heaven, the place of rapture high above the jets and the blue sky, was just another of the tales they told to keep people happy. And so was the argument against it all, thumped out on pub counters, "When you're dead, you're dead, and you don't know nothing about it."

But gradually—how long did it take?—he fancied himself a shade more solid. The sense of his own personality reasserted itself: Matthew Lurk, tractorman, in a donkey jacket and rubber boots and pea coloured cap. At times he was so sure of himself that he almost made Dolly aware too.

At first, he could not be certain. One day he stroked her hair again, and she put up a hand, absently, to smooth it down. Another time, she walked right through him, then turned, quickly, with a little shudder. It was a small triumph, but encouraging. He sang a little, and it was at least as effective as the mute groaning that used to pass for a song.

Dolly didn't like it. She didn't hear, but it upset her. Everything upset her nowadays. She told the doctor, sitting sacrilegiously on Matthew's chair, and the doctor said it was the shock of her husband's death, and her condition. Dolly cried again, and Matthew reasoned and counted, and realised that by dying he had missed the joys of fatherhood. And yet he would be there. He would see, he would know, he would miss nothing. Death takes away only life, not the observation of it.

So Matthew was there, yearning, his big hands stretched out to help. He was there when his son was born. For a moment, seeing Dolly lie with all her blood and energy drained, he half hoped she would die. It was not a cruel wish, because death was nothing, nothing at all, if only there were somebody else... Or maybe the baby would come to him, and they would live together—he thought of it as life—and comfort each other through the emptiness...

But Dolly only slept, and wakened refreshed, and the baby throve. His son throve. Matthew poked a rough finger into the cot, and the baby cried. Dolly always looked up sharply when this happened, so that it seemed as if she saw... "Dolly!" he called, his heart breaking. "Dolly!"

When the baby was able to sit up in his pram, she began to perk up, to smile and look in the mirror and hum to herself. A young man had come to the house about the Insurance money, and after the money had been paid, he kept coming. Matthew, hiding behind cupboard doors—he still felt it necessary to hide—felt furious and abandoned. The first time he saw the man kiss Dolly he drew all his thoughts together and forced his hands round the smart striped collar.

The self satisfied face turned crimson. "Something choked me!" he whispered. "A pair of hands..."

"Och, you're daft!" laughed Dolly.

"I'm not. It was—maybe it was your husband's ghost..."

"Matthew?" Dolly said his name with affection, but carelessly. "Oh, Matthew wouldn't hurt a fly!"

Of course he wouldn't; but that was in the old days. Even now, he didn't want any trouble. Dolly was innocent, because she knew that he was dead, and young Dickinson was innocent too. Matthew, better now at reasoning, because he had had plenty of practice, tried to work out his feelings, and came up with the decision that he still didn't want to hurt anybody. He only wanted to *show* them.

He worked harder. Once, a man at the garage had told him that gas, gathered together in small bulk by freezing, becomes a visible liquid. He hadn't understood this—"I never done Science at school"—but the fact stuck in his mind, and now the idea became relevant. With great stress and agony, he drew himself into a tautness, and nudged a teacup. It tinkled over with a splash of hot brown liquid, and he laughed as Dolly fussed about, mopping and grumbling.

After this he became more and more successful. He played gooseberry, and watched Dolly bloom as young Dickinson whispered things that made her blush. And he couldn't keep his hands off the baby. Matthew, Dolly had called him, after his father; but the child would call someone else Daddy, and would never know that he was watched so lovingly, so jealously…

Dolly was married, looking very young and fetching in a lilac dress and a big floppy hat. "I should have got dressed up for wedding," thought Matthew, in vague remorse. He stepped aside to let them pass down the aisle, and followed them, lost and out of place. He couldn't imagine himself other than in his donkey jacket and Wellington boots.

Dolly Dickinson sounded better than Dolly Lurk, and her new husband had more to offer than he had ever had. There was more money and more fun, and Dolly didn't have to work so hard. Matthew, standing forlorn by the bedroom door—even now he didn't have the nerve to intrude—was so worked up with envy and frustration that all his emotions coagulated into one vast effort, and for an instant he saw himself, the muddy trousers, the boots, the thick red hands; and in that instant Dolly saw too, or felt him, through the door, the wall, he didn't know how, and cried out in terror.

After that he never let them alone. He niggled at them continuously. Sometimes he did mean things, tormented the baby, *his* baby, kept him awake so that no one was able to sleep; and in this sad and peculiar way he sought some comfort and company for himself. At other times he actually appeared, and this was more effective because, once visible, he didn't have to *do* anything. The mere sight of him, clumsy and malevolent, was enough. Dolly screamed and cowered, and because he loved her and grudged her to anyone else it hurt him to see her terror. He went towards her, stumbling, awkward at using visible limbs again, and Dickinson, white faced, put Dolly behind him and stood with a poker in his hand.

You can't hunt a ghost with a poker. Matthew went away, of his own free will, but he materialised so easily now that he appeared again and again with almost spiteful glee. Soon everyone knew that Matthew Lurk's ghost had come back to haunt his young wife, and that Dolly and her husband were thinking of moving away.

This wasn't what he meant. All he wanted was to be with Dolly and the baby, and no matter whether they saw him or sensed him or whether he was forever lost and forgotten, it would be enough to be there, to see them and love them so much that he ached with the pain of it.

But of course, where Dickinson went, she would go too, and once they were gone, he couldn't follow. Somehow he knew that it was the house he haunted, tied by an invisible band which stretched so far and then snapped him back. Who would come in their place? And what would it be like, having strangers in his home? Nothing to live for... the weariness of knowing that he wasn't alive brought tears to his throat. Surely, if he felt tears in his throat...?

When he heard them talk to bringing in the minister he was almost grateful. Without belief in religion, he still had faith, and now although he had more knowledge than the men who preach and promise, Matthew Lurk was still impressed by learning. All ministers, he was convinced, acquired wisdom with their dog collars and degrees, and even the Rev Timothy Fergus would know what to do for the best.

So he listened, nodding, nodding in the background. The Rev Timothy had theories which he was obviously dying to test, and Matthew, so far as he could understand them, was in complete agreement.

"It's not an evil spirit we're dealing with," the Rev Fergus explained, his Bible at the ready, with little markers sticking out of the pages.

"No, no," agreed Matthew gratefully.

"A ghost is more a troubled spirit." He leaned forward and addressed them earnestly as in the preliminaries to marriage. His hands moved, his trousers were hitched over short nylon socks. "What we might call a lost soul," he went on. "I'd like to try to give this soul a little peace."

Dolly's eyes filled at the thought of her husband lost and wandering, but she had another husband, and she too wanted peace. No harm to Matthew; just to be rid of the tension, the fear of seeing him...

So they all knelt together in the parlour, rather self consciously, and Matthew stood beside them, very humble. When, after a period of pain and worry, he had gone into hospital to have his appendix out, he had never forgotten the peace of finding himself in bed, surrounded by people who were out to help him, and who knew what they were doing. He felt like that now, waiting trustfully for the words that would make everything all right.

He waited a long time. The baby began to cry, and Dolly pushed the pram back and forwards to quieten him. In his anxiety to have the crying stop, Matthew did not hear the words that were said. He waited and waited, eyes closed, and then he realised that there was no sound, either of crying or praying. He opened his eyes, but saw nothing. A thick mist was rolling up, thicker and thicker; the room itself was gone. Patiently, he stood, his head bowed at first, and then raised anxiously, peering, waiting for the mist to clear.

In hospital, there had been a period like this, white, swirling, going into the chloroform. That was what it felt like now; but then, there had been someone beside him to guide and comfort and tell him he would be all right. Now there was no one; and at last, Matthew Lurk, who could figure things out if he took his time, realised, with the same shocking certainty with which he had learned of his death, that there never would be anyone. Unlike the doctors, Timothy Fergus had *not* known what he was doing.

THE WOBBLY CASTLE

he castle stood by the esplanade, its towers like ice cream cones, its walls a lurid brick colour. It was made of rubber, and pumped up every morning to the proper pressure. At night, with the moon behind it, it really did look like a castle, its silhouette solid against the silver of the sea. In the daytime it was tawdry, a giant balloon with a painted doorway and an inner courtyard corrugated like an enormous li-lo; and on this rust coloured floor the children jumped and screamed and rolled about in ecstasy, while the whole structure shuddered and quivered grotesquely.

"Come and jump on the wobbly castle. Only 20p. Jumping time 5 minutes minimum." So said the big sandwich board on the pavement, and so said the big man in the linen hat, bawling against the din of the giant Whizzer and the chair-o-planes. Grey shingle stretched beyond the funfair, and the waiting children sat around, barefooted, ready to rush in when the five minutes was up.

"How about this, then?" said aunt Louisa. "Would you like to jump on that?"

Barbara nodded, and her aunt looked relieved. So far, Barbara had not behaved as a child on holiday should. She would not join in, she dragged back from violent roundabouts, she said "No, thank you" to everything. Louisa, who felt responsible for giving her niece a good time, was on the verge of irritation. Surely there was *something* the child would enjoy.

Even now, having agreed to five minutes in the castle, the child hung back. She worried about taking her shoes off, she was afraid of the rough, shouting boys who seemed to take up all the room; but her aunt promised to look after her sandals, and lifted her firmly on to the shaking floor.

The floor was hot, and smelt of new tyres. Barbara put out a foot carefully, lurched and fell, and bounced up again. It didn't hurt a bit. This time she jumped, and was surprised how easy it was. After a few more jumps, higher each time, she tried to stride forward, over the undulating floor, and falling and giggling like the others, she staggered, rolled, and lay on her back as the floor billowed and the walls wiggled like jelly.

"Can I go on again, auntie?" she said when the five minutes were up. "Can I? I want to jump right up to the top."

"Well, yes, I suppose so. But don't make yourself sick." At least, thought Louisa, I've found something she likes.

The second time round, she had more confidence. She fixed her eyes on one of the towers, the only one with a window, and tried to reach the narrow black cleft. It was harder than she thought. It was only in the last minute that she sprang right up and, for a long second, looked into the slit of the window.

She was so amazed that when her feet touched the tilting floor she ran stumbling to get off, just as the man was shouting, "C'mon, kids, your time's up. 20p. for another turn!" She gripped his arm, feeling the ground too flat and too steady. "Please sir, please—how did the lady get in?"

He looked down at her as he collected the money and shepherded the new lot of jumpers on. "What lady, love?" he asked. "And where?"

"In the tower. Looking out of the window."

He looked at the castle, already dipping and twisting as the children shrieked. "There's no lady there, pet," he said. "It's just a painted window."

"But it's not! I saw it! I jumped right up, and—"

Come on, Barbara!" her aunt called. "Come and get your shoes on."

"Auntie, I saw it! There's a lady in one of the towers. I jumped up and saw her. It's in the window there..."

"Just imagination," laughed the man. "If I thought there was a lady there I'd be up beside her. You bet your life!" Aunt Louisa ignored him. "Come on now, Barbara. We'll come back again another day."

"Auntie, the lady looked as if she wanted to get out. She said 'Quick, quick', and she sort of... beckoned to me."

"Now you're making up stories."

"I'm *not*!"

Aunt Louisa decided that the conversation should end there, and Barbara, being an obedient child, walked along till her aunt let go of her hand and began to fumble for pennies in her purse. "Would you like some ice cream, dear?"

"Yes, please." But she loitered as she sucked at her cornet and looked back over her shoulder to where the castle wobbled and gyrated endlessly; and when she went to bed that night she shut her eyes tightly and went over what had happened.

It was no good telling her aunt about it. Kind as she was, she obviously didn't believe it. Nor did the man, but of course *he* could be the one who was keeping her prisoner. He had seemed a nice kind man, but maybe he was only pleasant to children, to get them to spend their money.

As she grew drowsier, everything became clearer and clearer in her mind. She had seen right in, through the iron bars, into a stone flagged room, quite round, with a high carved chair at the window. On the chair sat a sad lady, dressed in black, with a sort of green headdress. One hand, a very narrow hand, crooked a pleading finger through the bars, and the other had what looked like an iron bracelet round the wrist; but when she moved it, painfully, Barbara saw that it was fixed to a thick iron chain, which was fastened to a ring on the opposite wall.

It had only been a glimpse, but she could see the picture in her mind as clearly as if it was painted on a page. It worried her. It was the sort of thing you expected in castles: she had seen plenty of pictures like that in story books, but she *knew* that the castle was only a gigantic balloon.

Next day she emptied her purse and counted her pocket money. She had plenty to pay for quite a few goes on the castle. Aunt Louisa told her to save her money; she'd want to buy things to take home, a present for her mother... but Barbara was quite firm about it. "I'm only using *part* of my money, auntie. I just want a good long shot..."

She did not waste time in aimless jumping or flopping about. She went straight to the tower with the window, and leaped as high as she could. Yes, she was right. The glassless window was barred with an iron grille, but this time there was no face at the window.

She leaped up again, and this time she managed to grab hold of the stone coping. In the few seconds she managed to hold on, she saw that the lady was slumped in a corner, her face in her hands; then she slid down, her hands and knees grazed and nipping.

"For Heaven's sake, Barbara, what have you done with yourself?" said aunt Louisa.

Half crying, half brave, Barbara looked down at the sore areas where the blood was beginning to trickle. "I got it sliding down the tower," she said, wincing as her aunt dabbed her with a hankie.

"The tower? But it's as smooth as a balloon!"

"No it isn't! It's rough, and there's a room inside, and the lady's sitting in a corner crying—"

"Right, that settles it," said her aunt brusquely. "That's the last time you go on there. And I'm going to see the man about what's wrong with his castle. There must be something dangerous about it for you to get scratched like that."

But there was nothing wrong with it. The man, impatient, offended, told her to take off her shoes and see for herself; so there was aunt Louisa, trying to be dignified as she lurched along the heaving floor and ran her fingers down every tower in turn.

"I'm sorry," she said, "but she *did* hurt herself on something. Don't worry, I'll get the truth out of her yet."

What Barbara told her, after a lot of firm talking and shaking, *was* the truth, she insisted, but understandably, her aunt didn't believe her. There was an atmosphere for the rest of the holiday, her aunt keeping her busy every minute, and Barbara, too polite to sulk and protest, co-operative but cold. When her mother came to take her home, aunt Louisa had a long talk with her, and after that everyone was bright and cheerful, with thank-yous and goodbyes ringing in their ears after the train had gone.

The castle haunted Barbara. She drew castellated walls and pointed towers in her drawing book, and she searched in her books for any pictures of prisoners in dungeons. At first, her mother did not object. Let her get the thing out of her system, she thought, and she'll forget all about it when she goes back to school. But Barbara did not forget, and so all talk about turret rooms and towers was forbidden. "Now mind, don't let me hear one more word about it. You should have something better to do than go on about it all day."

But they could not stop her thinking about it. At night, when the curtains were drawn against the still bright evening, she went over it again and again. She saw the castle against a background of blue sky, she smelt the hot rubbery smell, and she *knew* that the lady pined inside, tethered and maybe tortured. It worried her, got mixed up with her prayers and her mother's bedtime stories, and dominated her dreams. At last her mother, hearing her talk in her sleep, decided to take her back to the seaside, back to aunt Louisa's, so that she could get to the bottom of it once and for all.

It was wet when they arrived, and the fairground was half empty. "Wait till you've had your dinner," said aunt Louisa soothingly. "Wait till it clears up," said her mother, with less patience. "You don't want to go traipsing about in all that rain."

The rain didn't bother Barbara. As soon as it showed signs of stopping, she coaxed and badgered her mother to come out with her. She did not know that she was under observation. All she knew was that rules seemed to be relaxed, and that she was going to be allowed on the bouncing castle again.

The castle was deserted. Rain filled the creases of the courtyard, and dropped from the blue-capped towers. The man in charge was smoking in a little hut, and he shook his head when Barbara proffered her 20p.

"Sorry, love, no jumping today. Too wet."

"Oh, but I—"

"It's just an experiment," her mother said. "You see, she—she got it into her head there was someone held prisoner here, and I wanted to show her, just to make sure..."

The man looked at Barbara, and recognised her, none too pleased at the knowledge. "Oh aye! The girl that cut herself and said she'd scraped it on the wall." For a moment, his eyes looked almost vicious, and then he turned to Barbara's mother.

"Well, you see, the trouble is, if I let her on, all the kids'll want on too."

"Well, they'll pay, won't they?" This was aunt Louisa. "You're surely not turning away custom?"

"They'll get soaked," said the man, throwing away his cigarette. "I'll have their mothers after me. Still, if you say it's all right..." He took the 20p. and lifted Barbara on to the castle. "Now let's see what you can do."

The flabby castle didn't wobble so much when there was only one child to rock it. Barbara bounced up and down, self-consciously at first, but later with more confidence. There was no sea sparkling now, nothing but a wet mist seeping down from the sky. Drops of water splashed and trickled as she jumped, and her stockings soaked as she landed on her knees. "No, it's all right, Missis," said the man, when her five minutes was up. "Let her have a bit longer. Looks like she's going to be the only one today."

She was bouncing higher now, right up to the tower, her hands stretched out towards the bars, and her fingers squeaking on the wet rubber. There was nothing there. The window was a narrow rectangle of black paint, the bars a mere grey tracery.

Puzzled, desperate, she lurched off in her wet stockings and ran to her mother. "Oh mummy, she's gone! Even the dungeon's gone. But I did see her, I did, I did!" She turned to the man in the linen hat, pleading with him to believe her. "Where is she? *What have you done with her?*"

The man's eyes twinkled as he got into the spirit of the thing, "Oh, I set her free. She's working for me, now."

"Where?"

"In the amusement arcade." He winked at the adults, preening himself, the man who understood children. "She's got to behave herself, though. She's got to do what I tell her, or else I'll chain her up again."

"Oh." Barbara's eyes went from her mother to her aunt. "Could we...?"

"Oh come on, we might as well." Aunt Louisa sighed as rain came on again. "So long as she doesn't expect us to spend a fortune on her. *I* know these places."

Barbara dragged her mother along. "I know the way. It's in here..."

"My God!" said her mother. "Don't tell me *this* is where she spent her time!"

"Oh no!" Aunt Louisa was shocked. "I wouldn't allow it. Wait till you get inside. It's a lot worse."

It sounded like bedlam, a battlefield, an illuminated section of hell. Lights flashed, sirens shrieked, there was a taped cacophony of hysterical laughter. Long rows of gaming machines spun and clanked, and occasionally regurgitated a clatter of brown pennies. Flickering screens showed alien planes, bomb bursts, cars going "splat!" as they crashed off roads. Barbara retreated a little, and then crept in, deafened, mesmerised by the dizzying telegames and the incessant noise.

"Oh, look, mummy! Auntie, look!"

In one corner was an open log cabin with a row of rifles lined up outside. When different targets were hit, dreadful things creaked into motion; a falling window caught an old man by the neck, a corpse came to life and spat derisively, a skeleton reared from a coffin, a door sprang open and ejected a cowboy with a squirting water pistol. Barbara watched in giggling fascination, and even aunt Louisa seemed to enjoy it. "You know, I used to be quite a good shot," she began.

"Oh auntie, try it, please try it!" Barbara was now like an ordinary little girl, and her mother began to rummage in her handbag for money. "No, I haven't got any change."

"There's a machine over there," said aunt Louisa. "Take this pound, pet, and get ten tenpences."

Barbara skipped away and joined the queue. When her turn came, she clutched the pound and stared, white-faced. There, in a little kiosk no bigger that the room in the tower, sat a woman in black, with a green scarf over her head. She was seated on a high carved chair, and she seemed to have shut her mind to the screaming, bleeping racket around her. As Barbara stared, she put out a languid hand and beckoned desperately. "Quick, quick!" she said, as the queue behind pushed impatiently. Dazed, Barbara put up her hand with the pound note. The woman pressed a lever automatically, and a rattle of coins racketted down the chute. "Well, go on, then!" said a boy behind her. Someone scooped up the money and gave it to her, and she stood tranced with her fistful of coins. The woman had had a thick black chain round one wrist...

She was still standing there when her mother and aunt Louisa came to look for her.

THE MAN IN THE WALL

he friends I brought home after school were treated by my mother with a mixture of kindliness and suspicion. The best dressed, and therefore the cleanest, were the most welcome. Without being exactly snobbish, my mother preferred clean, well-mannered children—perhaps because, poised between poverty and respectability, the slightest tip would be enough to undo all the work she had put out on me.

Jessie McAreavy never came to the house. She was a bit rough in her speech, untidy in her dress, but otherwise fairly presentable. The fact that she was Irish was slightly in her favour. My mother vaguely equated the Irish with Catholicism, and that, in turn, with an exotic and more intense devotion, which was all to the good. On the other hand, there was the question of gullibility, the tendency to believe and to tell all sorts of far-fetched ideas and legends. In fact, I never knew the McAreavys to go to any church at all, but the religious idea was firmly implanted in my mother's mind.

As soon as Jessie told me about the old man in her house, I knew that my mother would not believe it. I didn't believe it myself, but there was something so compelling, so matter of fact in the way Jessie told me, that for long periods I found myself quite sure that it was true.

More than one girl in my class at school had a grandfather living as one of the family, but this was not a grandfather or any relation. Nor was he living *with* them. He lived apart, above them;

59

not on the floor above (Jessie's house, like ours, was a tenement room and kitchen) but literally over their heads, high up in a hole in the wall.

I was never allowed into the house. When Jessie asked me up to play we used to sit on the landing with a few toys, dolls which she carried about by one leg, a compendium of games with various pieces missing, and some grubby books. She herself was not a great reader. I was the one who leafed through the annuals, until she refused to let me read any more because for all the company I was I might not have been there.

By this time, I didn't care. Jessie's stories were much more exciting.

It started one day when, bored with the landing, I asked if we couldn't go into the house.

"Oh no," she said, pursing her lips and shaking her head. "He might be angry."

"He?" In my mind, her mother, like all mothers, was the one to be placated.

"The old man."

"Your father?"

"No. The old man who lives in the wall."

"The wall?"

"Uh-huh. There's a hole in the wall, high up, and he lives in there. It's like a cave."

"But why?"

"Well, we've got to put him somewhere, haven't we?"

"Yes, but—" I made a hasty count of the McAreavy family, and realised that there was hardly room for them, let alone a lodger. "Doesn't he ever come down?"

"Oh no!" She looked horrified. "Of course, he might, some time, but so far he hasn't. Just as well! I don't know what would happen if he came down."

"Why? Is he—fierce?"

"Oh, he's fierce! He grumbles about, and mutters to himself, and sometimes he lets out a roar. And he throws bones down."

"*Bones?*"

"Aye, bones. Once he's chewed the meat off."

There was something very impressive in the way Jessie told her story, casually, making light of the constant fear. I waited a minute, then, rather timorously, I asked her, "Can I see him?"

The lips pursed again, her head shook. "Oh no! My mother would kill me!"

"Why? Is it a secret?"

"Yes. She doesn't want anybody to know. So you'll have to swear not to tell anybody. If you do, the man'll come down and get you."

"W-what's he like?"

She considered a moment. "Pink," she said. "He's got a pinky sort of skin, and long white hair, and a beard like Santa Claus. And he wears a long white shirt thing."

"Has he ever come down to you?"

"No." Her eyes were wide and frightened. "But you can never be sure. My wee brother's the one that's going to catch it some day. He throws balls up into the wall, and the old man keeps them."

"To play with?"

"*No*, stupid! To punish him. And because—" she lowered her voice, "he thinks Tommy might climb up one day, and then…!" She drew a finger across her throat. "See?"

I nodded. Sceptical as I was, there was a kind of logic in Jessie's story. I got up to go home, and Jessie held the door open a crack, slid in, and shut it smartly before I could even try to peer in.

I did not tell my mother. Apart from having promised not to, there were so many things of which she would not approve, my sitting on the cold landing, instead of inside the house, the danger inherent in having a man living in a hole like a wild beast, and those bones—she would condemn the bones both on hygienic grounds, and on the ground of manners.

I dreamed about the old man all night. I visualised the McAreavy kitchen as immensely high, with a cave situated cosily in the wall, above the pulley, something like our recess bed draped with ivy instead of curtains. I saw the old man (something like God, I imagined him), crouched over a fire toasting crusts, picking bones, and looking down on the day to day life of the McAreavys like a moving picture. In a way, it seemed a pleasant kind of life; I tried to project myself up to the ceiling to see how our kitchen would look, and I felt it would be quite nice to have a den like that, private and inaccessible; but there was also a horror about it; not the old man himself, who probably had plenty to resent and grow fierce about, but the secrecy, the sense of shame and secrecy which Jessie and no doubt the rest of the McAreavys seemed to feel.

Jessie behaved normally, however, in school and out of it, as if she didn't have such a dark domestic burden. It was only with me, perhaps because I couldn't keep off the subject, that she dropped tantalising titbits of information.

"I thought he was going to come down today. He rumbled the walls with a stick."

"What was he doing with a stick?"

"Sure, all old men have sticks."

A question which my mother would not have liked me to ask formed itself in my mind.

"What does he do about... you know? Does he use your lavatory?"

"*No.* Somebody might see him."

"Well...?"

"I suppose my dad sees to that," said Jessie primly.

Summer came, and what with skipping ropes and other outdoor ploys, I didn't see so much of Jessie. We tended to play round our own doors; but when the clock was changed, and we were back in our school routine, the old man cropped up again.

"He's not well," said Jessie, sidling up to me in the playground. "He was groaning all last night."

"What's wrong with him?"

"Dunno. He won't say."

"Have you had the doctor?"

"Oh no! We can't tell anyone!"

And so I was off again, more curious than ever.

"Who washes his clothes?"

"I suppose my mother does. But he doesn't need much, see? It's hot up there."

On another occasion she had a new development to report.

"I came in, and there was a rope hanging down the wall. He pulled it up quick when I came in."

"What did your mother say?"

"She said I imagined it."

I didn't think she'd imagined it; I thought she was making it up. But a week later she came out with something so shocking I felt myself shiver. Jessie herself looked pale as she stared at me, whispering in terror, and yet still with a strange kind of pride in her story.

"He's dead."

"Oh...!" I thought of all the fascinating complications, more imagined than understood. "Will there be a funeral?"

"No."

"But you've got to have a funeral when somebody dies."

"But we can't. Somebody might see. Nobody's supposed to know about it."

"Well... what are you going to do with him, then?"

"Dunno. Leave him there. Fill up the hole. Plaster it up."

The whole thing was becoming so ridiculous that from then on I lost interest, and this, I think, was what Jessie intended. The story had been fascinating, so far, but Jessie had got out of her depth, and had timed the old man's demise with some skill.

I didn't see so much of her after that. The glamour had gone. It revived some while later, when police called at her house, but Jessie was off school at the time, and when she came back I was solemnly warned not to ask about it. I had the feeling that my mother knew more than I did, and this irritated me, the knowledgeable whispering that went on round the doors, when *I* knew more than they could ever guess. At last, I let curiosity get the better of me. "Was it about the man?" I asked.

"What man?" said my mother, rather defensively.

"The McAreavys had a man living in a hole in the wall."

If Jessie's information had startled me, it was nothing to the effect it had on my mother. She put up her hand to her mouth in a stunned sort of way, and when she took her hand away her mouth stayed open.

"How do you know? Who told you?"

I guessed then that there was more to Jessie's old man than an exciting story. My mother made me tell her everything, every single word, and mixed with my shame at letting out a secret was an undeniable pride in having such a tale to tell. My father was made to listen to it all over again, and when I had finished he looked even more serious than my mother.

They tried to make light of it; and then, more to impress on me the dire nature of the secret I had told them than to satisfy my curiosity, they gave me a sketchy explanation.

"Jessie McAreavy had a brother who was a deserter from the Army. It's not for us to judge what happened, but the police, and the military police, thought he might have got to his mother's place to hide. That's what they were looking for; but they found nothing. So it was true, in a way. Only Jessie had embroidered it, you see. Or maybe her mother made her think it was an old man so that she wouldn't know the truth. Anyway, you don't need to say anything about it. It's all over now."

"I know. He's dead."

"Dead?" This was another bombshell. "Why didn't you—?"

"Well, you kept interrupting. Both of you."

They listened to me more carefully, then, and when I mentioned about the lack of a funeral, and the plastering up of the wall, my parents became more serious than ever. They conferred together, in whispers, and then they closed in on me and warned me never, *never*, on any account, to mention this to a soul. If I did, something dreadful would happen, maybe to me, but most certainly to the McAreavys. "We don't really *know*," said my father heavily. "And we don't shop our friends."

My mother also thought that it might be a good idea if I kept away from Jessie in the future. Look what happened, she implied, when you got mixed up with people like the McAreavys.

They all moved away after that, and I lost touch with them, and gradually the scandal, and the burden of my secret, grew less. As I grew older, I looked back on the saga of the old man with humour and affection. An old man with a beard! And even my father's suspicions about Jessie's brother were somewhat far-fetched. The McAreavys had no room to harbour a deserter, or anybody else.

So I thought; but when they modernised the High Street, and demolished the McAreavys' old house, they discovered a skeleton up in the loft. The loft door had been nailed down and plastered over...

But it was a long time ago.

OBLIGE ME WITH A LOAF

"**M**ummy," said Rosemary at bedtime, "what will happen to me when I die?"

It was asked without fear or apprehension, a perfectly normal and natural question, cheerfully curious. When at Rosemary's age Roger asked the same thing, I was ready with the routine and reassuring answer about heaven, and living happily ever after.

Now I am not so sure. Suppose the dead go neither back to remembered joys, nor forward to some better or happier place? Suppose they keep pace with the living, year after year?

All this has been on my mind since my visit to Herdford Place.

This little place is neither a street nor a square. The gaunt wall of a church blanks it off on one side, and on the other is a small row of shops. The Place itself is roughly triangular, and there we used to play all the traditional games that children no longer know because traffic has left no room for them. We bounced our balls against the church wall, and scored the pavements with chalk beds for peever, and the only interruption was the milkman's cart, or the baker's van, with a horse that consumed an inordinate amount of its master's sugar turnovers.

I lived just around the corner from Herdford Place. To me it was a pleasant play area. My mother thought of it as a shopping centre. There was a draper, an ironmonger, a fish shop, and a grocer; and all of them we patronised in turn.

Each shop had its own characteristics. The drapery was run by a stately old lady with a black velvet choker and hair pinned up in a beehive. For all its comforting smell of warm paraffin and calico, I dreaded going in. Miss Mattock was kind, but impatient with fidgety children, and I was a child who found it difficult to keep still for long.

The ironmonger's stocked nails and tacks and knives and saws, and the fishmonger's was always cold, full of slippery, gaping fish and golden kippers; but it was the grocer's that benefited most from our trade, for what it was worth. It was the kind of shop that you see nowadays in museums of Victoriana: big brown canisters on the shelves, bags of potatoes on the floor, corned beef hand-cut on marble slabs, and a cat asleep beside the fire. Everything was sold loose, weighed out in paper bags, and the bread wrapped in soft brown tissue; and the counter held brass scales, with the weights lined up in diminishing size, and polished with Brasso every morning.

It was a good shop. It kept good-quality biscuits, beautiful Belfast ham, and what my mother called "a good class of sweetie". Having made brief experimental forays into the Co-op, with prospects of cut prices and dividends, she always returned, in penitence, to Coulter's.

Mr Coulter was a thin man with glasses, and black hair brushed across a flat, narrow head; his wife was a stoutish woman who looked like a cook. He was brisk and dashing, always clashing knives and rattling tins and slapping things on to scales; she was leisured and ladylike, the scoop poised as she weighed out lentils and registered delight or horror according to the gossip her customers relayed.

Mr Coulter *looked* busier, doubly prepared for work in an overall with a long apron over it, tied in two places so that his back view looked like a piece of meat ready for roasting, but his wife was the brains of the business. She kept the accounts in a two-foot-wide area of counter fenced off with a fancy iron grille, and laid out with pen, ink, and pink blotting paper in a chocolate-box lid, and here my mother's black book was made up every week, and the payment rewarded with a cake of chocolate as discount.

After my marriage, I kept on dealing with Coulter's. The war, however, was too much for them. Rationing harassed, coupons confused them. Eventually, they decided to give up, and settled down to a quiet life that ended, for both of them, peaceably, and with modest but respectable funerals. The shop was taken over by a rather flashy firm selling cheap furniture, brass long boxes, Long John coffee tables with scenes from *Swan Lake*, and orange-shaped lamps glowing seductively in corners. They ran "clubs", women paying their shoddy purchases at so much a week, and I never once entered the place.

But last week... I tell you this reluctantly, because I can't explain it... last week something happened that you're not going to believe.

I discovered, just before teatime, that I had no bread, and it was Thursday, the half-shut day. Why hadn't I realised sooner? There was a chance that some of the smaller shops, which stayed open on shut day, might have some left, but I would have to hurry; so I threw on my coat, and ran out, only to find that they all had their shutters up; and how was I to get bread now, not only for tea, but for tomorrow's breakfast?

It was then that I found myself near Herdford Place, and the thought came into my head, "Of course! The Coulters!"

I could remember sometimes, on a Sunday afternoon, when unexpected visitors arrived, being sent out furtively to the house door for some cold ham, or a cake, or a tin of fruit; and when I apologised, as I was told to do, they always said, "Oh, that's all right. We don't like to see anybody stuck." Surely they wouldn't see me stuck now. They'd oblige me with a loaf, even if they had to take it from their own table.

The shop was open; at least, a dim light shone in the windows, on sweetie bottles and sweetie boxes tilted temptingly forwards. The curved corner window had Panshine and bathbrick and zebra-striped tins of grate polish, and another small window was built up with old-fashioned pyramids of tins and jamjars; but the goods looked dusty, the glass smeared, and I was sure that the last of the summer's flies lay in the crevices, rolled on their backs among dead wasps and a mouldy litter of crumbs.

It wasn't like the Coulters to let things go like that. Uneasily, I crossed the worn step and pressed the old black latch. The bell tinkled. There they were, as usual, behind the counter, Mr Coulter wrapped round in his apron, and his wife with her white hair, queenly and ready to "oblige" me. But they had aged. God, how they had aged! His hair was thin and frosted, his face peaked, with a large white wart on his brow, and she seemed to have shrunk, bowed and flat-footed and slow. Their smiles were slow, and there was a restraint in their welcome.

"Well, Betty! It's a long time since you were in. I thought you'd deserted us." The voice came faint and reproachful.

"Yes," I said, embarrassed. "I'm sorry. I always mean to come down, but I seem to be so rushed, and I just slip down to the High Street..."

"Aye, we've missed you," sighed Mrs Coulter. "They're all away, all the old customers…" Her husband joined in, mourning, and the lament sounded like the thin wail of midges.

"Oh, but I'll come back!" I was desperate to reassure them. "I've never been so well served anywhere." I remembered the biscuits, sold loose, the Abdine powders on cards, and the sound of rice pouring into stiff blue bags; but all the time I was seeing ruin, rotting potatoes on the floor, cobwebs in the corners, and verdigris on the brass scales and weights. Did they wait here, day after day, in the hope that someone would call? And what did they live on? Who nowadays wanted blacklead, and Sunlight soap, and Monkey Brand?

But they were still in business. The knife that cut the corned beef was greasy, and a bottle of Rosebuds stood beside the scales, the lid off, and the counter littered with gritty pink crumbles. I leaned on the counter, guiltily chatty, trying to make up for the years of neglect and the shock of seeing them so frail and wraith-like. There was something almost transparent about them, a dim dustiness like the mist of dust in the shop; and the more fervently I promised to come back, and bring them my weekly order, the more eager I was to get out.

They did not want me to go. A hand like a hen's claw reached out, and a damp cloth made weak circles on the counter. Mrs Coulter was getting ready for business; and her husband creaked into action too, resting his shaky hands on the counter, poised on trembling finger tips. Slowly, his head tilted to one side in what was meant to be a stance of alert expectation; they were waiting to serve me.

"A loaf?" I whispered. "Could you oblige me with a loaf?"

She nodded. "Just help yourself, Betty. You mind where they're kept?"

I remembered. Opposite the counter, to the right of the door to the back shop, was a deep wooden box in which the loaves, steaming fresh, were deposited by the cheery vanman. The box was full; but the loaf I lifted was green on the outside, and freckled with mould, and all the others were the same. They smelled rancid, like everything else about the shop. Reluctantly, I selected one, and carried in to the counter.

"I'm afraid this one—they're all the same..."

Mr Coulter didn't seem to notice. In a gallant attempt at speed he took up a double thickness of soft brown tissue and enveloped the mouldy loaf. As he bent over his work, I couldn't bear to watch the dreadful parcel he was preparing for me. I fixed my eyes on the thick white wart on his head, and tried not to feel sick.

Mrs Coulter dragged my attention away. "... haven't my teeth in yet," she lamented. Her lips sucked and lisped. "He never told me he was going to take them out. 'Just sit there, lassie,' he said, and he went over to a case and took out his nippers. I saw them in his hand, but I never dreamed... next thing he had my head back, an' all my teeth went flying. It was terrible. I sat there for half an hour, the flesh streaming over the side of my mouth..."

I gaped at her. "But no dentist..."

"It was the doctor. I was bloodless, that's what I went about. But you know Morrison, the first thing he always says is 'Clear the mouth!' But he's not qualified to take out teeth. I've to go back in three months..."

Dr Morrison had died years before.

Mr Coulter advanced the loaf in my direction, and I pretended not to see. The wart on his head had moved... It wasn't a wart. It was a maggot, crawling from his head; and as I looked, horrified, at his wife, to tell her, to ask her what—I saw a long worm tunnel up her nose. I turned to run, and a rat moved from under the counter and scuttered away in front of me.

The awful thing was that, even as I ran, too choked with fear to scream, I half turned to assure myself that I wasn't dreaming; and the Coulters were still there, waving, their lips curling dreadfully into smiles, grateful in the midst of their decay that someone had come to visit them. The door juddered as I banged it shut, and I almost cannoned into a circle of little girls playing under a streetlamp.

> "Water, water wellflower,
> Growing up so high,
> We are all maidens,
> And we must all die..."

I hoped to God they had no pennies to spend in Coulter's. The window was greasy and green with gaslight, and all the other shops were shut. Half-sobbing, I burst into the High Street, where the pink fluorescents were flowering and flickering into brightness, and suddenly I remembered that the family would be in, the table not set, the kettle empty. That was when I pulled myself together and forced myself to walk, not run, home.

"Sorry," I said, when I arrived, far too bright and jovial. "I had to go and look for bread, and the shops are all shut."

"Where d'you get it, then?" asked my husband, without much interest.

"I didn't. The shops were shut. I needn't have bothered."

"Oh, really!" they all joined in, hungry and fed up. "What about the tea, then? Couldn't you make chips? I'm starving!"

I was glad to get into the kitchen, to think things over as I peeled the potatoes. I had seen, I had spoken to the Coulters, and yet there were no such people, there was no such shop; only the furniture store, enlarged, unrecognisable as the old shop it had supplanted. I had no doubt that if I went back tomorrow I would see the coffee tables, the plastic pouffes, and the framed, obligatory forest scenes on the walls.

That was why there was no point in saying anything about my experience. I had no proof. I hadn't lifted the loaf. If I had done, heaven knows what new complications might have arisen, paying— what was it?—3½d? Or would she have "marked it up", leaving me with an eternal debt in some small black book?

Nobody would believe me; and could you blame them? But it happened. I had seen and spoken to two old people, ageing patiently, long after death. And this is what frightens me: it could happen again. Some day, given the right circumstances, I might come on the fish shop, its wares putrefying into sea-slime; or the ironmonger's, all rust and dust; or the draper's—Miss Mattock was old, even when I was a child, only whalebone and a high collar keeping her erect. I don't want to know what she looks like now.

But what really worries me is what will happen to me, to Andrew and the rest of us. Parents grow old, and children grow impatient. If, years and years later, long after the funeral, Roger and Rosemary have to contend with us... I don't want to see the look on their faces; and I don't like to think of *them* going on and on...

So what do I tell Rosemary?

THE HEAD

he joug, the iron collar of penitence, was fastened to the church wall, four feet from the ground. It was too low for a tall man. He could neither stand nor sit, nor even lean in comfort. The gaolers forced him down by the shoulders, and the two semicircles of iron, cold and heavy, were padlocked round his throat. Then, half squatting, cramped already, he was left to the mob.

The first missile struck him—a wet cloth, which had soaked all night in the kennel. Its stinking folds wrapped him for a moment—as he jerked it off, the iron collar bit into his neck. An old woman, yattering and mumbling like a witch, emptied a pan of slops over his clothes, and he bit his tongue as he tried to duck from a clod of turf. They threw anything, anything which could soil or hurt him, stones, rotten food, and dirty water, till at last he sagged and nearly fainted; then they left him, for there was no fun to be had from a man who could no longer feel.

The sun was beating on to him, and he could not turn his eyes away. Above him, the steeple soared naked in the glare, and somewhere, behind him, a shadow steeple lay bent and prostrate on the roadway, and halfway up the opposite wall. The street was empty, the uneven roofs climbing like steps and stairs, up and up in a jumble of gables and chimney pots. Round his feet was a mass of filth and offal, and his clothing stank with what had dried on him. He eased his neck, and tried to move his legs to support himself more easily. At least, the crowd had gone; now there was the rest of the day to be borne, with the pain of his cramped body and bleeding face. He would have to endure the long burning hours till evening came, when they would free him, and he could stretch his legs, and maybe bathe his wounds and bruises before he crept home.

He did not turn his eyes when he heard the clop of hooves from the Westport, or the sound of a crowd following. Better to wait, and not anticipate what was to come. He closed his eyes, as the noise came nearer, the steps beating about him, the voices indistinct in their gabble. Then the man on horseback roused him with a deep, jovial hail.

"Hey, there, thief! Here's one to keep you company. Here's a friend for ye!" He edged his horse nearer to the wall, and unwrapped a stained, stiff sacking which rested on the saddle. The thief looked dumbly, his eyes screwed against the light. Inside the wrapping was a human head, hacked off raggedly, the eyes wide open, like grapes ready to burst.

He said nothing. He only stared at the head, and the man on the horse laughed roughly. "English," he said. "We'll see how he likes the view of Scotland frae the top o' the kirk. We'll keep him nearer the ground for the first day, though. The town will mebbe want to see him a bittie clearer."

The crowds were clamouring round the horse, pushing one another for a near view of the horror. The rider cursed, and cleared a path with his powerful voice. "Out the way, there, out the way! Plenty of room for you all!" He was in a high, roaring humour, aloft in the saddle, pleased to be the centre of attention. It was a long time since the town had had such a trophy, and he made the most of his position, playing with the head, delaying the moment when he would display it fully.

At the cross, just in front of the joug and pillory, was an iron spike, a little taller than a man. It was here that the heads or limbs of traitors and enemies were hoisted for public scorn, before being removed to a higher and more exalted position. Once there had been a leg, once a hand, which beckoned to the sky with a bent finger. Now the man on the horse cast away the bloodied sack, and held up the head like an offering. He hesitated. There seemed to be some doubt as to the best way of securing it; then, not wishing to show any inefficiency, he jabbed the neck stump on to the spike, and left it impaled.

The crowd soon tired of the curiosity, sooner than they had tired of baiting the man in the joug. They came to stare, bringing their children, and pointing upwards at the gory thing. Soon, however, they drifted away. There were more pleasant places to spend a summer afternoon, more pleasant things to see. The thief was left alone again, with the street bare and empty before him, and the shadow steeple soon veering round again with the sun.

A curtain lifted in a window near the church, and a face peered out, milky white against the pane. All the other houses seemed dead, shut up against the dust and the glare. He was a tenant of an empty town, with only the head to keep him company. He could not keep his eyes from it. Looking at it now, in the harsh sunlight, he saw it more clearly than in the quick glimpse he had had before it was hoisted. It was not a young head. The hair on top, standing up like rushes, was grey, and the skin was bristly and pale, bled white. The mouth was open in surprise, a black slit, the eyes dull and bulging. He wondered how the man had died. Perhaps he had gasped and grimaced as a sword entered his body; certainly, he had not been beheaded in one swift blow. The neck was too ragged, too mangled, the bungled effort of one with more zeal than aptitude.

An Englishman; an enemy. And here they were, side by side, held up to ridicule in the same town. A crow flapped a ragged wing over the church, wheeled, dipped, and circled nearer. It swooped near the head, its beak poised to peck, and the man in the joug called hoarsely, his voice not unlike the voice of the crow. The bird veered off, and again the curtain moved in the house near the church, and a woman's face glanced and retreated quickly. The man could not turn his head to see properly, but he sensed the furtive interest, the curiosity, the disgust, and perhaps the pity. He wanted to think about her, to dream of her, cool in her clean house, calm and kind and feminine; but his mind would not obey him. His interest was all bound up in the head.

He had, for a moment, been afraid for it, afraid lest the crow should strike, and pierce the grape-coloured eyes, or batter its beak on the bony skull. It became very urgent to him that the head should be protected, horrible as it was. It was like a friend to him, goggling with its startled stare, quiet and unmoving in its sufferings. He was so absorbed in it that he forgot his own pain, the numbing crick in his back, the stiff agony of bending legs. His eyes no longer sought the broad sweeping street, or the sun-mellowed jumble of gables. He could see no farther than the head, stuck on its spike. Tomorrow, it would rot high among the gargoyles; today, he prayed, it would be left unmolested. Surely the birds would have pity for one day!

And then the fly came, a large bluebottle, buzzing a stale, flat song in the heat. "Not on me!" he prayed. "Not on me!" Tethered, unable to move, it would have tortured him to screaming. But the fly only circled and droned, then made straight for the severed head. It settled, buzzed, and returned, settling on the bruised brow. The man watched it, fascinated. It began to creep, slowly, slowly, faltering over every blemish, darting in black, swift rushes, flying off in short circles to creep and creep again. The man flexed his face in sympathy, following the insect's progress with agony. It halted for a long time on an eyelid, poised like a plump currant, then crawled across the bulged eyeball. The man's eyes winked and watered, the fly teased him, hovering on the brink of every aperture, flying off, buzzing madly, but always returning; always, always returning.

The sun shifted, the shadow steeple veered another point. The man did not notice. His back, his legs, his chafed wrists were all forgotten. All his feelings were centred in his face, and his face twitched and contorted with the borrowed agonies of the face opposite. The black fly went creeping, creeping over a lip, into the black pit of the mouth, and the man spat, his tongue dry, like leather. The fly explored a nostril, and he sneezed till the iron cut into his neck again. It ran along a bloodstain into the ear, and he suffered till it trailed out again, creeping, creeping in sudden darts and pauses. He wept aloud. Sweat ran down his face, and he closed his eyes, so that he would not see; but always he had to look again, because his imagination teased him with the buzz and creep and the horrible fancies of his mind.

He was surprised when they came to set him free. He had forgotten that, sometime, he would be allowed to go. The keys jingled, the collar swung back in two halves. "Hey, steady!" said the gaoler, not unkindly. He walked off, swinging his keys, and the man staggered, and sank to the ground. His legs were too cramped to hold him, and his neck swelled so that he thought it would choke.

The shadow of the steeple was in front of the church now, the sun soft and red. Smoke drifted above the roofs, the quiet haze of fires in summer. The house by the church opened its door, and the woman came out at last, hastily, as if half ashamed of her mercy. She had a basin in her hand, and warm water, and a square of soft white cloth. "Here," she said quickly, "bathe your poor face before you go home. Leave the basin and I'll take it in when you've finished. You'll manage yourself?"

He nodded, too spent to thank her, or to watch her hurry away. He lay for a long time before he could move. At last he dragged himself erect, and bent to the basin. The water was cool now, fresh and cool and soothing. He lifted the cloth, dripping wet over his soiled hand. Slowly and stiffly he limped over to the spike, muttering to himself, "There, there," hardly knowing what he was saying. His dry lips cracked in a smile as, with fumbling, gentle fingers, he wiped the face of the dead.

SCOTS WHA HA'E

he lay awake in the darkness, hearing the town clock strike two. Something had jerked her out of sleep, leaving her skin scalded with fright. Her heartbeat was a little thrilling tick inside her, and her ears strained, listening to the remembered echo of the clock. It was a distant chime, not loud enough to have wakened her. What was it, then, that had stung her out of sleep?

Pushing back the blankets, she tiptoed to the bedroom door and listened. Stephanie was sound asleep, her side rising and falling gently, like a kitten's. She looked too peaceful to have cried out; and yet there had been *some* sound, thought her mother, loud enough to break a dream and set her nerves jumping.

She wasn't usually nervous. She was used to Eric being away all night. He worked nightshift every second week, leaving the house at half past nine with his flask and piece-box and his peaked hat with "SECURITY" printed on the band. He was at the new industrial estate on the outskirts of the town, transferred north from the Midlands. It had been a good move. At home, his name had been on the Council housing list for five years. "You've only one child, you see," they told him, when he protested about the length of time they'd had to wait; but he and Brenda refused to have any more kids until they had a decent home to give them.

They couldn't believe their luck when they were told that a house went with the job in Scotland; nor could they believe their luck when they saw the house. "You're lucky, son," his boss told him, as he handed over the keys. "You've got one down by the old castle. Half the folk would give their ears for one of those. They're old property, you see, gutted and rebuilt inside; bathrooms, central heating, the lot. We've even got people trying to buy them."

Castle Wynd was steep, clean and quiet, with cobbled corners and little gardens fronting the pavement. The houses were all different in style and level, and at the bottom, where the road dipped more steeply, they diminished to low, whitewashed cottages, which seemed to lie humbly in the very shadow of the castle. There was nothing left now but a low mound guarded by a broken wall; but the atmosphere remained, medieval, picturesque and feudal, as if the old nobles still dominated the land and its vassals.

Brenda looked round the room, the furniture half visible through the greyness. Something kept her from settling back to sleep; a flicker of light through the thick curtains...? No; that was imagination. It was the same noise which must have wakened her, someone banging a dustbin lid, or hitting with a stick on a piece of metal.

She lay still, puzzled and annoyed. A quarter past two! Nobody had any business to make such a racket at this time of night. It couldn't be any of the neighbours, surely. The noise was right out in the street, a whole crowd of people now, clanging and tramping and shouting. She couldn't make out what they were saying, but they sounded young and angry. Youths, probably; gangs with nothing better to do.

Prudence made her lie still. From her experience of this sort of thing in the city, it was better not to look, and certainly better not to be seen looking. It's a shame, though, she thought, that this sort of thing goes on even in a quiet little town.

The noise and scuffling came to a peak, passed the house, and went on down the hill. She heard it vaguely and intermittently till she fell asleep again; and next morning she could hardly believe it had happened; but later on she heard that one of the cottages had been disfigured by a splash of paint thrown at the gable, dark, reddish brown paint over the white wall and the neat cemented cobbles; and though the neighbours were shocked and indignant, none of them, oddly, had heard a thing.

"You'll be all right, then?" said Eric, next evening, "If you've any trouble, phone the police. And don't worry. I'll be home at the weekend."

The next two nights were quiet, though she wakened, or dreamed that she wakened, without knowing why. It was on Friday, the night before Eric's change of shift, that something happened.

It wasn't late—not really late, only about half past eleven, and Brenda had just finished putting rollers in her hair. The knock at the door was quiet but quick, and for a moment she wondered why whoever it was hadn't rung the bell. Then she thought, "Maybe they think I'm in bed. The living-room light's out." She tied a scarf round her head, went to the door, and opened it carefully.

It was a young girl, thin and frightened and terribly out of breath. She looked as if she had thrown a tartan rug over her white nightdress and run desperately into the street. She couldn't speak, and Brenda, looking quickly up and down the road, drew her in and shut the door.

The girl stood in the lobby and shivered. "In here," said Brenda, opening the living-room door and leading her over to the fire. "What's wrong? Are you in trouble of some kind?"

The girl didn't answer. She was dark and pretty, but so frightened that her breath caught painfully, like hiccups. Horrified, Brenda saw that she had nothing on her feet. "You'll catch your death of cold," she said, pushing her into a chair and stirring up what was left of the fire. "Look, let me give you something to warm you up. I'll heat some milk—"

"No," said the girl, cowering back; and when Brenda came with the milk, she wouldn't touch it. Her hands clutched the arms of the chair, and she shuddered.

"Oh God," thought Brenda, "why do these things happen when Eric's not here?" She didn't know what to do. Give the girl a shake-down on the couch? But it looked as if the girl was too frightened to stay. She kept eyeing the door like a cat ready to make a dart for it; and at that moment Stephanie came in, half sleeping.

"What is it, Mummy? I thought you were crying."

"It's all right, dear. This lady came in, and—"

The girl moved across the room, quickly, looking over her shoulder. She seemed so desperate that Brenda knew she couldn't keep her. "Let me give you a pair of slippers," she said.

"No!" The answer came like a scream, and Brenda thought she heard something like "English swine..." But it couldn't have been that; it couldn't possibly. She gave a little shrug, and turned to Stephanie.

"Mummy, what did the lady want?"

"I don't know, dear. She's very upset about something. Come on now, back to bed. Time you were sleeping."

"Well, I was. It was the smoke that wakened me; the smoke, and sparks coming in the window."

"Smoke? You must have been dreaming, dear. There's nothing like that here."

"No. I thought there was a house on fire." She yawned. "But I'd have heard the engines, wouldn't I?"

"Yes." Brenda, tucking her up, knew that there was nothing burning in the street; but that strange and terrified girl looked as if she had been running away from a fire...

It was better at the weekend. Eric brought Shane, his Alsatian guard dog, home with him, and between the dog and her husband Brenda felt safer; only, Shane growled a lot, and woke them up snuffling at the door, and Eric kept heaving up in bed and hissing, "Lie down, Shane!" He grumbled all through breakfast. "For God's sake, I get more peace on the job!"

And then, one of the Security men went off sick, and Eric had to do another stint of nightshift. "You won't mind, will you?" he said. "You'll be all right. I think you're a bit like Shane. Half of your trouble is imagination."

"I didn't imagine that terrified girl knocking at the door. Stephanie will prove that."

"Well, don't open it again. Don't open it to anybody."

As soon as she was alone, it started again, the howling and clashing and tramping of feet. She lay quaking, the old scalding terror on her, till it passed; then there were solitary footsteps coming up, quick but dragging; a thud at the door, and silence.

I won't go, she thought. They've thrown something, that's all. They know Eric's at work. But she couldn't settle till she knew, once and for all, what had caused that thud. Quietly, so as not to waken Stephanie, she put on her dressing-gown and opened the door cautiously.

Something was leaning against it. As she opened it wider, a heavy weight slumped inwards, and a man, haggard and bloody, lay at her feet.

She put her hands to her mouth so as not to scream; but the man was not wounded, only exhausted, and the blood was not his. Not the worst of it, anyway. What covered him and his clothes had come from somebody else. He got to his feet, looked at her blankly, and muttered, "I've killed him," and something else she didn't catch, something wild and desperate about "Mairn".

"Who—who have you killed?" she whispered, keeping her voice down for Stephanie's sake. She didn't want Stephanie to come through this time; but... it was not only concern for the child. This time, she wasn't going to tell Eric. He would get on to her for opening the door again—strange, how she always seemed to open it to trouble; but even that was not the real reason. This man... there was something desperate about him, blood on his hands and anger on his brow, but oddly, she was not afraid of him. She spoke again, more distinctly.

"Do you want to tell me about it?"

He looked up sharply, his hand making lost, groping movements as if he were searching for something. "You're English?" he said.

"Yes."

He glared at her, raised his hand as if to strike her, and then he stumbled out into the darkness. Shaking, Brenda went to the telephone and called the police. She'd had enough. She sat up till they came, nosing about and asking questions, and even then she didn't go to bed. She waited till Eric arrived with Shane; and Shane licked up something in the lobby, a nauseating brown patch something like the blood that had splashed the cottage wall. It *must* have been blood. She remembered the comments of the neighbours, "Yon was never paint. It washes off ower easy."

That was the end of it. There was peace at nights after that, and gradually Brenda settled down and forgot the first uneasy weeks in Castle Wynd. It wasn't till a year or two later that it all came back to her again in a terrible rush of recognition.

Stephanie had moved into a new class at school, and was flicking over the books she had brought home to be covered. Suddenly she looked up, pointing to a half-page illustration.

"Look, Mummy, there's the woman that came to see us that time, in her nightie."

"Eh?" Brenda looked, and caught her breath. That was her, thin, pretty—"Marion Braidfute," it said underneath. "Wife of Sir William Wallace..."

"It can't be," she said. "That was away back in twelve hundred and something. It's like her, though. Remarkably like her."

"We were getting about her in school," said Stephanie. "The teacher said I was lucky to live in the same street as Wallace. And do you know what, Mummy? The soldiers killed his wife, and burned down his house, and Wallace was so angry he gathered an army and marched down past this very door to the castle where the English were, and killed the governor in his bed. He left the sword sticking in his body," she said with relish. "And—and Mummy, I didn't want to stick up for the English, because I think Wallace was brave."

"Yes," said Brenda. The memory of those strange nights washed over her again, mingled with awe and disbelief and horror: the young girl fleeing for her life, the smell of fire, and Sir William Wallace himself—it must have been Wallace, fresh from his revenge, groping for the sword he had left in Haselrigg's body, the sword he might have used on her. "You're English?" he had said, recognising her speech, as his wife had done, and hating her for it...

Strange how it hurt, the unjustified hatred of a ghost! And strange how she hoped now for his return, so that she could explain... But that was daft. She blinked, and forced herself to answer Stephanie. "Yes," she said, "he was brave." And very softly, so softly that Stephanie didn't hear, "If I was a man, I'd have followed him myself."

GAS

he electric fire glowed dull in the brilliant sunshine. It had been switched on when Katherine arrived, and its dim red had not yet taken the chill off the air.

Katherine felt tired and cold. It was only nine o'clock. The dentist entered silently, smiled, breathing an antiseptic welcome. "Will you come now, Miss Lovegrove? Pleasant morning, isn't it?"

She smiled stiffly, her face numb. The dentist seemed to be looking forward to his task. "You've had nothing? Quite correct. You'll find gas much more pleasant, Miss Lovegrove, much more pleasant. Just relax—*that's* it—"

As he had promised, she felt nothing. She woke to the taste of scent in her mouth, and was surprised to find herself spewing pink mouthwash. The dentist's voice was gentle, like the hiss of the gas. "Rinse well, Miss Lovegrove. Not so very bad, was it, now?"

"No." She spoke awkwardly, spilling blood and pink water. Her tongue curled back into the deep black pits of her gum. "I didn't feel a thing."

"Spit now," urged the dentist.

She spat.

He bowed her out with antiseptic heartiness. "Just keep your mouth well covered, Miss Lovegrove, and try not to probe the cavity with your tongue. Yes, I know, a great temptation, but try to keep off. You'll be all right now, Miss Lovegrove?"

"Yes, thanks." Her voice was muffled in her striped wool scarf.

When she got outside, she spat a red gob into the gutter.

She still felt a little dizzy. The wind blew, and the sun was silver. The roads were dappled with snow, but there was a bright mildness in the air. At the corner of the street she met the priest, with his spectacles, his black hat, and his artificial hand. He stopped to talk, having visited her through the week.

"Good morning, Miss Lovegrove. You've been to the dentist, I see."

"Yes, father."

"How many?" He could not resist the question.

"Two. With gas."

She wanted to spit, but swallowed instead.

"Ah, yes. Well, my child, you must hurry home and not stand here talking. Cold is a dangerous thing, you know."

She left him, hating him for having made her stop and swallow. Her mouth was stiff, but not sore. She thought of the fire at home, banked with two briquettes, and she thought of the unwashed dishes. She came to a road which branched off downhill, beginning with cottages and ending between hedges, and the sun, the wind, and the spring washed away her sense of duty. She wanted to explore, to walk, not as a paid companion to her invalid aunt, but as an individual with life in her. Ten days of her aunt, ten days of toothache. They were the same thing. She set off down the road with the feeling that she could walk and walk for ever, and yet she was tired, and her head seemed to be swimming. Perhaps the fresh air would clear away the effects of the gas. She had heard of people being sick after it, but she felt fine. She would walk and walk—

There was pink gravel underfoot, with an odd glaring patch of snow at the roadside. The hedges were electric with life, tight pink buds swelling on the hawthorn twigs. There were cows in the field, licking the stiff short grass with mournful tongues. Katherine smiled, and shifted her scarf a little. The wool was damp at her lips.

The road dipped downhill, and a stream from the high meadows splashed into a stone trough. Where the trough overflowed was moss, green and sodden, and the clear arc of the water was like graven glass. She was thirsty, and there was a bad clotted taste in her mouth. She dipped her hand under the cascade and sipped with one side of her mouth. The water tasted like frost. Hastily, guiltily, she muffled herself again. The road was steeper now, between high banks. The roots of the trees were above her head, the grey, turnip-smooth roots of beech trees, and the marled branches of ash, dotted with buds like black pastel marks.

When the fields flattened out again there was a cottage and a bridge. Katherine passed the cottage for the greater delight of leaning on grey stone to watch a stream. The little river was broad with spring floods, and rushed by with a crest of cream froth. The edges lapped more gently, against a crust of snow melting grey-white like candle-grease. Trees leaned and interlaced level with her eyes, just out of reach. All the branches were hazed and netted with buds pushing to the strengthening sun, but cold air rose from the river, cold as the snow that was still thick on the hills. She turned away to look over the other side of the bridge; now the river was running away from her, towards a big house with two gaunt slated towers. A twinge of pain shot through her mouth, and her tongue touched the jellied gap. Two teeth together; it was a big space. She turned back, half tired, half dizzy again.

And now she had time again to see the cottage. It was white-washed and low, insignificant beside the incredible amount of ramshackle outhouses all round it. Some of them were mere collections of planks, green and grey, showing through the spaces old red flowerpots, rusty saws, and broken spades and axes. At the hedge, just beyond the gate, a short, rheumatic little man was poking around in the ditch. He turned round, and his pipe sent a cloud of almost royal blue smoke ripping away on the wind.

"Mornin'."

"Good morning," mumbled Katherine.

"You been to the dentist?"

She nodded.

"You're gey white lookin'," he said, peering at her. "Have ye far to go?"

"Into town."

"Well—"

"I wanted to go for a walk. I felt all right when I was going home, and I wanted to get into the fresh air."

"Aye."

She turned away to spit. "I think I'd better be going. My aunt will be waiting."

"Aye?"

"Aye—I mean, yes. I'm her companion. I don't like her very much, though. She'll be annoyed at me for being away so long." She liked this old man, and wanted to tell him all about the annoyances of her life.

He pushed back his cap and peered at her again.

"You'd better come in and have some tea. It'll do you good."

"Oh, I couldn't trouble you like that. Besides, I shouldn't be here at all. My aunt needs somebody with her, you know, but she let me off to go to the dentist. I haven't even tidied the house yet, and she won't bother herself to help."

"Never heed your aunt. You'd be the better o' a hot drink. You were daft to walk all that way."

"Well—all right."

The cottage was clean, but smelt earthy, like the old man himself. He was awkward in the house, taking tea out of what seemed to be a flowerpot on the mantelshelf, and spurting water from the shiny kettle. "Do you live by yourself?" asked Katherine.

"No. The wife's away up town for the pension."

"I see." She took the tea out of a pretty blue cup that had been imperfectly rinsed under the tap. She did not want to offend the old man, and the tea was refreshing. She felt again that she was strong and ready for anything. A strange idea came to her. She would leave her aunt and just walk away. There would always be people ready to feed her, ready to give her odd cups of tea. Even if that made her a tramp—time enough to think of that when winter came. Then she roused herself from the dark brown dream of the old man's kitchen. Of course she must go back; but not just yet. The man was watching her.

"Would ye like to see my dulcimers?"

"Dulcimers?" she said lazily.

"Aye. I make them."

He led her through a door at the back of the kitchen, into one of the outhouses. Green damp growths sprouted from the earth floor, and a pleasant mouldy smell came from old earthenware pots and broken garden furniture. Light came in through a cracked window, and through spaces in the rotting planks, bright stripes of gold and sepia moted with dust flecks.

"I sleep here in the summer," said the old man. "It's cooler."

93

"I believe that," said Katherine. "Isn't it damp, though?"

"Aye, but I sleep in the house when it's damp. There's snow-drops outside. I'll give you some afterwards."

"Where's your dulcimers?" asked Katherine.

"Here." He hauled a huge box from under the table, and opened it. He raised the lid, and lifted out an assortment of triangular flat things, which seemed to be made out of orange boxes, studded with brass headed nails, and laced about with some kind of horsehair stuff. Some of the dulcimers had a red border painted on them, and these were seemingly the best attempts, which the man handled lovingly.

"The earlier ones are a bit off tune. Aye, it's hard to get them right. The red ones are best. Would ye like a tune?"

"Well—"

"I'll play 'Rock of Ages.'"

He strummed and rattled away, and the strings whined and twanged tonelessly. The rhythm wasn't right, either, but Katherine nodded, and said it was very nice. He played several tunes after this, and the draught ruffled the leaves of the potted plants and stirred the loose mould on the table. Katherine wished he would stop. She wanted to giggle, and she wanted to spit. At last the man packed away his dulcimers, sighed happily, and looked at the cobwebs curtaining the edges of the sunbeam.

"Well, I'll need to get back to my work."

He shifted his cap, and looked at her for permission.

She moved towards the door and walked along the path which was steaming like hot bread. The old man, without a word, went to the ditch and started his task again, plunging something among the tangled weeds.

"What are you doing?" she asked.

"Cleaning the ditch." He lifted out a kind of scoop filled with mud and leaves and stones and waxy snow. She heard the faint treble of water, and the tinkle and drip of diminishing ice.

"Is that your job?" she asked.

"Aye, that an' seein' to the hedges. I'm a hedger an' ditcher."

"Oh." Katherine watched him raking and scooping. She wanted to watch him all day. Pulling her scarf down a little, for it was chafing her chin, she did her best to keep the conversation going a little longer.

"What's that big house by the river?"

The wind carried a smell of earth and tobacco from him as he answered.

"Yonder? Yon's the asylum."

"Eh?"

"Aye. You new here?"

"Yes, I've been here just over a week."

"Aye. Well, that's the asylum. A fine place."

She was feeling very much better now, and ventured to joke a little.

"You seem to know all about it."

"Aye." He stirred the rubbish from the ditch with his foot. "I used to live there."

"Working there?"

"No, livin' there; in the madhouse." He braced his stiff shoulders, and pride straightened his spine.

"You—you were discharged, though?"

"Aye; discharged incurable."

Katherine's inquisitive tongue rambled on.

"But—"

"That's how I got this job. All them as are discharged incurable get a job as hedger an' ditcher. The asylum's famous for hedgers an' ditchers."

"Are there many?"

"Och aye. It's no' a good asylum for curin' folk, but it turns out rare hedgers an' ditchers. There's about a hunner in the county."

"All mad? All the hedgers and ditchers in the county are mad?"

"Aye."

"But why?"

"Because the asylum canna cure them."

"But—you're not mad," said Katherine, not knowing whether she believed it or not. She was not yet frightened, but the conversation was getting very deep, and the incurably mad are easily offended.

"Have it your own way," said the old fellow magnanimously, "but wait till next summer. You'll see."

She muffled her mouth, but listened, curious.

"It's a conspiracy. We're goin' to grow thistles in the ditches."

"Thistles?" said Katherine. She did not want to stay much longer, but she had to find out this mystery.

"Aye. We're goin' to plant thistles as thick as hedges. Then we'll cut down the old hedges, an' put ditches in their place. I'm tellin' you, it's a great plan! Every hedger an' ditcher in the county's on to it; an' when that's over, when that's over—over—"

"What?" she said. His voice was fading.

"That's over!" It was queerly loud and reassuring, close to her ear. The cold spring landscape cracked across, all but the patch of snow at the ditch, which stayed like fluffed cotton wool. It *was* cotton wool; she wiped her lips with it.

"That's over," said the dentist. "Not too bad, was it?"

"I was dreaming," she said awkwardly, rinsing her mouth with pink mouthwash. "I thought I had gone, and was walking down a road."

The dentist smiled indulgently. "Yes, that must have been the gas. Not so very bad, was it now? Just spit, Miss Lovegrove."

She spat.

She wrapped herself up, and tried to curb her morbidly exploring tongue. Outside, she spat a red gob into the gutter. The wind blew, and the sun was silver. The roads were dappled with snow. At the corner of the street she met the priest, with his spectacles, his black hat, and his artificial hand.

BARLEYRIGGS

We've been house hunting all day. Vincent has been given a new area to cover—the boss says he thinks it's time the firm broke new ground—so we're going to settle down in Scotland. I must say I'm quite looking forward to it. We could do with a bigger house anyway. Jean and Roger are still young enough—technically—to share a bedroom, but the way they carry on they'd both be better for a den of their own. Then there's the question of friends and relations. Once we move, they'll all be looking for holidays in Scotland! It's a good time to make a break, before the children get too involved at school, and Vince and I are both enjoying our forays over the Border. Luckily, the firm gave us time off, and a good removal allowance.

MAY 14TH

It isn't so easy as we expected. We've looked everywhere in the area, but there just isn't a decent-sized house for sale; one or two new bungalows, but at the most they run to three tiny bedrooms, and the living-room's crammed with only a TV set and a three-piece suite. Not the thing at all for growing children.

MAY 17TH

Got a note from Rankine the lawyer today. He says there's a house on the market called Barleyriggs. It's going remarkably cheaply. Probably too big for most folk, and a bit remote; but, he says, if we'd like to make an appointment to see it...

MAY 20TH

It's *exactly* what we want! It *is* big, it *is* remote, and I've a feeling we'll have to spend quite a lot to make it habitable, but never mind. At the price they're asking, it's a gift; and with what's left over from the sale of our own house, we'll be able to spend quite a bit. I'm not keen on all the upheaval, mind, but if we start now we can have it done before winter; and I'd rather have Barleyriggs than a staid terrace house with no personality at all.

JUNE 14TH

We finished the formalities today. I've a feeling that Rankine looked relieved. I can't say I blame him. Vincent had the house checked from top to bottom, and asked so many questions, even after the report came in, that I was beginning to feel embarrassed. I wanted to butt in and say, "Oh, look, Vince, can't we just sign and be done with it?" but I have a very careful husband. He feels that if the house is going at what Rankine calls a bargain price there must be something wrong with it. I'm so taken with the place that if there are snags, I don't want to know; but of course, I'm not business-like. Perhaps it's better that one of us should keep both feet on the ground.

Now I can start packing and getting ready. We're not going to rush things. We'll tackle one room at a time, and make up our mind about things as we go along.

JULY 2ND

It's happened at last! We've moved into Barleyriggs, and I'm writing this letter before I put out the light and call it a day. I'm so tired I'm beginning to twitch. Vincent has been camping here for two days while I organised things at our end. We got the carpets down, in the rooms we've carpets for, and the beds are up, but all we've unpacked are the necessities.

Jean and Roger, thank goodness, just keeled over after tea, and we put them to bed without washing. I didn't hear any complaints! Skidlum, though, is pretty unsettled. He keeps whimpering about and looking for all the familiar things. I thought it was cats who were attached to houses. Still, he's only a pup, and he'll soon grow to like his new home.

JULY 16TH

Things are looking quite reasonable now. We've got a milkman, a butcher and a grocer. We didn't have to do anything about it. They just arrived, and introduced themselves very civilly and pleasantly. You'd think that our arrival was an event. They all asked the same questions, whether we wouldn't be nervous with no near neighbours, and so on. I assured them we wouldn't be; but I've a feeling that when I'm not so busy (if I ever get to that stage!), and when Jean and Roger are at school, I'll be pretty glad of vans calling to break up the day.

JULY 21ST

Life is getting positively hectic. As well as the grocer and the milkman, we'd a visit from a man in a small red van. He said he'd called about the gas fire. I told him we didn't have one. That was his chance to make a sale, if he'd been quick enough, but he only looked at his list and muttered something and left. Oh well, maybe that wasn't his job.

AUGUST 30TH

I know now why they call it Barleyriggs. The fields around us are all a silky cream colour, and they hiss when the wind strikes them. I'll be sorry to see it all cut down. There's a nip in the air now, morning and evening, and we've loaded up the shed with logs. I'm looking forward to having fires all over the house.

OCTOBER 30TH

This is a very intermittent diary! I thought I'd have more time, with Jean away most of the day, but I seem to be busier than ever.

One snag about this house is that it's terribly difficult to keep warm. I take back what I said about having fires all over the house! It's a full-time job keeping them going, and even then they're not all that efficient. Vincent keeps muttering about central heating, but it seems daft to go through all that upset when we've just finished decorating. Still, it would be a lot more comfortable.

NOVEMBER 8TH

We've decided on storage heaters; not too difficult to instal, and no stoking. Just the thing.

NOVEMBER 12TH

Heard Skidlum barking hysterically at the gate. A red van with GAS on it was parked outside. Before I could call Skidlum in, the van had moved off. Whatever they wanted us for, it couldn't have been all that important.

DECEMBER 3RD

A real cold snap, and we're delighted, because we can test out our heating. It's super. Skidlum loves it. He lies curled up against the heaters, and I'm sure he thinks they were put in for his special benefit.

A funny thing happened today, though. Another gasman came, a different one this time, with a bag of tools on his shoulder. He said he'd come about a leak. I tried to explain we'd no gas in the house, but he didn't seem to believe me. His mate sat at the gate in the little van, and he shouted out to him something about "Barleyriggs", and the mate came out and nodded, and hung about and argued. I was going to ask them in, and show them, once and for all, that we didn't need them but Skidlum made such a fuss that we couldn't hear ourselves speak. I know we need a watchdog in a lonely place like this, especially when Vincent's away so much, but he gets too enthusiastic sometimes. I just had to let the men go, waving and grinning at them to show there was no ill feeling.

DECEMBER 7TH

Roger came up to me today when I was making a steak and kidney pudding. "Mummy," he said, "what's that lady doing in front of the fire?"

"What fire, dear?" I said.

"The sitting-room fire."

"There isn't a lady..."

"Yes there is. She's sitting on the sofa. She's all pale and thin-looking, and I came away because I thought she was going to cry."

Of course, I didn't believe a word of it. Roger's got a very vivid imagination, and I think he misses Jean since she started school. But—"Skidlum doesn't like her," he said seriously. "He growled and bristled."

"Oh, Skidlum's a daft wee dog," I said, but I slipped in a minute or two later, and had a look. There was nobody there. Of course there wasn't. I'll be glad when Roger's old enough to go to school.

DECEMBER 18TH

A week to go to Christmas. I spent all day getting in holly from the woods—I'm pricked to bits!—and at night Vince and I put up the decorations. Nothing elaborate or trendy, just old-fashioned paper chains and cotton wool and balloons and a few pictures Jean did at school.

Great preparations for Santa Claus! I'm glad we've kept the coal fire. It's so much more traditional. I only wish we were nearer the centre of things, so that other kids could drop in on Christmas morning.

DECEMBER 25TH

Phew! So that's over! It was the most marvellous Christmas ever, but I feel completely whacked. The children are sound asleep, and Vince and I won't be long till we go upstairs too.

Thank goodness it went so well! I was beginning to worry on Christmas Eve. Roger started this business about the lady in front of the fire again. We were laying out ginger wine and biscuits for Santa, and Roger said, "What if the lady eats them?"

"What lady?" I said.

"The lady that sits by the fire."

"Of course she won't eat them! There isn't any lady anyway." I was a bit sharp this time, but Roger didn't seem to notice. He looked thoughtful, and then he said, "No, she's too quiet. And too sad…"

Jean heard him, and told him not to be silly, but she was too quick about it, as if she wanted to cut him off before he said more.

She looked scared too. I wonder if they've been talking about things together? You can never tell with kids.

Anyway, I got them off to sleep, and then just as we'd got to bed ourselves Skidlum started, yap, yap, yap, quite hysterical. He wakened the children, and I had to try to keep them in bed while Vince went down to try to quieten the dog. "No, no," I kept saying, "it's not Santa. Santa hasn't been yet, and he won't come so long as you're awake." And there were the stockings, hanging filled, and the big toys piled up round the Christmas tree... I was terrified they'd go down and find out!

"It's all right," said Vince, coming back. "He's just being silly. There's an awful smell of gas down there, though."

"Gas? But there's none, Vince. You know that. You're as bad as those workmen who keep calling..."

And of course there was no smell. I checked it myself. He'd imagined it all.

FEBRUARY 12TH

I'll be glad when winter's over. It's bleak, black, and very cold, and there's something uneasy about the place, a kind of hostility I never noticed in summer. What do I mean by hostility? I don't know. Something in the air... Skidlum is uneasy. They say these highly bred dogs are apt to be nervy. Maybe we'd have been better with a mongrel. And the children spend far too long whispering and pointing. This game about a woman at the fireside is going too far. It gives me the creeps.

The red van called again. Reports of a gas leak... more muttering and checking of papers, then they apologised and went away. Till next time, I suppose.

FEBRUARY 29TH

An awful thing happened. Shouts and crying, two voices raised in the night, but nobody there. Skidlum was right against the wall when we came down, snarling. And then... it went quiet, all except Skidlum's whines and whimpering. We waited and—we both smelt it; gas, hissing... and suddenly, vague, at first, but growing clearer, lying on the rug, The Lady...

A quiet, thin lady, elegant but untidy, her hair in wisps, her hands thin... no sign of the man with whom she'd quarrelled. He must have gone out, and she had laid herself down, and turned on the gas fire...

But there was no gas fire, and no one beside it. Maybe we had imagined... but the smell was there, sickening and heady...

"Shut the door," said Vincent. "Open the windows in the children's room; but don't waken them! I'll ring the gas people. There's an escape somewhere."

We opened the door and the windows, and the cold damp air blew in. I made a pot of coffee. If a man was to be hauled out of his bed at this hour of the morning, he'd be glad of a hot drink. Fidgeting about, I waited for the familiar red van.

But the van that came was grey, and the man with it was a stranger. I expected him to look annoyed, but he was more puzzled, and something else.

"You're *sure* you smelled gas?" he asked.

"Oh yes. Not for the first time."

"But there's no gas in this house."

"Your lot don't seem to think so," said Vince. "They've been turning up regularly with the same bit of paper, telling us we've got a leak. And now *we're* telling *you*, and you turn round and tell us we haven't."

"Nobody came from our lot. I can assure you of that."

"They did!" I insisted. "A wee red van…"

He licked his lips, and shivered slightly. Relenting a bit, Vince shoved the door shut, and poured out the coffee. The gasman shovelled in sugar, and gulped.

"Our vans aren't red. They're grey. And I know—and all my workers know—there's no gas at Barleyriggs. It was taken out years ago."

"The pipes under the floor…?"

"No. We took them out too. And…" he put down his mug, and looked from me to Vince and back again. "Have you—did you… when you bought this house, did nobody tell you…?"

Without answering, we waited for him to go on.

"There was a suicide—well, they think it was a suicide, but there might have been more to it than that. The woman disappeared, you see. Then the next people who came in kept complaining about a smell of gas, and we could never find anything—we did have red vans at that time, Missis." He gave me a little nod, like a detective praising smart observation. "Well, the tenants got fed up, and at last they got us to take the pipes out. We lost a customer, you might say; but we found something else…

"She—the lady who was missing—she'd been buried under the floor. Gassed; they found that out, the way they investigate these things. And nobody wanted the house after that."

*

So that was it. We haven't smelt gas since, and nobody has mentioned the unfortunate woman by the fire; but I don't think we can stay here much longer. I've a feeling that the drama we saw may be enacted again.

There's no particular hurry. This is February 29th, and it was leap year, according to our friend the gasman, when the tragedy took place. That gives us four years...

We'll need it. It took long enough to sell the house last time.

HELP THE RAILWAY MISSION

he museum at Tinnock was built in the likeness of an old Victorian street. It was craftily and skilfully done. Old lintels were let into new but artificially aged walls, concrete floors had patterned vinolay cobbles, and the neon lighting simulated daylight, a grey colourless daylight like an eternally suspended afternoon.

But the shops were the thing. When the windows were lit, the street darkened to the mirk of a winter evening, brightened by the comfort of gaslight and lamps. Peer in at the shop doors, and the lights in the glass globes were gas mantles, you could have sworn; but of course they were small electric bulbs; and the low, economical fires in the iron grates—remember the iron grates in wee shops?—were also electric, a red bulb, a flicker rotor, and a piece of crumpled fibreglass. The lighting set the mood, an elusive mood of nostalgia, expectation, sudden recognition... and something else, I don't know what it was. Something which gave me a pull at my stomach which was not entirely pleasant.

The first time I visited it was just after it had opened. Lorna and I, newly married, went along on a Saturday afternoon. We went into the strange dead afternoon light, and there were the shop windows, gay and brilliant—dim by modern standards, but the suspension of disbelief was so complete that they shone as brightly as they must have seemed to do at the beginning of the century.

The draper's was a prosperous, up-to-date shop; you could tell that by the large panes of glass, the vivid display of scarlet uniforms, the elegance of nipped-in waists and whorls of beads and embroidery. I looked down at Lorna, in her blue jeans and jacket. She suited tight trousers. Would she have looked any more feminine in a bustle and bow?

We couldn't go in. The shop was a sham, a window only; nor could we enter the jeweller's, though we could look in and see the interior and almost hear the tick and scurry of clocks and watches, or the whirr and chime of time passing as slow pendulums waved it on. We went into the chemist's, though, with its gilt-labelled drawers, and proprietary labels from old advertisements. A stone jar marked LEECHES stood on a shelf, and there were nasty little powders in dusty packets...

The grocer's was more cheerful. Here was a great treacle barrel with a jug beneath it, and black and gold canisters, and brass scales on the counter. Inside, people were moving and exclaiming, lifting up odds and ends as if they were greeting long-lost friends.

"Do you mind Zebo?"

"Oh, *yes*! My mother used to have a tin in the cupboard, with her blacklead brushes and emery paper..."

"Here's Monkey Brand!"

"My, I don't know when I last saw..."

"I'll bring my mother next time," I said. "She'll get more out of this than me."

"Your granny, more like," said Lorna. "Fancy living like that, everything to do by hand. It's a wonder they'd any time to themselves."

"I think," said a very smart lady with grey hair, "we'd more time than you have nowadays. The days seemed longer; time went more slowly. Or maybe it just seems better for being farther away…"

That's what struck me about all the elderly people there. They were so eager to get back. They yearned over the old irons in the ironmonger's shop, the packets of pins in the draper's, the magazines on show in the printing shop. I had a look at them, and shuddered; deathbed scenes, chapter-headings with wreathed flowers, moral exhortations… Lorna and I walked back along the street, past the Bank where an old couple were enthusing over the linoleum square on the floor, past the doors with their polished knockers and nameplates. "Skinner and Bone, Notaries", and "The Misses Annand, Dressmakers".

"You'd think they were real, wouldn't you?" said Lorna; and then we were outside, dazzled by the sun, and somehow relieved to be back in the present. There was nothing there that I actually remembered; but I had the peculiar feeling that there was much I had been glad to forget.

Next time I went to Tinnock was in winter. It was my mother's birthday, and, choosing her card and present, I realised that she was getting on. She had married late, and she was over forty when I was born. That would make her… well, never mind. She was old enough to look forward to a visit more than to a present. I decided to take her to Tinnock to see the museum.

It was quiet, out of season, but the museum was open, sparsely heated, but with the shops all lit as usual. Mother's eyebrows went up as we went in the door, and she gasped a little. I hadn't told her the kind of place we were visiting, and I think she had expected a suite of polished rooms with ticketed exhibits in sealed glass cases.

If she was surprised at the revelation, an authentic-looking street *inside* a building, I was more than surprised at her reaction. She seemed to fit into the time and the environment with something more than memory. The grocer's sent her into ecstasies, the old enamel signs on the wall, Van Houten's Cocoa, Mazawattee Tea, and the dark varnished wall covering—what was it called—Lyncrusta? There was a sort of wrought-iron screen with a ledger behind it, and she remembered the scrapy pens and pink blotting paper that went along with it. "I used to think we got groceries for nothing, but it was all written down, and we paid every week. They made up the books in there..." There was a hungry, remembering look about her.

"Not *there*, Mother. You didn't live in Tinnock."

"I know. I'm not daft, son!" She sounded irritated, but she looked confused, just the same. "It was just that—there must have been wee shops like this all over..."

The chemist's shop fascinated her too. "Fancy, Scott's Emulsion! I hated it. And Steedman's Powders... my mother dosed me every Friday to 'cool my blood'. She gave me jam to take away the taste—eugh!" She shuddered, and I laughed. I didn't know I'd had a hot-blooded mother.

We passed the Solicitor's, and the door with the dressmakers' nameplate. "No, you can't go in there," I said, as she put out her hand. "It's just a door."

"No, it isn't." She lifted the heavy knocker, and hammered out a brisk "V" signal. Amused, but exasperated, I looked round again. For a woman of her age, my mother got up to some terribly juvenile tricks.

But the door opened. A grey head peeped out, straight grey hair parted in the middle and dragged into a bun. "Come in," said a quiet, resigned voice.

My mother went in politely, and just a little patronisingly. As for me, I was the one now to be confused. My first thought was that the museum was really going to town on authenticity. Not only were the exhibits spot on, but the staff were dressed in character. And then it struck me that this was not one of the staff, nor was it a museum room. The two old ladies—there was another sitting by the fire—lived there, and carried on their trade.

"I'm sorry," I said. "I thought—"

But my mother was not put out at all. "And how are you keeping, Annie?"

"Oh, we can't complain. We cannie complain." She smoothed her hands over her long apron, and I saw that she had a tape measure round her neck.

"And Mary?"

"Just the same. She manages up, part of the day. Here's Ruth to see you, Mary."

The other old lady looked up. She was very like her sister, but softer looking, more frail. She seemed to feel the cold, and after she had nodded she leaned forward again to the fire, her feet on the steel fender, her hands stretched out to coals smoking blackly and without heat. Weakly, she reached for a poker and raked between the bars.

"A bit more coal, Annie," she murmured. *For the visitors*, her tone implied.

"Yes. Well..." Reluctantly, Annie lifted a lump or two from the scuttle with enormous iron tongs. I was fascinated. What a bother, what a *mess*, for so little result! No wonder the women in the grocer's shop had gone on so much about blacklead! There were so many surfaces to be polished, doors and bars and trivets, a swee with an iron kettle, and an assortment of heavy ironmongery cluttered round the fender. Every movement of the coals or the poker brought more dust to dull the polish; and yet the polish was not so bright as I guessed it could have been. Either the sisters hadn't the energy—or the time.

"You'll take a cup of tea…?"

"Well…"

That was my mother again. I didn't want to stay. There was something about the room that depressed me; but mother sat down on a hard chair, the kettle was swung over the fire, and Miss Annie fiddled about with cups and saucers and lifted the kettle lid—Heavens, she'll let smoke in, I thought—and then muttered something about slipping out to the shops. She took a black cloak from a hook on the door, pinned on an enormous blue tammy, and went teetering out into the dark afternoon.

"She's not needing to get anything for us," said my mother belatedly.

Mary mumbled something about not having had time to bake.

"You're busy, then?"

"Oh yes. Annie does it all nowadays." She coughed, and sighed, and poked the fire under the kettle. "We're very fortunate, taking all things together. Very fortunate."

I didn't think they were fortunate at all. I had never seen such a depressing room. The gas hissed in its yellow mantle—real gas, this time—and a paraffin lamp stood on the sill, for emergencies, I supposed. Even with the lamplight added, the room would have been dull. There was a rag rug on the floor, navy blue, and in the corner was the sewing machine, with something black under the needle. The brightest corner was where the dresser took up more than its fair share of space, a dresser crammed with so many dishes you could hardly see the shelves. Cups, saucers, teapots, every monstrosity of Victoriana was there; and on the extreme edge, a wooden collecting box with a picture of an engine on it. "Help the Railway Mission," it said.

The lid of the kettle lifted, and water poured into the fire and sent up a stoury stream. "Oops-a-daisy!" said my mother, swinging the swee aside, and in that moment the other Miss Annand came in with scones and crumpets in a paper bag. She put the odd ha'pence from her purse into the collecting box, and put the teabread on to two plates.

"You shouldn't have bothered," said my mother.

"Oh, but we're glad to. We like visitors. It makes the days shorter."

"The days seemed longer." Who was it had said that...?

With the best will in the world, it was a meagre meal. The two old ladies tried to be hospitable, but you could see it was a strain. Something was dragging them down, Mary's health, or Annie's responsibilities, or merely the general atmosphere of the house. How in the world did Miss Annand find customers, when there were gay and cheap clothes in the chain stores and boutiques? She didn't charge much, of course. There was an account book lying open nearby, and she seemed to work for next to nothing; in old money, too. That was perfectly in keeping. I wondered if she'd ever get round to metrication.

But whatever she charged, her clients must belong to an older generation. Older than my mother. *She* likes bright colours, and she's up to date in her tastes. She seemed quite at home, though, with the Misses Annand. When tea was over she excused herself graciously, and I let my breath out in a loud sigh when the door closed behind us.

"Well!" she said, with a little laugh of appreciation, "that was a lovely surprise. Come on and I'll treat you to tea at the café. We might as well make a day of it."

"Tea? But—"

"Don't argue, Jim. It's my birthday, remember."

I gave in. My mother loves having her tea out—and neither of us had eaten much in that dreary little kitchen.

Over our tea I tried to clear up some of the things that had been puzzling me.

"Mum—I didn't know you knew those two old ladies."

"What ladies?" She selected a fern cake, and poured herself another cup.

"You know. The Misses Annand. The dressmakers."

She stared at me.

"*You* know," I said, exasperated because I was worried in case she was growing old and forgetful. "In the museum Annie and Mary."

She laid down her cup and frowned, her head on one side. "You're getting all mixed up, son. You've heard me talk about your Aunt Annie and your Aunt Mary. And you know my own name was Annand."

"Yes but—those two—they weren't—"

"*What* two?"

Half angry, half worried, I reminded her of what she shouldn't—couldn't—have forgotten, and all the time she kept her eyes on me, her face growing white.

"Son, I don't know what's got into you, this last half-hour, but—what you're saying, all this about the two sisters—it's all true. But not this afternoon. Never this afternoon!"

"We went—"

"You wouldn't remember your two aunties. They were a lot older than me. Your grandpa worked on the railway, and he was killed when we were quite young. When Mother died not long after—she'd never been strong—the two girls were left on their own. Or the three of us, I should say. I was a good bit younger, and I didn't have any responsibility."

"Do you remember them dying? Your parents?"

"Not really. All I can remember was the room, all cluttered with dishes and dresses, and the black fire that never seemed to warm the place, and the sewing machine going all the time—I hated that machine, and I hated my sisters for never stopping, never playing, never enjoying themselves—"

"That's what it was like," I said. "Dreary and miserable... and those Victorian dishes on the dresser, and that big tammy on the back of the door—"

She stared, her face grey. "How did you know?"

"And the collecting box," I went on. "The Railway Mission."

"That's right. I hated it too. If they'd just once spent something on fun, just once enjoyed themselves... but every ha'penny they could spare went into that damned mission box. As soon as it was emptied, they filled it up again, all those hard-earned ha'pennies..." She stirred her cold tea, shame in her face. "And then Mary took ill. Consumption. I hated her for that too. And yet she'd worn herself out, working for me—"

"Well, if you were too young—"

"I cleared out," she said. "As soon as I left school, I went away. I just left them on their own. I couldn't *stand* their life."

"Mum," I said, afraid she was going to cry, "those women we visited—they've upset you. You're mixing them up—"

"We didn't visit anybody," she snapped. "And stop acting the fool. You've trapped me into saying too much already."

So we went back again to the museum, to iron it all out.

There was no room. Of *course*, said my mother, there was no room. The door with the brass knocker gave on to an outside wall, and the owner of the museum told us he'd found the nameplate in a junk shop.

We didn't tell him about the Misses Annand; nor did I tell Lorna. After all, the dressmakers were my mother's ghosts, not mine, though I was the one who had to see them.

Which is why I haven't been back since.

BLACK CHAIN

he island was three miles out, by the small motor boat which took trippers to look at the monastery. On a rough day the boat didn't sail. The island hid itself in a veil of spray and seemed to retreat farther into the Atlantic; but at odd times of the year, when the tides were low, the Black Chain reared up from the sea bed and linked the monastery to the mainland.

So once or twice a year it was possible to walk to the island, but local people knew the dangers and wouldn't take the risk. The half-mile of stepping stones was longer than it looked, and the chain was not easy to traverse. If a man fell, no boat could put out to rescue him until the tide turned, and if he took too long on his journey he would find the rocks suddenly submerged, and a strong current carrying him round the point.

Brother Thomas knew the tides as well as he knew his prayers. Day after day he sat in his little office waiting for the tourists to come straggling up the path: the elderly ladies, the young girls with the sunglasses, and the men in coloured shirts with their maps and cameras and binoculars. He led them over the island with his hands muffled in his robe and his feet dusty in their sandals. An hour, the tour would take. He had done it so many times that he could judge it to a second.

It was very hot. The fields rose up and up to where the monastery dominated the island, and then fell away to the sea on the far side. The sea was everywhere, reached too quickly from every direction.

"At first," said Brother Thomas, staring abstractedly at the thick bar of haze which hid the horizon, "at first you feel trapped. There is nowhere you can go to escape. And then, gradually, you realise you're on an island, and you resign yourself."

"Personally," said a grey-haired lady, with a hearty, metallic directness, "personally, I'd get demented. But I suppose you've a sort of vocation."

He didn't answer her. The word "vocation" which the visitors always bandied about had come to set up in him a violent eruption of discontent, a feeling sour and familiar. He had battled with it for a long time before telling the dogmatic old confessor about it, and then the routine prayers had given no help.

It was worse, too, at this time of the year, when the boats came over with the visitors. There was something unsettling about them. He could never get down to work or meditation till the last load had gone and the last voice faded over the water; and even then the voices came back to him, more real sometimes than the sounds around him.

It didn't do to think about it. "Yes," he said quickly, snatching at a question with relief. His stretched arm took in the brothers dotted about the field. "Yes, we do everything ourselves. We bake our own bread, catch our own fish, preserve the eggs from our own farm—"

"I thought you did nothing but pray," said one of the slim brown girls.

"We pray the clock round. We rise at two in the morning—" He smiled at the expected gasps, the incredulous respect on their faces. "It's a hard life, but we weather it well. Two of our brothers are over ninety—this is the chapel. Each of us has his own place—" He smiled again at the old and somewhat bitter jest. "You will see that we don't go in for comfort. There's no danger of our falling asleep in these seats. There is no heating."

They shivered, thrilling at the thought of it, and the sun fell on them solidly as they left the church. Brother Thomas blinked, and there was sweat on his brow and the white circlet of his skull.

"And now," he said, leading them seaward again, with the tide falling and retreating all the time, "you're in luck today. The Black Chain's just coming into view."

They craned and jostled as he explained the phenomenon. "St Samuel, our Founder," he said, "was the first man ever to cross the chain. His preachings had roused the mainland folk against him, for he was a plain speaker and did not spare his audience. He had to run from the mob. It was low tide, and the rocks were his only way of escape. The islanders, even then, were a different race, cut off, more gentle in their ways. They took the saint in, and he lived among them and found followers. From them he created our Order."

There was no longer any romance in it for him, but the visitors found it thrilling, and a young man in a tartan shirt took his field glasses from their case and began to twiddle with the lenses. His lips sucked in with concentration, and a little muscle jigged in his jaw. Suddenly Brother Thomas felt an insane desire to possess the binoculars. He looked at the strait, like a blue ribbon threaded with black velvet, and the fawn-speckled rocks beyond. And then he touched the young man on the elbow, and said, "I wonder—would you mind if I had a look?"

"Oh, not at all!" The youth started, half ashamed at not having offered the glasses, and thrust them quickly into the monk's hands. Brother Thomas worked clumsily, altering the focus, and the party crowded round as if trying to share his vision.

The sea was crawling, splashing gently against the black stepping stones. In just over an hour, the tide would be at its lowest, so that if a man wanted to cross, he should start a little before. He swung from the flat shore and the cliffs to the town, pale colour-washed, and frighteningly close to a man who had not set foot on the mainland for twenty years. The only monk who left the island was the steward, who went over once in a while to order the stores the community could not produce themselves. He paid accounts, he took sick monks to hospital, and ferried visitors over for an occasional retreat; but always he came back to his prayers and his piety, and he never spoke of his privileges.

"If only I could have been the steward," thought Brother Thomas. "Even that little pleasure... but they live too long here." He was bitterly jealous of the steward. Sometimes he found himself quoting venomously,

Grr, there go, my heart's abhorrence...

"Thank you," he said, almost pushing the binoculars at the boy. "It's a bit difficult to focus, when you wear spectacles."

He stood on the little jetty, waving off his guests, and watching them pick up again their tourist jocularity. The grey-haired lady was being exaggeratedly careful about choosing her seat, and the boy with the checked shirt had hooked a girl with the strap of his binocular case. Soon, thought the monk, he would put his arm round her. He raised a hand as the boat puttered away.

Strange, he thought, how poignant it was, this farewell after an hour. In some ways, the trippers seemed more real to him than the people he lived with. He waved again; and it was then that he saw the binoculars, lying on the jetty steps where the boy had left them while he handed the girl into the boat.

He could have shouted. He could have signalled to them, held the glasses aloft, done something to attract their attention; but he let the boat go farther and farther away, till the waving stopped, and the wake had faded to nothing more than a shadow on the water; then he bent down, his hands shaking a little, and raised the glasses again to his eyes.

The boat was clear again, and the youth in the tartan shirt was whispering into the girl's ear. And beyond he could see the town. There were gulls hovering over the chimneys, and people walking on the quay. He let the binoculars dangle on their cord like the cross the Reverend Father wore on his breast. Then he turned and began to run furtively round the island.

There was no-one to see him as he hurried down to the shore. The next boat, the last one of the day, would not arrive till the turn of the tide, and he would not be missed till then. He went slithering down the grass tussocks to the broad crescent of sand, and began to make for the first stone. The cold of the water was like a shock to his feet. It swirled above his ankles, so that he had to pause for a moment to lift his habit and tighten the cord round his waist to pouch the grey material over it.

Sand silted over his toes and sucked at his sandals as he pulled them clear; and the rock, when he reached it, was warm with the sun, dried after long months of cold soaking beneath the sea. It was only a step to the next stone, and a short leap to the next one, but after that he paused, seeing the way more difficult. The rocks were farther apart than he realised, and it would take a clever man to judge each jump with no room for a take-off.

He had never been much of an athlete. Prayer, and the daily walks over the island—he looked back, a guilty glance over his shoulder, but nobody was there. The monks would all be labouring at the other side of the hill; and as he thought of it, the two steps he had traversed seemed far more of an accomplishment than the miles and miles he had walked on his religious duties. He drew back, leaped, and almost over-stepped himself. Careful now; steady. There was no time to waste, but caution would pay.

He measured the next gap, his eyes screwed shrewdly, but his knees trembling. The rock was higher this time. Wait till my nerves settle, he thought; but he could not regain confidence in himself. Time, too, was flustering him. The tide was at its lowest ebb, and soon it would be on the turn. He made three more leaps, quickly, almost carelessly, and then he had to stop. He had made the mistake of looking down at the sea.

It was not the sea itself that he feared. If the rocks had been level with the water, he would have felt as safe as a child playing hopscotch. What frightened him was the ascending height of the black pillars, and the sheer drop to an ocean hardly moving, a heavy slow drift of indigo and silver. Sometimes there was a quick flash as a fin of rock broke the surface, and it seemed as if the rock, not the sea, was moving; the whole chain riding and gliding against the slow silken tug of the swell and the vertigo of high rocks toppling...

He was riding through space, the sky and the sea racing past him. This was the narrowest rock yet. There was room to stand, if he could resist the giddy swing of the sea, or room to kneel, as he was doing now, with hands clinging and head bowed, looking backwards and downwards. He raised his head quickly, away from the topsy-turvy turmoil of water. Better to sit, perhaps... he edged himself round, keeping his eyes steady and straight ahead. The next rock was lower, and broader. Without thinking he launched himself forward, his mind purposely blank against terror, and a long strand of seaweed squelched under his sandal and sent him sprawling on the slaty slabs. His wrists stung where they had been grazed, and his ankle was numb with pain.

"Oh, Lord," he thought, feeling the tender puffiness round the bone, "suppose I can't walk? Suppose it's broken..."

He tried his weight on it, and the ankle held him. It was only a strain, a slight injury which would pass after a few minutes' rest. He could do with a few minutes, anyway, to get his breath back. He touched the binoculars swinging at his waist, and their presence was a comfort to him. Moving as far as he could to the edge of the rock, he lifted them to his eyes.

He did not look at the island. It was clear, far too clear in his mind, the green fields running down almost to the water, and, dominating everything, the cross on top of the monastery. What he wanted to see was the mainland.

From where he stood, the town itself was almost out of sight, but he could see enough to tempt him: a few houses, pink and lemon washed, and a little road running uphill with a figure toiling up on a bicycle. Where the road turned to the right there was a cemetery. Fascinated, he worked at the focus till he could make out the individual stones, the birds and urns and crosses, and the chained-off lairs. It was so different from the austerity of the monks' burial place.

On one of the graves, a child was skipping, crossing her feet and singing to herself. He could not make out her face; she was too far away for that; but he watched her bounce up and down, more and more slowly as she grew breathless, and then stop as her tired feet tripped her. She swung the rope again, after a minute, and then began skipping in a new rhythm. Suddenly, there was another child dancing with her, the two children face to face, the rope going over and over.

Blinking his eyes, for he found that the glasses strained them, the monk began to breathe the words he remembered from long ago, "I—call—in—my—sister—Betty!" He laughed, half ashamed, even in the silence. His sisters used to sing that rhyme, and he and the other boys used to tease them, throwing stones to knock them off their count. The two girls' rhythm was becoming irregular. One faltered a second later, and then they were both down, rolling and giggling and waving their legs in the air.

He swung the binoculars away, back to the road. The cyclist had dismounted, and was lounging on the verge, munching something from a paper bag. It was so free, not wicked at all, not anything to be renounced; the freedom to skip and dance, to eat and enjoy life instead of always meditating upon death.

He sat for a long time, watching the road, and seeing the traffic creep up and down, the cars and cycles and once a bus, a green bus with yellow lettering on the back. A girl went up with a young man, both taking slow, exaggerated steps, their arms twined, their heads leaning together. The monk sighed, and looked away again. It would not do, this senseless spying and wishing. What he should do was get across, and reach the paradise he saw so clearly and tantalisingly in the little circle of glass.

As he lowered the binoculars, he felt the first cool wash of the water at this feet.

He could not believe it. He was not yet halfway across. He looked down, drawing his legs up, as if he could halt the tide by avoiding contact with it. The sea was racing swiftly, with a wicked blue and white sparkle. The only thing now was to make a run for it, and get back to the island as quickly as possible.

But he hesitated. The whole rock was submerged. He could not see the beginning or the end of it, and he was afraid to go nearer the edge. How could he jump, out of this mounting flood, without room for a take-off? The hem of his habit was wet now, heavy with water, and the curve of the current made the sea look as if it was turning, turning, with himself the hub, spinning round and round.

This was the end of it. There was time, only just enough time, to resign himself and make his peace with God. But his mind cavilled, even now, at the necessity for prayer. He had prayed so long, and to such little purpose. Surely life could not end like this, mock humility on a rock, the last minutes wasted in hypocritical repetition? He rebelled; but even then, feeling the water at his knees, prayer was forced from him, the automatic crying of the soul in panic, the cry for life. He did not want to die; and in a few minutes more the life he had despised became desirable. If he could have got back to the monastery, he would have fallen on his knees and kissed the stones in gratitude.

But of course he would never get back. He was numbed, too numbed to think properly; too numbed now to be afraid. A listless despair and misery filled him. Why had he imagined that he could escape? Suppose he had reached the mainland, what then? What could he have done? Where could he have gone, an elderly, monkish figure, ridiculously dressed, and out of touch with the world? He was a childish man, a man entranced by the sight of two children dancing in a graveyard; a man who would be by turns prudish or sensual, unbalanced by isolation.

Oh, he got on well enough, speaking to people, shepherding them for an hour, and repeating his well-learned pieces; but to them he was something out of a picture book, picturesque, but no more real to them than the three wise men; and if he did live and work among them, how could he settle to it? He would waken in the darkness to pray, and—well, the question didn't arise now. He was going to die, and no-one would know what had happened to him. When the next boat arrived—

The next boat. It came into sight, shearing through the water, abob with heads, an arm waving, pointing out the monastery.

"Ahoy!" the monk shouted, his own arm waving, signalling wildly for help. They would not hear him, of course; and even if they did, they would not be able to help him. He raised the binoculars again, following the boat in anguish. There was a young man in a tartan shirt—the young man coming back for his binoculars.

"Here! Hoy, there! Look! Help!"

The man's face was so clear, it was inconceivable that he could not see. Brother Thomas kept the glasses trained on him, willing him to look, praying for a glance, the slightest second of recognition. It became very important that someone should know about him, even if only to shake a helpless head and wave farewell. But the youth did not look. Of course, thought Brother Thomas, he can't see without his binoculars.

It was very funny, so funny that he laughed lightheadedly. Quite ridiculous. He was laughing in great sobs as he braced his feet against the current and felt the water pulling at his shoulders; and the boat went lifting on the waves, round the corner and out of sight, taking the last load of visitors to look at the monastery.

THE BOOREES

remember, when I was very young, I used to sit on the fender and listen to the boorees.

I was afraid of the boorees. They lived high up in the chimney, away up where it narrowed to a round "O" like the end of a tunnel. All summer, when the fire was low, blown up only for cooking, and damped down again between meals, they kept quiet, squatting on sooty ledges, with their feet tucked in and their heads on their knees, half asleep. When autumn came, and we stoked the fire, and gales swept through the air, and the air was full of leaves, the boorees wakened and stirred. At first they only muttered a little, and sent a patter of soot down on to the boiling pots; but later, they seemed to grow stronger and more angry. Winter saw them howling and roaring, and sometimes Spot, our old dog, would turn up the whites of his eyes and growl before he settled down to sleep again.

"It's all right," said my mother, when I inched away, "it's only the boorees. They won't do you any harm."

I found this hard to believe. Creatures who wailed and roared like that were fearsome things. "What do they *do*?" I asked my mother, and she said: "They don't *do* anything, as long as you behave yourself. They're just there."

"Are there boorees in all the chimneys?"

"Oh, yes."

"Even when there's no fires?"

"That's right."

I had hoped she'd say no. The room where I slept was a wee box of a place, with a tiny grate which was never lit because of something called "back smoke". This meant that smoke blew down the cold chimney from someone else's fire. "It's the boorees again," said my mother, bringing in a paraffin stove when the nights were coldest, and I pictured them craning malevolently, sucking in deep gulps from other chimneys, and blowing it into our room like an evil breath.

Once my sister upset fat on the kitchen fire, and the chimney went up in a blaze. Oh, then the boorees were angry! They roared and rumbled, and threw down great clods of hot soot; and then the fire brigade came, clang, clang! and men in navy blue, with big belts and boots and heavy helmets. They rattled ladders over the roofs, and sent a solid jet of water down the chimney, all hissing and smelling, and there was steam all over the place, ash on the shiny furniture, and rust on the bright fender; and I was terrified the boorees would come down too, washed into the middle of the kitchen to snap and flap, or whatever they did to show their spite.

Another thing that worried me was when the sweep came. What a great palaver that was! Rugs were rolled up, ornaments put away, curtains taken down, furniture covered. The two men arrived at the door, their faces black, and sooty caps on their heads. Their clothes, too, smelt of soot, and they had black cloths with them, dreadful black cloths that they unrolled at the hearth. "Are you going to clear the boorees out of the chimney?" I asked them once, and they laughed and said, aye, that's right, that's what they were going to do. I was never easy after that. I wanted them to take the boorees away, but I didn't want to anger them.

They *must* have been angry. I watched the whole thing from a corner, ready to bolt if anything black came at me. But the men were very skilful and very brave. Only brave men could have done what they did. One crooked his hand over the mantel and keeked sideways up the chimney. "Aye, there's a good lot there," he said. He must have counted them, sitting on their ledges, all huddled up like bats in the velvet soot. Next, he took his black cloth and nailed it to the mantelshelf, and then looped it under to make a bag to catch the boorees.

By this time, the other man was on the roof, getting his spiky brush ready, walking duck-footed along the ridge, and clinging to the chimney pot, when he reached it, like an old friend. He called down the chimney, a muffled, eerie noise like "Heeh!" and the man in our kitchen called back, to let him know that he was at the right one. Then there was the most awful rumble and thudding, and things began to bounce and thump against the black cloth.

My mother always looked anxious at this point, watching the soot puff and trickle out at the edges, and I caught her terror, and nibbled my fingers, and made little whimpering noises.

"It's all right, missis," the man said, easy and comforting. "Nothing to worry about. We'll be all clear in a minute."

Sure enough, what he said was true; but I didn't like to see the way he gathered up the corners so carefully, holding them in so that nothing could escape, and slipping out of the door quickly with his nasty black parcel. And what a pile of soot was left in the fireplace! The man on the roof came down and swept it gently with a soft hearthbrush, and shovelled it with great care into a bucket; and still I wouldn't come near in case a stray booree reared from the blackness and broke loose into the room.

I don't know when I got over my obsession with chimneys and their occupants. Gradually, I suppose, I realised that, in spite of my fears, nothing happened. Christmas, too, did a great deal to calm my fears. Not even the most malevolent booree, I was sure, would dare to tangle with Santa Claus. At some point or other I realised that there was a rational explanation for all the noises which took place in our chimney, howling winds and hissing rain, and the roar of flames licking at soot and sending it tumbling down in red, smouldering embers. Then we became modern, and had an electric fire with moulded coals and a little wheel and a red bulb, all of them adding up to a clean, artificial and characterless fireside. The boorees retreated to a dim corner of my mind, smiled at indulgently, sometimes, when I remembered them, as I smiled at the memory of my dolls and teddy-bear.

I resurrected them when I became a nanny.

I used to read a lot of stories about nannies, plump, plain old ladies who lived with the children they cared for in comfortable nurseries while the parents lived upstairs, tended by servants, and seeing their children only once a day. These Victorian nannies had practically no life away from their charges; nor did they want any. They doted on their titled and hyphenated darlings, and years later, old and wise, ruled them still from cosy cottages where they listened to confessions, soothed, judged, advised, and kept their elderly hands as tightly as ever on the reins.

Victorian nannies were stricter than parents, but not nearly so smart. Not for them the easy confidence of cheap and changing fashions. What they wore was almost a uniform: dowdy, but worn with pride. And their employers treated them almost as equals. Almost, but not quite. A nanny was an acquisition, coveted by other families, but not to be lured away by gold or better conditions. Genuine nannies had a built-in resistance to bribery; they were hooked by the first cry of the newborn.

I was not that kind of nanny. Mine was only a vacation job, taken between terms at the university, and I would have gone over to anybody who tried to tempt me. Most of the other women on the estate would have loved to hand over their offspring to somebody else, but none of them could afford it. Mrs Yates reckoned that it was worth paying me so that she could take up work again as a pharmacist, and so reduce the mortgage a little. The rest could only rise to baby-sitters.

Mrs Yates certainly treated me as an equal. I had colour TV in my room, the run of the house and the pick of the freezer. If I baby-sat in the evening, she paid me overtime; and all she asked was that Dennis should trouble her as little as possible.

Unlike the Victorian nanny, I did not love Dennis Yates. He was only my summer job, and many a time I would gladly have strangled him.

To begin with, he was defiant; not cheekily defiant, but in a sly, persistent sort of way. If I told him not to do something, he would say nothing, but stare as if he didn't understand, and then do the same thing over again as soon as my back was turned. If he left the hot water tap dripping, and I told him to turn it off, he would do as he was told, but go back a minute later and turn it on again so that the water ran cold. That sort of thing. Add to this a cool stare, and condescending, middle-class voice, and I could understand why his mother preferred dispensing medicine to mother love.

Mostly, by nagging, vigilance and expending a great deal of energy, I managed to keep Dennis under control. Often I was tempted to try a good clout on the ear, but this his mother had absolutely forbidden. "I'll smack the child myself," she promised, though obviously she never carried out her threat. She did nothing more than shake her head at him when I told her he was too fond of the fire.

It was then that I remembered the boorees.

One day he had been leaning over the guard, pushing the poker into the coals till it was red hot. I smacked his hand for this, and he dropped the poker on to the hearth with a bouncing clatter. I smacked him again, and he said he'd tell his mother. Ten minutes later, when the poker was cool, he was at it again.

"Distract his attention," said all the articles I'd read about this problem. "Give him something better to think about." So I put away my ironing, sat down by the fire and, with my arm around him, told him about the boorees.

All the time, I kept my voice down. I told him bare facts, as dispassionately as I could. "The boorees live in the chimney," I said, "way up high in the chimney when the weather's warm. But in the winter, they come down lower and lower, so that they can feel the heat. They like to be warm, but not too hot. That's why they don't like you to poke the fire and make the flames shoot up."

"What are they like?" he asked, interest springing up in spite of himself.

"Well..." I hesitated. "Black. They would be, of course, living among the soot. And... well, you wouldn't like to see them. You're better not to know. They're very fierce..."

"I'm not afraid of them." He turned to the fireplace and began to yell. "You hear me, boorees? I'm not afraid of you! You can't touch me—"

"Sshh!" I clapped a hand over his mouth, and held him tight. "Don't let them hear you! They don't like boys to speak to them like that. So long as you behave, and don't bother them, they won't do you any harm."

"Wh-what could they do to me?" He was beginning to sound nervous.

"Well..." Again I played for time. "I wouldn't like to tell you, Dennis. You wouldn't be able to sleep at night, worrying about it. Just you be a good boy, and you've nothing to worry about."

I thought it was beginning to work. For the rest of the day he did as he was told, but next afternoon I saw him throwing sheets of newspaper on the fire. I snatched him back, furious. "*Stop* that, you little fool! Do you know what you're doing? *You'll burn the boorees' feet!*"

"The flames won't reach up—"

"They will! You'll burn their feet, and they'll be very, very angry!"

I wish now I had put him over my knee and skelped him good and hard. I wish I had taken him out with me, played a game, asked him to help me in the kitchen. I was baking a cake for tea, I remember, and I went back to my mixing, checking that I hadn't forgotten any of the ingredients. I hate being interrupted when I'm baking.

I'll never forget the screams that came a moment or so later. Leaving everything, I rushed in, sticky hands and all, and...

I don't want to tell about it. I don't think anyone should ever see a sight like that. Dennis was a mass of flames, big forked flames shooting six feet over his head, and the whole blazing, screaming thing *whirled* round and round like a top. But that wasn't the worst of it. All round him stood the boorees, the boorees I had once believed in, and called up again for the sake of a few minutes' peace.

You don't want to know what they're like, do you? I'd rather not. Well... they were black, hopping things, like frogs, with leathery wings, but men's bodies, leathery caps on their heads, and big ears, and—and claws...

I had always thought they'd be black, and so they were, eventually, but to begin with they were red, as red as fire, not flame, but dull crimson coals. They hopped and fidgeted and poked at the pillar of flame that still managed to scream, and their claws were like forks, sharp garden forks... As Dennis's cries grew weaker, the boorees became dark and darker, till they cooled down to ebony black, then... withered away to what looked like the feathers of soot you see trembling in the draught of the fire...

It was me that screamed, then. Once Dennis was silent, I heard my own voice, so high and ringing, scream after mighty scream, that I didn't recognise it. They came, then, from all over the estate, all the young wives and mothers. Their faces went sick white, and there was so little they could do. The fire brigade arrived, but there was no fire to put out. The doctor came, but it was too late. Mrs Yates... I don't remember her coming, but by then some of them had taken me away, and sat with me till the doctor stuck a needle in my arm and everything went as black as the boorees I kept screaming about.

I was a long time in hospital. They called it the psychiatric ward, but I knew in myself it was really the madhouse. Well, what of it? What happened was enough to drive anyone mad.

I never went back to university. What was the point? I didn't want to be a teacher, and, let's face it, nobody would have employed me. I just wasn't "suitable", they would say, to be trusted with children.

I'm all right now. I got work in a department store, where I would always be among people, and now I'm understudy to the head buyer. I've done well. If anyone knows what happened to me, they accept it and keep quiet. It doesn't affect my work.

There's only one thing. I can't stand a room where there's a chimney. Every room I go into, I look round quickly to make sure. It's no use telling me they never use the fireplace, and, look, the chimney's been blocked up for years, and they have a carboy of flowers where the fire used to be… I just can't stand it. I can't even go down to the basement, at work, when they're building a generous big chimney for Santa Claus to sit beside; even if I know it's only plasterboard and paper.

And I wouldn't want to see the children anyway; demanding little boys with middle-class voices. I know what I hope nobody else will ever find out: how loud a child like that can scream.

DON'T LOOK IN
MY WINDOW

o, I know you didn't mean to be rude. I know the bell wasn't working, and you wondered if I was in; but couldn't you have waited? Couldn't you have knocked? You've no idea what it does to me, to see a face peering in at me like that.

I *have* got a grip of myself. And no, it'll take more than facing up to it to put it out of my mind. I faced up to it long ago, and I still—

All right. Now that you've asked, I'll tell you. But you'll have to listen to the whole story...

What happened was that once, when I was coming home from school, a man chased me. To begin with, he just followed me, step for step, until I began to feel uneasy. I'd a long way to walk, and I'd never been followed before. I kept going faster and faster, and all the time the footsteps behind me kept on, getting a little nearer, a little nearer...

There was a dark bit of road coming, a bit with no houses and a lot of overhanging trees, and I knew that, by the time I reached it, he'd be almost up to me. So I started to run.

In a way, it was better then, because I didn't have to hold myself in. I could admit I was terrified and trying to escape; but the faster I ran, the more terror became panic, and I would have screamed if I'd had the breath. The man behind me was out of breath too. I could hear him panting, and his boots thudding on the road...

Never once did it occur to me to look round. It would have wasted time, thrown me off balance, maybe, and certainly frightened me more. I didn't *want* to know what he looked like. All I wanted was to get home and slam the door in his face.

We lived, at that time, in a little cottage tied to a big house on the estate where my father was gamekeeper. Once or twice a week my mother had to work at the house, and this was one of the days. I knew she wouldn't be in, and this in itself didn't bother me. So long as I could get round the back, to get the key of the back door from under the flowerpot where it was kept...

I made it, only because as I turned the corner, I jicked through a hole on the hedge. Sobbing, I ran round the house, grazing my arm on the roughcast, and clattering the flowerpot over as I groped for the key. It took me all my time to get it into the lock, but I managed to get the door open, pull out the key, and lock myself in. The front door, I knew, was safe.

So was I. This was home, strong walls, locked doors, the windows snibbed... it never occurred to me that the man, whoever he was, might persist. Surely he would give up when I vanished. Even if he knocked at the door, I knew better than to answer it; and Heaven help him if he was still hanging about when my father came home!

And then he looked in at the window.

It was dark, but not so dark that I couldn't see him. He pressed his face to the window, shading his eyes against the fire which I'd poked into a blaze, and I looked at him for a long minute before I screamed. There was nothing *wrong* with his face, nothing grotesque or threatening. It was its very ordinariness which made it so terrifying—and so memorable; nothing but a red face, amiable enough, comical, even, with a red gash of a mouth, clownish eyebrows, and short grey hair. He was needing a shave, I remember, and the hair was strong round the beginning of a double chin. Somehow or other I knew that he had a thick neck, with boil marks in the creases, and little bald bits where his hair was cropped short at the back. He wore one of those shirts without a collar—you know the kind you used to get, with detachable collars, and there was always a lot of both with collar studs. This man had no collar. It was as if he'd taken it off as my father did when he came in—he looked the sort of man who might come home at night, take off his jacket and collar and boots, and settle down to play with the children. There was absolutely nothing you could point to and say, I don't like this, or it's this or the other that frightens me. Nothing at all; and yet I knelt there on the hearthrug, feeling my skin go white and cold, and absolutely petrified with horror.

He was only there for a minute, and when he had gone, I thought at first that I had dreamt it. Certainly it came back to me many a time afterwards in nightmares; but this was no dream. I had seen his breath dim the pane, and then the dimness vanish. You don't get details like that in dreams.

For a long time I was uneasy when my mother was out of the house, and the thought of my father's gun was a comfort to me. I dreaded every day that I had to walk home from school, but, oddly, I never said a word to my parents. Why? I don't know. There was something so horrible about the whole experience that it made me somehow feel tainted. And how could I have proved it? No-one else was chased on the way home, and there were no reports of children being molested, or "interfered with"—I wouldn't even have known what the phrase meant. The man had made no threat.

I retreated into a secret silence, and when the days grew longer, I forgot some of my shock and obsession.

Later, we moved into a house on the outskirts of town. My parents were tired of living in a tied cottage, and my father made the break before he was too old to try for another job. I was almost finished with school, studying for my A levels before making up my mind what to do; and one day, coming home from school, I saw this man working with a gang who were doing things to pipes in the road.

There was no mistaking him. He hadn't aged at all. This time I saw him first from behind, and there were the boil marks on the fat neck, and the little bald spots on the grizzled head. Then he turned round, an ordinary working man, wide mouth, half smiling, eyebrows raised, so ordinary, but... so awful; and when he saw me staring at him, he simply put down his pick or whatever he was holding and came towards me.

You wouldn't believe, would you, that a man could simply leave his work and walk away like that, to follow a stranger? But that's what he did, in his dirty dungarees, with his hands soiled with work, and thick mud on his boots. This time I should have felt safer. It was about four o'clock, the streets were crowded, and a man can't just chase a girl and grab her in broad daylight...

Can't he? I didn't wait to find out. I ran, hardly seeing where I was going, bumping into people till they turned and made irritated noises. "These High School girls..." and I couldn't look round to see if he was following...

Maybe I should have stopped, faced up to him and asked what he wanted, but I couldn't bear to. I kept on running till I got home. Once again there was nobody in the house. Once again I ran in and locked the door; and then, peeping round the corner of the curtain, I saw him coming up the path.

Oh no! I thought. If he peers through the window at me, I'll go mad! So I ran up the stairs and into my bedroom, where I could look down on him, and see what he was going to do. I could just bear to look at him, so long as he couldn't see me... I was halfway towards the window *when I saw his face at the pane*, the same face, wide mouth, clown's eyebrows, the hair, more grizzled now, standing up like a brush.

No, he hadn't climbed up. There was no way he could climb. He had stretched, made himself taller, far taller than a man on stilts, so that he was walking easily, his head level with my window, and *smiling*—

I didn't know what to do. If I went into another room, he could follow me round the house, looking in at every window—any window. Eventually I stood on the landing, between the doors, where I couldn't see him—but suppose he climbed in? The upstairs windows were all slightly open. All he had to do was to slide them up and heave himself over the sill.

I was hysterical when my mother came in, so hysterical that she sent for the doctor. Neither of them could make head or tail of my story. No man could possibly grow so tall, so quickly. It was all imagination. My mother remembered vaguely seeing a working man roughly like the one I described walking along the road away from the house, but there was nothing unusual about him, certainly nothing alarming. "You'll forget all about it in the morning," said the doctor, giving me an injection to make me sleep; and later, downstairs, he asked my parents if I was in any way worried about my exams?

Nobody referred to the man after that, and for myself, I was sorry I'd mentioned it. I felt silly and shamed, as if I'd acted like a child, and yet more deeply afraid than ever. It had been bad enough the first time, that dreadful face smiling in; but how much worse the second time! And no-one believed a word of it.

As the weeks passed, though, weeks and months and years, I became more easy in my mind. I became a teacher, and teaching gives one confidence. Then I met Frazer, and that was it. We married, after a year's frantic saving, and set up house temporarily in a couple of attics near the school. We'd put our name on the Council housing list, and later—how much later we daren't think—we might even manage to buy a house of our own.

After we'd been married about three months, the man looked through the attic window.

It was late at night. We'd fallen asleep in each other's arms, and I'd wakened, my arm cramped and dead with Frazer's weight. There was the face, smiling easily, staring in, so near, so very near—

I screamed, I gibbered, I clawed at Frazer to wake him and, thank God, oh thank God, Frazer saw him too! Half asleep, his heart blooping so loud I could hear it, he said, "What the Hell!—" and started towards the window. The face vanished—snap!—like that. Frazer leaped up and leaned out of the window, and there, down below, was an ordinary man, middle-aged, grizzled, walking away—

"It couldn't have been him," said Frazer. "He couldn't have jumped. He'd have been killed."

"He stretched—"

"He couldn't. It's fifty feet. He *couldn't* stretch."

"He *must* have."

And there was no way of settling it.

143

*

We gave up the idea of buying a house. Sooner than we expected, our name came up on the housing list, and we were allocated a flat on the top of a tower block, 100 feet high. The housing manager wasn't sure if we'd want it. We were young, we were liable to have a family, and then, no doubt, we would start to complain.

Frazer and I, however, were delighted. It seemed the answer to my phobia. Nobody, surely, nobody at all could look in at the window now! There wasn't even a balcony. We took the flat, and with the money we'd saved we made it into a beautiful little home.

We'd only been there six months when—when—

It was a Saturday afternoon. Frazer was marking some history papers, and I was ironing. I looked up, casually, and—the man was looking in again, smiling.

This time he was lower in the window, his head resting on the sill like a big turnip. I screamed, the iron clattered off the board, and Frazer jumped up, swearing, and picked it up before it could singe the carpet. Then he saw the face, and went pale.

He didn't hesitate, though. He took his chance. We had those windows that tilt inwards and turn over, so that you could clean them, and Frazer quietly unlatched the fastening and tilted the pane so that he could get his arm out. Then he clutched the grizzled hair. The man winced a little, and blinked, but kept on smiling. Frazer leaned forward a bit, and then let go. "Oh my God!" he said, coming in and looking as if he wanted to vomit.

"What is it?" Why didn't he bash the face, squash it, take away that terrible smile…?

"He goes all the way down to the ground. Look!"

"No!" Nothing would have made me advance to that head, lying so amiably on the sill. I didn't want to see him, stretched long and thin like a drainpipe. I believed it. I could believe anything—

Suddenly, Frazer went mad. He got hold of the head again, tugging and wrenching and straining. It must have been agonising. The face twisted, ugly, and yet pathetic in its suffering, and a hoarse voice grunted "Don't!" It seemed to make Frazer worse, and I remember yelling at him, because, for God's sake, we didn't want that long thing in the house.

Suddenly there was a loud *snap!* like a cracker going off, and Frazer staggered back, with the head in his hands. We both stared at it. A man's head doesn't come off so easily. And there was no blood. And then we saw that it wasn't only a head. Under the chin, snapped back, shrivelled and tiny like a burst balloon, was the man himself, the workman's clothes, the body only an inch or two long, with heavy boots on the end...

The face was smiling again, like a Hallowe'en lantern, though it was paler than usual. Snapping him back like that must have taken it out of him. We stared, silent in shock, with the placid obscenity in our hands, and then, as if realising what he held, Frazer went to the window and threw it out.

It was a pretty mangled thing once it hit the ground and burst, and for a while there was quite a stink about it in the papers. You remember now? I thought you would. Of course, nobody ever heard the truth about it.

Everything was suddenly hushed up, you see. You know how you've got to have a head before you can finally identify a mutilated body? Well, in this case there was nothing but a head, and it was in such a state... There were enquiries, of course, and a great deal of what they call "police activity", and then suddenly it was called off, and the newspapers never did get the full story. They could only make guesses, but Frazer and I could have told them what had happened. They had discovered the "body", and didn't know what to do about it.

For a while after that we haunted the libraries, both of us, doing as much research as we could into monsters, but we didn't learn anything. The elastic man, please God, was the only one of his kind. We moved, of course. We couldn't live in the flat after that, and, all things being equal, we felt we'd be as safe on the ground floor as anywhere. So far, nothing has bothered us. There was only one of these monsters, and he won't come back. I'm quite sure of that; but please, please, *never* peer in at the window…

DOROTHY DEAN

hen Mrs Dean called at the Remand Home, shamefacedly and on foot, she was surprised to find it both respectable and anonymous. It was the kind of house where you might expect to find a brass plate, a doctor's or dentist's or architect's; but only the brass bell glinted, and worn gilt on the fanlight scrawled the signature "Tintagel".

The door was unlocked to admit her, and locked behind her again, and the superintendent looked a cross between a hospital matron and a gaoler as she led the way to her room. Mrs Dean sat in the warm study, her white gloves screwed to grubbiness, her jersey suit smudged with train dust. Already she was on the verge of breaking down. Only her indignation kept her going, a resentment against everyone concerned with placing Dolly in this halfway house between court or prison, or perhaps, if one dared to hope, a second chance in life.

"I can't understand it," she said peevishly, forgetting that she had come to plead for help rather than to excuse. "She's always been a good girl. She's highly strung; but what she did to Mrs Stanley, and then carrying on like that afterwards—well, I mean, it's just not *like* Dolly..."

"That's what we want to investigate," said Mrs Gallacher gently. "We want to find out *why* she did it." She felt that, at short notice, it was too much to expect her to unravel her charges' kinks for the benefit of persons who should have seen trouble coming a long time ago. The girls were here for such a short time. Some you were glad to see the last of, some you liked on sight; but you learned to distrust the lot of them, Veronica, with her bronzed hair turning to mouse, Barbara, who stole, Jean, who lost her head whenever a man looked at her, and Dolly Dean, who wouldn't talk, and who rejected all offers to help her.

"We're having her checked up, of course," she said. "There's this nervous tic that she's got—"

"She can stop it if she wants to," said her mother sharply. "You don't need a doctor for that. It's not the first time I've smacked her out of a bad habit..."

... She had always had some mannerism or other, like jerking her head or flicking her hair back. "My hair gets in my eyes," she complained, and so her mother clipped back her fringe and put the long mane into a pony tail. Next there was blinking, screwing her eyes to squeeze the blackness till it ached ecstatically, but by this time she was at school, and they sent her to the eye clinic and made her wear glasses.

The blinking stopped, but it gave way to yet another habit, an uncomfortable twitch to keep the glasses from sliding down her nose. She indulged in it when she was reading, and her mother would watch in exasperation, breaking in on her with complaints. "You read far too much. Wasting your eyesight, that's what you're doing. No wonder you have to wear glasses."

She sat reading all day in a dark corner, newspapers, comics, or catalogues, whatever she could lay hands on. She spent long hours with Mrs Beeton; but her mother's library was limited. There was a more fascinating selection at Mrs Stanley's and Mrs Stanley's house was itself an attraction. She lived across the landing, on the sunny side of the building, and her kitchen was bright with geraniums and green linoleum. Dolly went across sometimes to see the budgie. "Wee Joey. Kiss wee Joey!" it chattered, and Mrs Stanley chattered back; and when they were both chattering away, Dolly would slip away from them and go into the parlour with the dark chenille curtains and the glass bookcase. There were old annuals there, *Chatterbox*, and musty bound volumes of *Atalanta*, and the *Home Doctor*, banded with gold, and too heavy to hold.

Dolly went through them all. The first time she opened the *Home Doctor* she was fascinated. There were men with stumps and moustaches, enduring terrible things; and then a folded diagram opened to show networks of nerves and arteries in a man stripped of skin...

She shut the book and locked the glass door, and for a long while she would not go back. Her mother could not understand it, nor could Mrs Stanley. "I don't know," she said. "She just walked out without a word, as white as a sheet. Did she say anything to you?"

"No. Just that she didn't want to go back."

But she went back, eventually, because she had to have another look; and when the first horror of the *Home Doctor* had spent itself, she discovered the book about martyrs, and this time she did not run from it, though it frightened her even more. The saints suffered willingly, too willingly, but they did not hide their pain. Wide mouths yelled, eyes rolled to Heaven. The pictures were red with fire and blood, but the saints did not die. They stayed screaming; and reading about it was worse than looking, because it told *everything*, the pincers and the burning, and how they dragged themselves about. She gnawed at her nails, trying to get the thought of it out of her mind.

"Don't bite your nails," her mother said to her, "*and don't suck your thumb!* Honestly, Dolly, if it's not one thing with you, it's another!" She went to Mrs Stanley to escape, and there, in the bookcase, was a scissor man, lean, leaping, and a child screaming in a shower of blood, or sprouting flames from every finger. "Struwwelpeter," said the sprawling letters, and she dreamed about it at night, but she did not tell her mother why she wakened and screamed. Her mother would have blamed it on her reading, and forbidden her to go to Mrs Stanley's again.

It was about this time that Mrs Stanley had what she liked to call, with a certain amount of pride, "her accident." A car battery that her husband, who was a garage attendant, had put, for some reason, on the top shelf of the cupboard, overturned and showered her with acid. She was alone at the time, but she managed to get to the door and shout for Mrs Dean. There was a great crying and running to and fro between the two houses, and for a while the doctor came every day; and then Mrs Stanley appeared again, as cheerful as ever, and looking almost the same. She had a tendency, however, to dwell on the accident, and Dolly saw her draw her blouse down and show the red weals on her breast before she covered them up tenderly again. She noticed the wry pull on her mouth as she touched the scars; and there was a blouse, a white blouse, eaten into holes, that was shown off sometimes to the gloating neighbours.

Dolly could not get the accident out of her head. Her mother and the other neighbours had taken turns at nursing her when she was in bed, and their whispers rolled down the echoing stairs: "... couldn't bear the blankets over her... marked for life. If you'd seen what I seen, Mrs... Oh, I never knew a woman to suffer like that!"

Somehow, because of this, Dolly could not feel the same towards Mrs Stanley. She was always afraid that she would draw her blouse down and show her scarred bosom; and yet she wanted to see...

She was always drawn to forbidden things. From the landing window, three storeys high, she could see into the next backyard, uneven with stones, and with great coarse dockens sprouting in the corners. Her mother called it "the dirty yard" and warned her not to go near it; but one day she stared and stared till she couldn't resist it any longer, and at last she climbed over the crumbling wall and into the forbidden yard.

Her own window was high, high above her, her own yard looked strange and unfamiliar. Here she could see into doors which from above were only shapes to her, wash houses with dripping taps and broken tubs, and a dirty lobby stretching into darkness. A sour, soupy smell came from the lobby, and suddenly there was a man at her side, a thin, high-shouldered man in a dirty pink jersey.

She knew who he was. She had seen him from a distance standing in the yard, with his high shoulders and dingy grey head. He was deaf and dumb, and nobody cared what happened to him. "It's a shame," her mother said. "Three women next door, and not one of them sees that he gets a decent meal. He'd be better off in a home somewhere."

For all that, she warned the child not to speak to him, never to speak to anyone from the dirty yard; and here he was now, his hand on her arm, grunting and making queer noises. His eyes were cold blue stones in a tiny skull. She screamed, and a fat woman in a rubber apron came and pulled him away. He shuffled over to a stone stair in the corner, and the woman shook her fist at him.

Before Dolly could make up her mind to run, the woman had gone into her house and came back with a chunk of bread and rhubarb jam. "Here, love," she said coaxingly, and Dolly was afraid not to take it. She carried it back to her own yard, and there she dropped it in the dustbin.

She wanted to tell her mother about it, but she knew she would get into trouble for going, so she kept quiet, though she could not get the thought of the man out of her head. The house up the stone stairs had dirty windows, and she knew just what it would be like inside. She would lie in bed, seeing it, and where did the images come from, a furnace room with a black boiler taking up nearly all the space, and the floor all ashes? In the middle of the ashes the man would lie on an iron bed, blinking at the grey dark.

She did not know how she knew this. She did not like knowing. Then one day the bed was outside, poised on top of the stairs, and the man still in it. Rain fell on him, wind plucked at the covers, but he didn't move. With a sick horror on her, Dolly ran crying to her mother, and told her to make the man go away. Her mother took one quick, astounded glance, and shook the child till she was stupid. "There's no bed there, do you hear? There's nothing. Telling lies like that—you try that nonsense again, my girl, and I'll have something to say to you. The very idea!"

It was never mentioned again. Her mother did not believe in encouraging nonsense, and Dolly was afraid of her mother. She loved her, she ached with love of her, but somehow she could not talk to her. There was never time. Her mother had been rushed off her feet ever since she had been left a widow, and Dolly came back from school now to an empty house. The house was growing more and more neglected, dust on the dresser, spiders' webs in the corners, cold grease in the frying pan. The mirrors were dim, and Mrs Dean never swept up the crumbs until Dolly was in bed; and Dolly was always glad to go.

Hunched up, eyes screwed, she would lie tense with a terrible pleasure, imagining things, the things she was afraid of, Mrs Stanley sizzling away in acid, the high-shouldered man doing horrible things, the saints with their eyes turned up and their mouths yelling. The pictures would come to her small, miles away, but so clear that they *rocked* with intensity; then they would rush together and explode in a black star, and she would feel herself trembling and somehow ashamed.

"Why don't you go out to play?" her mother said irritably. "Mix with the other girls. Haven't you any friends at school?" She could not explain that at school the other girls laughed at her. Where authority saw her as a quiet child, sweet-faced and docile, her classmates saw only lank hair, glasses, and a tendency to fidget. Even the teachers could not ignore her fidgeting. "For goodness' sake, Dolly, sit still. You'd think you had St Vitus' Dance!" Who was St Vitus? A long, deranged monk, continually on the twitch? Sometimes, as she walked home alone, he jerked and hobbled beside her; and when she got in she would sit quiet, so still that her mother noticed it; and dull as it was, she would wish that things could always be like that, because it pleased her mother.

She had a great and touching urge to be good. Sometimes she was happy, in a peculiar sort of way, as if she was living each day with a touching devotion to everyone she loved. Surely, then, things had been happier, the times long ago, when she was small, and her mother took her on her knee and sang to her

"Oh, Dorothy, Dorothy Dean,
Oh, Dorothy, where have you been?
She's suddenly flown
To regions unknown,
Along with a man in a flying machine!"

Funny how it came back to her now, the old-fashioned song, through the racket of records the girls played in the Common Room, the heartsick crying of the Top Twenty and the pop charts. Funny how it frightened her, the Regions Unknown, sadder than anything wailed out by the boys with guitars.

"I just can't understand it," said Mrs Dean querulously. "She's had every chance. Of course, she's been left on her own a bit, but who hasn't? You've just got to trust them. You can't be around all the time."

"Do you have to go out to work, Mrs Dean?"

"How else do you think we'd manage? It could be done, I suppose, but it would only be a bare living. I wanted to give her nice things, things I could never afford myself. And they *need* so much nowadays, record players, school trips—you just can't keep up with them. Not that Dolly ever asked for anything. She was quite happy, just reading and imagining things. I know some have said she'd too much imagination, but I saw to it that she kept it under control. I soon knocked the imagination out of her."

"What did Dolly do when you were out, Mrs Dean?"

"Oh, she went over a lot to Mrs Stanley's. That's why I can't understand it. Ever since she could walk she's been in and out as if it were her own house. And Mrs Stanley wasn't the one to stand for a lot of nonsense either. There's no imagination about *her*. That's why I always felt she was so good for our Dolly..."

It was Mrs Stanley who first put the idea into her head. Dolly had gone over quite happily—but she did not look happy. She had a new mannerism now, a habit of peering round and rubbing her chin on her shoulder. There was no pleasure in it for her, nothing but an uncomfortable desire to do it once and for all and be finally rid of the temptation; but the temptation grew with every indulgence, until her mother sometimes slapped her in frustration, and the teachers checked her at school. It was time, everyone agreed, that Dolly grew out of that sort of thing; and Dolly knew it better than anyone.

That morning, Mrs Stanley took it on herself to do something about it. She started as soon as the girl came in, before she could lift a magazine from under the cushions. "Do you know this, Dolly? People will think you've got something on your shoulder if you keep looking round like that. I knew a girl once that had a black imp on her shoulder. Nobody but her could see it, but she knew it was there, and she was always looking at it—"

"What happened to her?"

"The girl? Oh, I don't know. They took her away, I think. But she used to look round just like you—"

"I think I'll go back to my own house now," said Dolly, her mouth tight smiling, her heart nearly choking her.

She did not really believe there was an imp on her shoulder. She could not see it in the mirror. She stared in the smoky glass, and the room looked odd and fascinating, all the furniture back to front, and her face not at all as she imagined it. Her cheeks were red, guiltily red, her hair dark, and her tongue sly, pointed at the edge. Suppose the imp *was* there? She jerked her head sideways, to surprise it, and thought she saw the flick of a black tail; but it was only her hair, flung round. There was nothing. Of course there wasn't. Then, sitting quiet at the fireside, reading her book, she felt it on her shoulder, the slight weight and warmth of it, and a sweat came out on her as she sat rigid, waiting for it to move.

"Will you set the plates for me, Dolly?"

"Mummy." She said it experimentally, her voice casual, but with screaming undertones. "Mummy, there's something on my—"

"What, dear?" Her mother was at the sink, pouring the potatoes, her mind already on the next task, and Dolly knew that she would never be able to tell.

"Nothing," she said, and went carefully, steadily to the table.

In time, her mother noticed it. "What are you holding your shoulder like that for?" she asked, irritable at always having to criticise. "Your left shoulder's higher than your right. Have you got a stiff neck, or something?"

"No. No, it's all right." She relaxed carefully, so as not to disturb the resting fiend.

"If it's not one thing, it's another. Why you've got to get up to all these capers, I don't know..."

She walked at a slow, gliding pace, because she was afraid that a jerk might send the invisible thing flying. Or would it dig in its claws? She was afraid to put it to the test. It was like having an animal that could be vicious, but what kind of an animal she didn't know. Black, maybe, with sharp ears and a bat's wings and a tail like a devil's?

Her mother poked the fire, and flirted the brush from the companion set.

"Do you *feel* anything wrong with your shoulder?"

"It—it feels heavy. As if there was something on it."

"Well, there isn't. And the quicker you get those ideas out of your head, the better."

But her mother was wrong. The weight shifted, the clutch of small feet tightened, and sometimes there was a warmth of breath at her ear. Once or twice she put up a hand to feel, but there was nothing—unless it had edged away. It seemed able to move. At night, reluctantly, it let her undress, but in bed it sat, touching her, on the pillow. And all the time, she wanted to tell about it.

There was sun in Mrs Stanley's kitchen, and she blamed her mother because their house was at the dark side of the building.

"Oh, come in Dolly. My, what's wrong with your shoulder?"

"It's nothing." She walked in, casual and cautious, but her voice went high with the effort of not tilting the fiend. "Any magazines, Mrs Stanley?"

"There might be one or two. Go and have a look." She handed her a biscuit from the tin, pink mallow and coconut. "You're a great girl for the books. How are you getting on at school?"

"Fine, thank you." She chewed the biscuit, but the crumbs went dry in her mouth. "Mrs Stanley, remember that girl with the black imp?"

"What girl, dearie?"

"The girl that used to look round like me." Her voice broke, and she swallowed. "And you said she'd an imp on her shoulder."

"Oh, that one? I don't know. Nobody knew for sure that there *was* an imp. It was just the way she kept looking round, and people said—"

"Mrs Stanley, I think there's one on my shoulder!" It was out now, in tears and wild panic. "I know I kept looking round, but it wasn't for that, honest it wasn't! I just did it because... I just did it! But now I feel one there..."

Mrs Stanley smoothed her skirt, and swallowed two or three times. Her eyes, fearful suddenly, looked over the child. "Tell me where it is," she said nervously. "*I* can't see anything."

"No, but neither could the other girl. And neither can I. But I can *nearly* see it. Just here..."

"Oh, get away with you!" Mrs Stanley was becoming more confident. "You've far too much imagination. I—I was just kidding about that other girl. I said it to get you to stop that habit you've got."

"I can't stop. I can't stop now it's there."

"But it isn't there! Did you tell your mother about it?"

"No. She'd have been angry. She shook me when I told her about the man in the bed—"

"What man?" said Mrs Stanley, sharply, almost eagerly.

"The man in the dirty yard. He used to lie in bed, on the stairs. I could see him... there was a furnace in his room, and he used to get burnt squeezing past..." She could not stop herself, the horrors mounting, crowding out of her mouth to the woman who did not want to hear—

Mrs Stanley went white, and the sunlight in the room seemed to sicken. Jerkily, she went over to the window and craned out. There was the shabby yard, the stone stairs and the iron railing; but there was not a bed to be seen, and no room for one on the landing; and the deaf man had been taken to a home long ago.

"You're making it up," she said. "You imagined it."

"I know," said the child. "But it comes into my mind and frightens me, and it's *there*! And now there's this imp—you shouldn't have *told* me—"

"I know what'll happen to you." Mrs Stanley picked up her duster nervously, and inched her way among the ornaments. "There's a place for people who let their imaginations run away with them. I remember one girl who was always making up stories. She got so she didn't know what was real and what wasn't; and one day they came for her in a black van—"

"NO!" Dolly screamed, seeing the van draw up, knowing that, if Mrs Stanley said so, it would be so. There was desolation and terror in knowing that now, at last, she had gone too far. She lifted a knife, a poker, a candlestick, she didn't know what it was, and screamed and screamed as she went for her; and somehow there was a queer pleasure in it, the twisted pleasure of the martyr book, and the cruelty of Struwwelpeter.

Nobody scolded, everyone was very kind as they took her, Dolly, back to her own house, and her mother, and the people who came for her in a closed van. And now all she felt was the desire to be safe and good. She was played out and weary, and chastened at the thought of what she had done. But it would be all right. She could behave if she wanted to. She sat quiet and conscious of her self-restraint, and there was nothing on her shoulder. She looked around, she moved her shoulder, but the imp had gone. Surely that was a good sign? Surely, if she did what they told her, they would let her go home... she thought of her mother, her face tired, her hands tired, and her mouth squared with the strain of not crying. All she had to do was run into her arms, and never let go as her mother petted her.

"Oh, Dorothy, Dorothy Dean,
Oh, Dorothy, where have you been...?"

Her mother was standing with Miss Gallacher, all dressed up for visiting, with her pearls on, and her navy suit, and her gloves all grubby with train dust, and as soon as Dolly saw her she knew she was angry. "Well? I hope you've been behaving yourself. You'll have to pull yourself together, you know, if they let you out of here..."

It went on like that all the time. She did not cry when the visit was over, and her mother gone, still indignant and hurt. Stiff, icy cold, she sat alone, and there was nothing behind her, nothing good or bad to remember, and nothing to look forward to or dread. And then, suddenly, there was a slight pressure on her shoulder, a warmth of hair or fur on her face. For a moment, she almost saw it; and then it settled down, invisible but familiar, the fiend, the friend; its weight no longer a burden, and its touch a caress.

DAY OF WRATH

he child worked gently, with a kind of timid reverence. It was dark in the mortuary, with the altar at one end, and the windows covered with wire netting. "Dust the bier," Nurse had said. "Wash the floor, and polish the altar brasses." Ella had wanted to hang on to her, to beg her to stay in case Mary Vincent or any of the other dead ones should come out of the gloom and smile; but she was almost more afraid of Nurse than of the dead, so she had folded her duster into a pad, and touched the wood as if it would burn her.

Now, working more quietly as the fear left her, she was almost glad to be on her own for a while. Nurse had a soft, cruel way with her which cured her patients because they were afraid to stay ill. She threatened castor oil, and administered it in the dispensary with the door shut; and she laughed when a dressing was to be pulled off...

Ella had only worked in the Infirmary for a week, and already Nurse had called her the laziest and most inefficient child in the orphanage. Now, lifting down the cross and the candlesticks, she felt for the first time an inclination to work well. With no-one to hurry her, she would linger over her task, so that Nurse, coming back to inspect and lock up, would surely admit that the brasses were brighter than ever before.

But she could not work in the mortuary. It was a holy place, but Mary Vincent had laid there, and when they had come to screw her down, she had smiled at them. Annie Sneddon said so, and she had been at the orphanage longest, and ought to know. They had buried Mary Vincent in spite of her smile, and perhaps, even now, if you dug her up...

So she lifted the crucifix and candles, and carried them to the door. There was long grass by the path, and a sprinkling of long black nettles. A bee went past on a high whang of sound, and the sun was hot, as soothing and golden as syrup. Carefully, she sat herself down in the grass, and lifted the crucifix on to her lap.

With the rag ready smeared with polish, she looked at the brass Christ. It was a strange, contorted image, heaved awry with suffering. The face, the small carved face, was twisted and distinct; the eyes were black sockets of agony, the beard jutted as the jaws locked in pain. Here there was no drooping languor, no sighing commendation of the spirit. It was crucifixion, the Christ convulsed, the cry lamenting, "*Why* hast Thou forsaken Me?"

She breathed heavily, her tongue lolling at her lips. The cross was heavy, but the Christ was small as a toy. He would lie on the palm of her hand. She traced a finger round the curve of His body, and the body shifted a little and settled again. The Christ and His cross had been fashioned separately, and joined in a real crucifixion, and now the screws were loose, and God lay on a bed of dried Brasso. Tenderly, the child twisted the screw heads, and the brass figure slewed sideways and was tight in her clutch like a lizard struggling to escape.

It did escape. Sideways in the sunshine, it lurked and darted, flickering through the grass with a twist and a rustle. It looked like a yellow flame, low among the grasses, and the girl sat in a fixed horror, her hand at her mouth. She could not move, and the little

Christ dipped and fluttered, farther away, almost out of sight before she realised it.

She did not want to go after it. She could not believe it had gone. There had been no moment of relinquishment, no wrench and wriggle to mark the striving for freedom. But the cross was gaunt and bare without its burden, and from a distance she saw the small Christ flat like a discarded toy. "If the Nurse comes…" she thought, and pulled herself up to retrieve it; and the image started off again, all humped and squint, and the sun flashed on it as it bobbed along the ragged path to the graveyard.

"If it's alive," she thought, "If God is only…" She could not reason or collect her thoughts. Beneath her fear was disappointment at the triviality of the Trinity. Nurse was still the avenging God; but the little figure moved again, like a crocus low on the path, and she saw it bob and flutter towards the yew trees and the shorn green turf of the graves.

And suddenly, her thoughts tumbled over one another in revelation. The ideas were bright and sharp in her mind, like the image in a smashed mirror. Nurse was nothing, nothing, that is, for a child to hear, unless she feared the sight of her cast away, screaming, to an eternity of pain and fire; because Nurse was wicked, and the wicked, when judged… she saw the woman, ludicrous, going down like a doll thrown from the window, red face rigid, fat legs straight, and her white starch stiff as marble; and a horrid yelling would come from the red face, poised above the flames in one of the eternal moments of eternity…

She did not want to see it; but she had set God free, and He had said that, as His second coming, He would judge the world. The graves would open. The crooked Christ poised on a stone cross like a butterfly, and, suddenly released, she ran towards Him, her hand stretched out to prison the Deity in five fingers. He had settled on Mary Vincent's grave, and Mary would rise smiling, because she had been a good girl; but after all the years, Mary's smile would be terrible to see, the awful stillness and peace of a soul going up to Heaven.

The Jesus jerked free, and she chased it with the polishing rag still in her hand. She was humble in her fear of Him. She had set Him loose, and now she was chasing Him, but there was no irreverence in it at all. Fear wiped out everything, and she prayed like a parrot to the God who eluded her. "Oh God, please! Oh God, let me catch it!" The metal glinted, hither and thither, like a crackerjack, and she zigzagged after it in her sack apron, clutching and snatching at thin air and disappointment.

It went into the church, cool, dark, the smell of stone and candle-grease. It was so quaint and unseemly, God dwarfed to the level of the hassocks, and no sound in church but the sound of boots tramping, and a child sobbing under her breath. She wanted to catch Him before He reached the altar. There was something about sanctuary... but what of the Christ *there*, the gentle soul sagging between the Communion candles? She looked up from the floor, dragging her eyes fearfully over brocade and white linen. The cross was bare. There were black holes where the nails had been, and a smear of polish where the body of Christ had hung.

Weeping, she clutched the empty cross. Her hand was tight round it, tight and clammy. Outside, the day of judgement went past, quiet, still, all sound shrunk to the whisper of a summer day. When she raised her head from praying, the church, too, had shrunk. But it was not the church, it was the mortuary, and on her lap lay the

Christ, bright and glittering; and Nurse was angry, looking at her watch, and the Brasso tin tipped over on its side.

"A whole hour! Sitting there, sound asleep—what have you been doing to the cross? You'd no business to meddle with it at all! There you are, now! Just as I expected. You'd better find them screws, my lady, or it'll be castor oil tonight before you go to bed!"

Bewildered, she groped in the grass, and searched in the folds of her apron; but it was Nurse who found the screws, and finished the job in her impatience to be gone. Fiercely, she snatched up the Christ, fitting His hands to the cruel holes. The body heaved awry with suffering, the beard jutted from the wracked face. "Don't..." said the child, putting out a hand to stop the crucifixion.

"Don't what?"

She could not explain. The Nurse gritted her teeth as the nails went in, deeper and deeper through the cupped palms, and it was good to know that the suffering thing was only a graven image. It could not feel the pain it postured, or mark the venom in the woman's eye. Only the child could do that, calculating her own punishment by the sufferings of the brass Christ; and as she thought of it, the agony in the dispensary, the castor oil going grey and gelid over her throat, the fear of judgement was nothing more than relief that she need not see Nurse go howling into the Inferno, or Mary Vincent rise smiling from the dead.

THE MOONBOW

he last thing I ever expected to do was consult a medium, or go to a séance; but then, the last thing I ever expected was for the Tressels to be dead only a year after their wedding.

Julie and Edward Tressel were friends of mine—very good friends. I was best man at their wedding. Edward had a business, a small factory which made pottery and things, and he painted a bit as well. Julie gave up a librarian's job to help with the factory, doing the books, and generally looking after the business side. On the face of it, things seemed to be going well, and when they married they scraped together as much as they could and paid the deposit on a small cottage in Clovyrigg.

Clovyrigg was a hamlet set among gentle hills, sheep country, green and lush except where the heather took over. One or two farms, a church and tiny hall, a post office, grocer and gift-shop—that was Clovyrigg. The Tressels loved it. "We haven't a minute," they said. "The social life's terrific. You wouldn't believe all that goes on. The church is the centre of everything, and we're all roped in; and then there's the W.I...."

"And what about you Ted?"

"Me? Oh, I'm roped in too. I never thought living in the country could be so hectic."

They were so happily involved that I made a point of ringing them up before I committed myself to visiting them, whereas at one time, when they were in town, I would have dropped in in passing. But don't get the idea I wasn't welcome. An evening with the Tressels was something to remember, not because they made a splash—they were too hard up for that, anyway—but simply because they were such good and genuine people. I always felt better for having been with them.

And then things began to go wrong. Orders fell off, costs and wage demands began to rise, and the factory had to close. It closed at a bad time. Edward couldn't find a job, and there was their mortgage hanging over them. One night they came to see me, and I'll never forget the look on their faces, worried, guilty, and yet proud, a look as if they had a prize coming which they felt they didn't deserve.

"Don't tell me," I said. "You've got a job."

Ted shook his head. "Wish I had, Tom. No, it's Julie—"

"Well, so long as one of you has a wage coming in."

They looked puzzled. "I haven't—" Julie began.

"Oh, she's getting a job all right," said Ted, "but not a paying one. We're going to have a baby."

He looked so comical, his expression all mixed up between chagrin and delight, that I couldn't help laughing at him. Julie sat and hugged herself, and laughed too, with a kind of blush on her face.

"You're pleased, then?"

"Oh, we're delighted! Actually, we're worried to death. I don't know how we're going to manage, but—"

"We'll have to drink to this."

"No." Ted never drank when he was driving; so we made coffee, and sat by the fire, and we discussed ways and means of getting work for him, even if it was emptying dustbins. They left about nine o'clock, as cheerful and indomitable as ever, and I was sentimental enough to act the old bachelor and say something corny about the baby being like a rainbow shining through the clouds.

"Ah well, let's hope there's a crock of gold at the end of it," said Ted.

That was the last I saw of them. Their car crashed on the way home, and because of the circumstances, everyone assumed it was a suicide pact. There was nothing wrong with the car, nothing to cause it to crash. It had been raining, but the road wasn't greasy, and there had been no skid. There had been no traffic. They had simply driven straight on at a bend, run into a wall, and been killed instantly.

I couldn't stand this talk of suicide. It made them out to be defeatist, and that was one thing they were not. They had had so much to live for. All they needed was money, but without it they would have battled on and managed somehow. I was sure of that; and because no-one would listen to me when I argued against the rumours and suppositions, I took what to me was desperate action. I enquired about until I traced a medium who seemed to be reliable, and I arranged to attend one of her meetings.

I suppose I could have had a private session, but I had reasons for preferring to meet her in public. One reason, frankly, was that I was nervous. I wasn't too sure what would happen. The other was that I wanted witnesses.

It wasn't an easy decision. I went so far as to go to see the Rev. Michael Brand, the minister at Clovyrigg, to ask him what he thought about it. He didn't commit himself. He was inclined to agree with me about the Tressels, but not too keen on the medium angle. "However, go if you really want to," he said. "Get it out of your system, and come back and tell me how you get on."

Mrs Bligh—thank goodness she didn't call herself *Madame* Bligh—was an ordinary sort of woman, plumpish, in a crimplene two piece, with a slightly purple look about her hair. I could imagine her taking the chair at meetings, or organising home helps—the kind of woman that always frightens me a little. She rubbed her hands with a managing kind of modesty, and I found that we, the seekers, the audience, whatever we called ourselves, were expected to prepare the room under her supervision.

There were about six of us, men and women, and they all appeared to be regular visitors. They knew where everything was to be found. They placed chairs, they drew curtains, they showed me where to sit; and, acutely uncomfortable, I cleared my throat and put my hands on the table.

For a long time, nothing happened. I didn't know what to expect, but I felt that if there was any sign of ectoplasm I would break away and run. It wasn't that I was afraid. It was just that it was so damned embarrassing, sitting waiting, minute after minute, for something to appear, and I was so keyed up that I wouldn't know how to tackle a materialisation.

And then Mrs Bligh spoke, the chairwoman calling the meeting to order.

"Mrs Sullen. A message from Patrick."

"Yes?" Mrs Sullen, a heavy lady with a grey moustache, sounded as if she had been called to the phone.

"Patrick says you've to remember the pork chops. Does that convey anything to you?"

"Oh yes," said Mrs Sullen, as if she'd heard it all before. I felt that the chops had come up on other occasions, and that she somehow resented Patrick's harping on them.

"Mr Trout. Your wife is worried about you. She says you've to have the operation. No harm will come to you. Have you been worried about your health, Mr Trout?"

He nodded.

"Well, your wife wants to comfort you. She tells you to take her advice."

"She would," murmured Mr Trout. I wondered why he bothered.

So far, Mrs Bligh, though apparently asleep, had spoken in her own voice. I watched her, a dim shape in the semi-darkness, and wondered if her name was Nellie. A rhyme came idiotically into my mind, a tune picked out with one finger on the piano.

> "Nelly Bligh
> Caught a fly,
> Tied it to a string..."

I jumped, and almost lost contact with the hands on the table. Julie Tressel was speaking, a light laughing voice, a voice I would know anywhere.

"Tom! Hello, Tom!"

"... and a message for Mr Ogilvie," said the medium, like an operator cutting in to a phone message.

"Is—is Ted there?" I heard myself asking huskily.

"Of course. Come on, Ted, speak to Tom. He looks so worried!"

And then a peculiar thing happened. I had thought the spirits, or the voices, or whatever they were, would speak through Mrs Bligh, but that didn't seem to be happening. The two voices spoke at once, breaking in on one another, in a perfect duet of bliss and laughter.

"It's wonderful here, Tom. All blue and misty, and the sun shining through, and the colours coming out so strong when the sun shines—you've never seen anything like it! And there's flowers—such flowers as you can't imagine! Everybody's happy. There's nothing to worry about now. We're different. We don't need things... there's music..."

The voices tailed away, Julie's in a characteristic little giggle, and I realised that I had never asked them what happened that night. Not that I wanted to, now. The light went on, the curtains were pulled back, and everyone began to congratulate me on what had happened. Not everyone, I gathered, got such good results at a first meeting. Sometimes they had to wait weeks and weeks for one word.

I couldn't wait to get out. In a way, I wished it had never happened. Those voices definitely belonged to the Tressels—but surely they might have come across with something more original. The same old guff about brightness and flowers...

Well, I'd asked for it. And now I had to admit it all to Mr Brand.

I drive slowly on the road to Clovyrigg. It was just a month since the accident. They had been in good heart when they left me, going home... I looked at the fields and the hills, as they must have done. It was quite light, the moon almost full, but a light smirr of rain making everything ghostly—

Then I saw it, for the first time in my life. A moon rainbow—a moonbow; not so clear, not so substantial as an ordinary rainbow, but unmistakeably coloured. It shimmered ahead of me, straddling the fields, and I remembered Ted saying something about a crock of gold.

It was ridiculous, of course, but I got the idea that maybe there was something in it. One foot of the rainbow rested on the road. There, just there! I put my foot down, and gained on it a little, but it eluded me like the path of the moon on a lake. I went faster again, before it faded, and then stopped with a jerk that nearly sent me through the windscreen. I was only a few inches from a stone dyke, the very spot where the road curved sharply, and where Ted and Julie had crashed.

I sat trembling on the quiet road, puzzling it out and wondering what the Rev. Brand would say about my explanation. Because I thought I could see what had happened. I had started it with that daft remark about rainbows; then, driving to Clovyrigg, with the moon almost full, and in a light rain, just as it had been tonight, they had seen a moonbow, and tried to catch it…

It was a triumph for me, in a way. I had known all along that their death had been an accident. But what about all that hackneyed stuff in the séance this afternoon? That was what I had to think about seriously, so that I could put my case to Rev. Brand with some kind of conviction; because it all tied up, the beauty, the joy, the freedom from care. A month ago, Ted and Julie, driving too fast, and with lack of care, had done what I had just stopped myself from doing. They had found the foot of the rainbow.

VOCATION

he was alone in her cell, praying. It was so still that her fidgeting fingers made little noises, dry noises like crickets in the grass. Tomorrow she was to make her vows, and as she prayed, she let her mind go back to the start of it all, seeking a sign to show her that the way she had chosen was the answer to her prayer.

It had happened two years ago, when she was on holiday.

"Put your two fingers on the glass, dear," Miss Mather said. "Lightly. Just make your mind a blank, and let the spirit guide you."

They were alone in the lounge, bent over the coffee table with its tumbler and its ring of letters. Miss Mather had put the light out, and the standard lamp, with its shade tilted towards them, covered them in a parchment-coloured glow. It was silly, Susan thought. She didn't believe in it, but in these small hotels one had to be sociable.

"Don't think of anything," Miss Mather said, coughing over her cigarette. "Just relax, and It'll do all the work."

The clock ticked, and the woman opposite breathed hard through her nose. She was like a man, Susan thought, with her tie and her striped shirt and her smoker's cough. She looked at the fingers, square-nailed, and the sleeves with the pearl cuff links, and suddenly the tumbler lurched and jigged erratically. "You pushed," Susan said, watching it slither and pause.

"No, I didn't. Hush. Concentrate and see what It says."

The glass was stubborn again, poised in the centre of the circle. Throwing away her cigarette, Miss Mather spoke in a firm, masculine voice.

"Who are you? Tell us your name or your initials."

Slowly, the glass veered over to the letter C, touched it, and slid across to V. Susan raised her eyebrows, and Miss Mather frowned for quietness. "C" it said again, and "V, CV, CV, CV" over and over again.

"Two names," said Miss Mather. "Let's ask for more information. Have you a message for us?"

"S-U-S—" The Glass faltered and stopped.

"You. You ask It, my dear. It's you It wants."

"Oh, but—all right, then." She laughed suddenly, letting her disapproval go. Enter into the spirit of the thing...

"Male or female?" she said, edging a little nearer.

"S-I-S-T-E-R-S."

"Well! You must have the gift, Miss Simpson. Ask their proper names. See if they'll tell you."

"C-H-R-I-S-T-I-N-A V-E-R-O-N-I-C-A."

"I bet they're nuns," said Susan, and then she started, scared at herself. What had made her think of that? It was not even a question. But—

"Y-E-S," said the tumbler definitely.

"You're sure you're not cheating, now?" asked Miss Mather, lighting another cigarette. "You mustn't decide on the answers beforehand, you know."

"No, I didn't. It just came to me, somehow, that they might be nuns. I don't know why. You ask the next question, and see."

Miss Mather thought for a moment before asking, "Where are you speaking from?" as if she were dealing with a deaf person over the telephone. There was a clatter as the glass careered in circles, scattering the letters out of place. "Mischief," said Miss Mather, removing her fingers. "Too much noise. Find out which one's talking."

Strange how easy it was to be serious about it. Susan waited, as Miss Mather took over again. "CHRISTINA," said the glass, and then, without a pause, "HELL."

"Good Heavens!" gasped Miss Mather, affronted and a little afraid. "There's no need—"

"Let me, now." Susan was eager, a great power and curiosity surging inside her. "Are you in Hell? You must have done something wrong. Tell me what you did."

There was a long pause, and then the glass faltered slowly, as if in shame. "L-O-V-E..."

"What...?"

"That's enough now," barked Miss Mather, sweeping up the letters and setting the tumbler upright with a bang. "You've a vivid imagination, you know. Too vivid, I don't think we should do any more of this tonight."

Next evening, however, they started again, with an audience grouped round the larger table in the middle of the room. "Don't pay any attention to them," Miss Mather whispered. "Concentrate. Just forget about yesterday and concentrate."

She was serious about it, serious and rather perturbed, but to Susan it was still nothing more than a joke. Miss Mather had been cheating. It had been easy to feel the pressure of her fingers on the glass. But when the glass started its C-V careering all over again,

Miss Mather frowned and said, "Don't push, dear. Don't anticipate what It wants to say."

"H-E-L-P," it spelled, without any prompting. "S-U-S-A-N HELP."

There was a murmur all round the table. "That's what It meant yesterday," said Miss Mather, with relief. "Got Its spelling wrong."

"How can I help?" Susan asked, speaking coaxingly. "What can I do?"

"C-O-M-E."

"Come where?"

The tumbler went berserk in an orgy of communication. "WHERE I BURN."

"I don't like this," said Susan. "If you're playing a trick—"

"I wouldn't dare." Miss Mather looked sickly in the parchment-coloured light. "Do you want to stop? It's up to you."

"Ask It—no, I'll do it. How did you die? What happened?"

"W-A-L-L..." The tumbler faltered and stopped.

"Walled up!" Miss Mather's voice was almost shrill, pushing the tumbler away as if it were a reptile. "I knew it! Love," she said. "That's how they punished them..." She looked at Susan, then round at the watching audience. "Just keep out of this," she warned. "You don't know what you're playing with."

Had she tried it, pulling the answers from the wish of her subconscious mind? It was easy enough. The glass spelled Y-E- and the fingers pushed automatically towards S. But what had started the story? Veronica and Christina had come unbidden. The nuns were her own idea, but who had put the idea into her head? And she had never thought of them as being in Hell. Were they both in Hell, or was it only Christina? She tried one night, after she was home, sitting at the kitchen table with her sister, but the glass would not co-operate. Not, that was, to the extent of anything new. "Who is Christina?" she asked, and got the answer, "NUN." But when she asked about Veronica, she got nothing but a jumble of phrases, SUSAN HELP, DAMNATION or COME...

Sometimes she laughed at it. Sometimes it worried her. The game cropped up at parties, and she played it, joking dreadfully. "Let's see what Christina's got to say today." The answers were all the same, her finger pushing out the letters with too much assurance. It was only with Veronica that she drew a blank.

"Leave it alone," her mother told her. "It's enough to make anybody daft." But her mother could not know how it obsessed her. In bed, with the light out, she would go over and over the nun's last hours. She lay with the agony dragging through her own mind, far too vivid and detailed, the bricks earthy brown, damp-looking, and the trowel going lick, lick like a grey tongue. At first the doomed one would stand quiet, contemptuous, knowing that a step could mount the structure. Suppose she struggled...

But it would not happen that way. The wall would mount brick by brick, and there might be prayers from the mouth which could still breathe and articulate. Breast high, the hands might forsake the rosary, and rest a moment, almost lovingly, on the soft mortar; and then a brick would bruise the nails, and the hands would retreat in quick pain; and soon the wagging, trembling chin would thrust forward in a last look, and the mouth scream in sudden realisation...

But it was when the light went that the cries would be most anguished. They would ring out, astonishingly loud, beating and fluttering in that small place, the narrow place without air; and the other nuns would listen, a sickness sucking at their hearts and thinking, in death she will be upright. There was no room to fall; and how did she keep silence so long, knowing the dread death only an hour away, and the more dreadful judgement to follow?

"Damnation," Christina had said, and Susan would not follow her that far; but in dreams she hung over a Biblical Hell, the steep-sided pit with its sulphur fumes and fathoms of searing fire. She could see the nun there, tossed in the tide, a small triangular face and a shorn head not yet burned away. It took eternity to burn. The face pleaded, tortured, above the white hot flux of the body; and there was a piteous beauty about it, pain and a twisted innocence...

But she kept her conscious thoughts away from it. Hell, to her, was a tumbler sliding, the black letters being nosed out of place. She brooded, and refused her food; the man who used to call on her had gone away long ago. When her mother, worried, showed irritation or dismay, she sprang into a ghastly sprightliness, but she found the effort more tiring than it was worth. Gradually, she was beginning to lose touch with her mother, her sisters, her friends. The girls in the office were growing tired of her moods, and she didn't care. All she wanted was to be left alone.

Prayer soothed her. Sometimes at the dinner hour she would slip out to a church, and come back late for work. Her fingers fumbled in the typewriter, her lips muttered, and peace was already slipping from her soul. So quickly... there was never enough time to store up peace...

There was a convent near her home, a small place with a tower rising over the high encircling wall, and sometimes the sisters let visitors in to look round the grounds and the less private parts of the building. She went in one day, with a handful of people. Strange how she had never been interested in it before. How quiet it was, quiet and narrow and peaceful! It frightened her, the stern discipline moulding the peace. The faces seemed all the same, like masks...

The sister who was guiding them smiled perpetually. She smiled even in the graveyard, among the worn crosses with the names, Sister Benedicta, Vocation 21 years, Sister Martha, Vocation 15 years, Sister Perpetua, Vocation 10 years—

"You hadn't—you hadn't a Sister Christina here?" asked Susan. "Or do you not...?"

She had not wanted to say it. The words had come out unthinkingly, before she realised that this was the name she had been seeking all the time. "I just wondered—maybe long ago...?"

The nun did not answer. Only, her smile faded a little, and a closed look came into her eyes, as if she were seeing with dread, and almost with satisfaction, the horror of justice which comes to a woman breaking her vows. "It was nothing, really," Susan murmured, sick at the mute confirmation. "Only a name I heard..."

"You see all the graves here," the nun answered.

She visited the convent again and again. The place fascinated her. She did not want to become a nun. She had a horror of eternal renunciation, the boredom of penury and penance; but at least there would be peace, time to meditate, to let her mind go till it reached the mind lost and damned... She forsook prayer, and consulted the tumbler again. Her mother, sceptical but resigned, went out of her way to help her, one worn finger to the glass, and the letters moved in little nudges, "COME", and more slowly, "W-H-E-R-E I B-U-R-N."

"It's wicked!" The woman scattered the letters, and left the glass upturned among the little cards. "You'll have to get rid of these notions. Are you *listening*? How long is this going to last?"

"I don't know," said Susan. "I don't know."

She became a novice. There was no love, no joy in her decision. All she wanted was time to meditate, to bury herself in her vision and so sate herself into peace. But there was no rest at all. The body suffered and shrank a little, and the soul was steered into paths even more strait. Work and prayer loaded the hours, and her sleep was at the mercy of bells which dragged her from her pallet to pray again. In the boredom of eternal obedience, her purpose weakened. How had she been trapped into this? She should have confessed her fantasies, had them explained away and exorcised. Her belief in them was fading; and so there was now no point in her dedication.

But she could not draw back; and now, making her last prayers before the bonds were tightened and the body tethered to the dominant soul, she went over it as if she were memorising an old story. "Put your fingers on the tumbler, dear..." The laughing acquiescence became the cancer-like growth of her dread. The dread had borne fruit now. She was here, swaddled and shapeless, and tomorrow the key would turn on her.

And what good would it do? In the tight bitterness of relinquishment, she prayed for an understanding of her sacrifice. All through the long months there had been no sign, nothing to help her; and now, only half resigned, she repeated her plea.

It was so still, as she knelt, that she could hear her blood pounding out eternity. Her hands sweated, and there was sweat on her brow, and the haggard runnels of her face. If there is any purpose, show it to me, she prayed. Make Thy ways plain, O Lord...!

She was still kneeling when the old nun came in, shuffling on chilblains, and more than half blinded with cataract. So that was how it ended, a name on a tombstone, the modest boast, Vocation—how many years? Strange how she had thought of them all as young... but one renounced youth here. One even renounced one's name. The old nun placed a slip of paper on the bed, and went shuffling away without speaking, and the novice reached out her hand and unfolded the paper, still on her knees. It was there now, the sign, the direction, she had pleaded all night; and as she read the two words, she knew that prayer could no longer help her. There, in black letters, like the letters the tumbler had chosen, was her new name, and her destiny; her obituary, and her only epitaph,

SISTER VERONICA.

THE MEMORY

"It was my father said to me, 'Bessie, there's a man being hanged in the street, and if you're good, I'll take you.'"

Her voice warmed as the girls leaned forward to listen. Her black hair was short to her ears, and she wore it in the plain orphanage way, strained back from her sallow face, and held in place with one kirbigrip. Rain danced in the puddles, and the windows were misted with wistful breath. The scrubbed floor was a labyrinth of wet bare footprints, as if a colony of savages had danced in the common room, and the girls sat in secretive little groups, their bare feet tucked under their pinafores.

There was so little to do at the orphanage on a wet day. The *Schoolgirls' Annuals* had been read over and over again, till the gaudy covers hung by a thread; the jigsaw puzzles were always scattered, and the same crowd commandeered the patience cards. The only recreation left was snakes and ladders, and the girls had tired of that long ago. Now they fell back on conversation, and, as always, the conversation grew nostalgic, stretching back into the past with roots which were so often rotten.

Bessie Borthwick had only one tale to tell, but she could always command an audience. She never contradicted herself, never changed her way of telling it, unless she added here and there a detail to make it all more clear. The girls believed every word of it. Doubtful at first, they listened and grued, and forbore to contradict her; and afterwards, whenever they thought of Bessie Borthwick, they remembered the awful thing she had seen...

"It was my father said to me, 'Bessie, there's a man being hanged in the street...'"

How often had she told it? Hundreds of times; and each time, she saw it more vividly, imagination brighter than memory. It was a close, still afternoon, with the sun just out and no more, shining with a dusty flatness on the houses opposite. The door and windows were open for air, but no air came in, and the big geranium on the sill sucked up what was left till there was hardly enough to breathe.

Down in the square, all day, there had been hammering and banging, with women leaning from windows to watch, their houses neglected, their hair uncombed. Bessie did not know what the high wooden edifice was for, but she guessed it would be some kind of stage on which the day's performance would take place.

Her father made her wear her Sunday dress, dark brown, with a touch of lace at the collar. She took his hand, and skipped along beside him. There was a murmur somewhere, like bees swarming in the heat, but there was not a soul to be seen. A queer fiery light shone on the empty streets, and all the houses were shut up.

"Where's everybody?" she asked.

"You'll see," said her father, and wiped the sweat from his brow. "Come on now, hurry! We want a good place!"

When they came round the back of the church, the sound broke on them suddenly, as if cotton wool had been pulled from their ears. The crowd buzzed and bumbled, jammed together, but moving in itself like a swarm dazed with smoke, and scattered at the edges as people hovered about trying to find a vantage point. All the tenements around were cram-jam with heads and faces. Even the roofs were full. The only clear space was the platform itself, and even there, a few boys were clambering up the struts and being knocked down again by hectoring policemen.

Everyone was sweating and uneasy, but hysterically eager. The women at the windows yelled to their friends on the ground, making rude coarse jokes, and screeching with laughter. Bessie's father began to nudge and edge a way to the front of the crowd, a few paces at a time, so that no-one could say definitely that he was moving forward. It was frightening, squashed among the big people. Bessie was suffocated in a tunnel of shifting humanity, fearful of being crushed or separated from her father, of looking up and seeing nothing but strangers. She kept her eye on his broad grey back, and clutched his cuff with tight fingers.

When they got to the front, right opposite the platform, people muttered resentfully, but nobody protested outright, because Bessie's father was a big man with a scowl and a heavy jaw. The sun had gone in now, and purple clouds were piling up behind the chimneys. The whole sky had darkened, and a little wind sprang up, swinging the rope on the gallows, letting everyone see the black noose hanging from the beam. The clouds moved slowly, and thin wisps of steam seemed to drift over the darkness. "Thunder," muttered the crowd, passing the word from mouth to mouth. "Thunder..."

When the cart came, cutting a slow way through the heads and tossing arms, those who could not see it traced its progress by the howls and catcalls and derisive cheers which followed. "Look! Look, d'you see?" Bessie's father lifted her up on his shoulder, but the men behind growled, and she had to be put down again. "We were here first, see? Got as much right as her to our places, haven't we?" "All right, all right!" grumbled Mr Borthwick, and put her down, and smoothed the clothes which had rumpled round her waist.

Bessie could not see who was in the cart, but she clapped solemnly as a man was half dragged on to the platform, his brow bleeding and his arms tied behind his back. The priest was helped up, an old, white-haired man with a red face, then the hangman, with a black mask as if he was dressed for Hallowe'en. He seemed to enjoy the attention which was paid to him, and waved his hand jovially to the mob.

"Daddy, what—"

"Sshht!"

It was time. The priest had prayed inaudibly, and those who had removed their hats kept them off and mopped their brows. The prisoner stepped forward, mouthing, pleading, evidently, but he could not make himself heard. Then the hangman came up with the rope, and the prisoner started at its touch, as if he had but then realised what was going to happen. "No—no!" he screamed. "*No!*" A great wave of laughter echoed round him as he struggled and blubbered.

He had no chance. There were many hands on him, dragging him back, and his heels made long scores on the new wood. After they had put the noose on him, he stood quite still, snivelling a little. A spot or two of rain fell, and the heads turned up, diverted only for a second. Suddenly, the man was swinging out over the crowd, a wild jerking thing against the boiling sky. The men's voices were like wild beasts.

"He's dead now, see?" said her father.

She could not believe he was dead. It was too sudden. The wind was colder now, playing with his hair, and his legs were still jerking about like mad. His face was as murky as the sky.

"I could hardly walk, I was shaking that hard," said Bessie.

Still the rain held off, and still the crowd massed and roared. She began to cry, and asked her father to take her away, but they had to stand still, their heads craned back, watching the dead man's eyes bulge farther and farther, as if they were on stalks…

"Bessie Borthwick, you might come to my study for a moment."

All the girls jumped when the matron spoke. Bessie shook her head, half dazed. There was the common room, the empty grate, the ragged annuals, the rain dirling and drumming long streaks on the window…

"Yes, ma'am," she said.

"Now, Bessie," said the matron, "I've been listening to you, more than once. What was that story you were telling the girls?"

"Please, ma'am, it was before I came here, my father took me to see a hanging."

"Really?"

"Yes, ma'am."

"Oh? I don't suppose you know that people are never hanged in public nowadays? That sort of thing was stopped long before you were born."

"Please, ma'am—"

"And another thing, Bessie. How long have you been at the orphanage?"

"I—I think twelve years."

"And you're nearly thirteen now. That means you were a baby when you came?"

She thought for a minute. "Y-yes, ma'am."

"Well! How is it that you were able to walk about and do all these things before you were a year old? It's rather premature, isn't it?"

She stood quiet, blushing. There seemed nothing to say.

The matron tapped on the desk with her keyring, and smiled, not unkindly.

"I see that you realise what a silly girl you've been. Oh, I know you're not the only one who tells stories. I hear some very strange tales when you think I'm not listening; but yours is—it's not a healthy kind of story, child. It's morbid to think of all these horrible things. Forget about them. Make up something else—but be sure you know you *are* making it up. There's no harm so long as you know yourself it's all make-believe. Now I want you to promise never to mention that subject again. Forget all about it, will you? Put it right out of your mind."

"Y-yes, ma'am."

"That's right. Remembering a hanging! It's so ridiculous! Run along now and don't be silly."

It was all very well to say, "don't be silly." Now she thought about it, she realised that the matron had been right. She had been a baby when she came here; and yet—she *could* remember it! She could see the man twitching as he swung, and feel the hot thundery air, the press of the crowd, and the sickness at her stomach as she saw the man's tongue thrusting from thick lips as if he were mocking her. She could remember every detail of that day. After the hanging, with the rain coming on...

But it stopped there. She knew what the house was like, the dark kitchen, the scrubbed floor and the wool rugs with the lace curtains clean but frail. She remembered her mother at the sunken doorstep, watching them go, but reluctant that the child should see such sights. She had worn a print apron and a dustcap. *That* was all clear, as vivid as the musty smell of the geranium; but before the hanging, and after, there was nothing.

"Forget all about it, and don't be silly." But, if she did forget, everything would be as blank as the emptiness which surrounded the one bright picture. She was afraid of the blankness, afraid of the great spaces of oblivion. The way to security was buried deep in her dream.

Back in the common room, the windows were completely misted over, and another girl had taken her place in the circle. Bessie hardly heard them move up to make room for her. She was remembering something which had escaped her up till now. During the hanging, a stray dog had pushed up to her and she had automatically fondled it. She could feel its nose cold in her hand, and the draught of its tail as it beat against her leg...

UP, LIKE A GOOD GIRL!

hey had never had a funeral at the orphanage before—at least, not so far as any of them could remember. There was one old matron who must have been there when Daisy Dyke died, but she had said nothing about it. The legends that had sprung up after Daisy's death were partly due to imagination, and partly to the long empty nights when there was nothing to do but talk.

The orphanage was short on entertainment The few books they had were falling to pieces, the ludo and halma sets were incomplete. It was easy, then, to huddle together and hand on orphanage lore, how Daisy Dyke, dead in her coffin, kept whispering, whispering, to try to tell how she hated being dead. People passing by the mortuary had heard the low whisper, but had been afraid to stop and listen. Everyone was glad when the earth on her coffin silenced her, because—what could anybody *do*? Better to cover her up, stamp down the soil, and get away quickly.

But though they all carried the picture in their minds, nobody could remember it, nobody knew the secret of her death—if there had been a secret; so Barbara Gordon's funeral was a new experience, anticipated, though no-one would have dared to say so, almost as eagerly as a party. Dinner was early, that day; then there was the almost festive donning of Sunday hats and coats, each sleeve adorned with a black armband, sewed on laboriously the day before. There was the solemn parade to the chapel, where Barbara's coffin stood on trestles, covered in flowers; and each child, going in, was given a single lily purchased at God knows what expense, much as at Christmas parties they were handed a bun going out the door.

It was *very* impressive. Angela-Marie sniffed her lily and listened to the Dead March rumbling out of the organ pipes. Here and there a child sobbed, overpowered by the atmosphere, and Angela-Marie bowed her head self-consciously. Everyone was looking at her. Barbara had been her friend, her best, in fact her only friend; and now Barbara was dead.

They carried the coffin out to the graveyard, six gardeners in their best suits, concentrating on keeping in step. There was a low smirr of rain, making the choirboys' candles fizz a little, and the earth looked as if it was steaming. One or two of the matrons dabbed their eyes, and a few of the children blubbered out loud. The rest looked frightened, curious, or in some way envious. Barbara Gordon, who had not been at the orphanage for very long, had suddenly become the centre of attraction. They were even carving a tombstone for her, and flowers would be laid by it every Sunday.

The gardeners paid out their ropes, the coffin touched bottom; and now every child filed past and threw in her lily. Some of the little ones didn't want to part with their flowers, and were divested of them, then led off howling. Angela-Marie, looking down at the tossed flowers, paused for a moment, half dreading to hear a whisper, but there was not a sound. One more hymn, and then they would all go home; and as a consolation (or a celebration?) there would be jam for tea tonight.

Angela-Marie felt she deserved the jam. For three nights now, everything had been fine.

*

Lying awake, long after the whispering in the bedroom had stopped, she went over it all in her mind, her first meeting with the girl who now lay in a litter of lilies.

She went down the passage with the slightly pompous air of one who has permission to be out of bounds. Inside the kitchen, in front of the range, cook and the kitchen maid talked to each other, their faces to the fire, their voices low. There was a smell of grease and soup and sour milk, and sheets hung from the high pulley, swaying slightly in the heat. She did not look at the sheets. She only said, briefly, "Please, Cook, the new girl," and went over to where a figure sat alone at a large table, tears dripping into a mug of milk and a plate of bread and jam.

"I've got to look after you," she said with institutional politeness. "My name's Angela-Marie Bartleman. What's yours?"

"Barbara Gordon."

"Don't you want that bread?" Her hand darted out and palmed the last slice under her pinafore. "Come on and I'll show you what to do."

The new girl went after her nervously, and Angela-Marie put out a hand and decked her companionably. "Why were you sent here?" she asked. It was the standard opening, the first question anyone was asked at the orphanage. It opened the door to all kinds of drama; but new girls didn't always rise to the bait. Their answers tended to be prosaic. "My mother died," or "My father died, and my mother had to go out to work." It was only later, when the child realised the potentialities of a good story, that she would elaborate, and come out with confessions guaranteed to raise her status and the hair of those who listened.

Barbara was one of the reticent ones. She mumbled something about "consumption" and hung her head.

"My father cut his throat," said Angela casually. "Matron says you're to have a bath."

There was something obsequious about Angela-Marie in spite of her brisk and bossy manner. Her hair was scraped back, her eyes were nervous, but she became more confident as she dragged Barbara here and there, throwing open the locker where she was to keep her clothes, bouncing on the bed to test the laths, showing her how to take off and fold the red blanket on top. "You and me'll be friends," she announced; and then, less certainly, "Will we? You'll be my best friend?"

"All right," said the new girl obediently.

Angela-Marie watched closely as her best friend undressed.

"You put your clothes at the foot of your bed, and they go to the laundry. You won't need them again, anyway. You'll get new ones."

"But I don't want new ones!" Evidently Barbara had observed and condemned the long dark dresses, the heavy boots, the pinafores frilled over the shoulders.

"Oh, but you'll have to wear the same as everybody else." Angela-Marie began to undress now, unbuttoning flannel petticoats, stripping down to navy blue knickers and a striped calico chemise. "Come on," she said. "Take your towel. Hurry up before the hot water's all finished."

The stone floor of the bathroom was dappled with damp footmarks. Hot steam belched from brass taps, girls shrieked four in a bath, their knees up to their chins. Angela stood by as Barbara entered the bath, and helped her to scrub her back with a loofah; and then, back in the dormitory, she led her off to bed, bewildering her with information and warnings about rules. It went on till Matron ordered them all into bed, and they all sat erect in their clean sheets and rough blankets to sing their evening hymn. The gaslight flickered, two fishtail burners turned down low. Matton said, "One, two, three!" and the orphans sang, rather drearily,

> "Now the day is over,
> Night is drawing nigh..."

No-one was allowed to talk after the bleat of the final "A-a-men!" Only a few daring or garrulous characters whispered from bed to bed. The new girl put her head under the blankets and wept, and Angela-Marie curled herself up and prayed. Tonight she had a new friend, yet another friend. "Please, God," she prayed, "let me keep this one. Please, God, let everything be all right, this night and forever more, through Jesus Christ our Lord, Amen."

She prayed with desperation, but without faith; and, as usual, the nightmare came. In the middle of the night, the fat nurse came shush, shush along the bare floor, her grey hair tumbled over her shoulders, her pink dressing gown tatty. "Come on, now. Up. Up, like a good girl." She was so kind, at first, and if everything was all right she tucked you up and gave you a sweetie. Oh, to go back to bed with a sweetie! Stumbling with sleep, Angela-Marie got out of bed and groped underneath for the enamel chamber; but while she was using it the woman began to hit her in sharp, sore slaps, telling her she was a bad, bad girl, in shrill, screaming whispers; and then she went away, shuffling down the corridor with her candle, while Angela-Marie, crying drearily, climbed back into her damp bed to wait till morning.

*

"Wet, ma'am," she answered, as Matron met her eyes; and then there was the routine of puddling the sheet in the bath, rubbing the stains with carbolic soap, and rinsing it out in cold water. It was difficult to wring the sheet out single-handed, and no-one would help. "Eugh!" they shuddered, backing away in contempt. If it was raining you couldn't hang the sheet on the green, so you had to use the pulley in the kitchen, and then Cook railed all the time about smelly sheets dripping where she had to prepare meals.

And now, probably, Barbara wouldn't have any more to do with her. As soon as she left the dormitory, they would all have enlightened her.

"Didn't you know? She never tells anybody. She's a pee-bed. Every night."

"Every single night. That's why she always runs after new girls. Nobody else wants her."

"You don't want to go with a pee-bed, do you?"

"Well... no..."

But Barbara showed no signs of avoiding her. She seemed more at ease, more self-possessed this morning. Sitting in the dining hall, she turned and looked curiously at Angela-Marie.

"*Why* do you wet the bed every night?"

So she knew. When she didn't get an answer, she pressed on with another question.

"Don't you know you're doing it?"

"No. If I knew, I wouldn't—"

"Why don't you see a doctor?" She spoke like one accustomed to life outside, where one "saw" doctors instead of being sent to them.

"He said—he says I'll grow out of it."

Barbara shrugged, as if to say, "Yes, but when?" Then, chattily curious, "Isn't it awful when you wake up and find it's happened?"

Angela hung her head, and munched the lumps in her porridge. Apart from quarrels, when they called her names, none of the girls mentioned her affliction to her face. Barbara Gordon, now, was both frank and inquisitive, and Angela felt there was something disquieting about her interest. Almost, she would have preferred to lose her friendship rather than suffer her inquisition.

When they filed out of the hall, Angela tried to slip off on her own, but Barbara followed doggedly.

"Where are you going?"

"To Miss Struthers' study."

"What for?"

"I get the strap."

"Every day?"

"Yes."

"But you don't *mind*?"

She didn't know what to say. She was used to it; something to be endured and forgotten. Today, she allowed herself to feel the punishment as another might feel it. One stroke numbed her fingers, the other lashed her wrist, and as she walked out, she could feel the hot sting increase, so that she wanted to bend over, her hands under her arms to ease the agony... but she couldn't. Barbara was there, watching her.

"Where are you going now?"

"To the Infirmary. I've got to see Nurse."

"You've to get castor oil!" The voice was eager and gloating. "They told me you get castor oil."

She didn't answer.

"I wouldn't take it. I *couldn't* take it. I'd spit it out."

"I'll have to go." It was like hasting towards sanctuary.

"I'll wait for you!"

Again it was like a new experience, throbbing hands clasped behind her back, the obligatory pose for dosing, the large grey spoon clattering against her teeth, the grey gelid stuff oily over her tonsils. The spoon jerked up, soiling her lips, and she swallowed desperately, gagging, but keeping it under control. Don't think, don't breathe... Barbara watched her keenly as she came out, her face wrinkled.

"I'd be sick."

No answer.

"Doesn't it make you...?"

It did; but she had learned to control the griping pains, to put them to the back of her mind.

"I've never heard of anyone like you before," said Barbara, falling into step, almost happily. It was as if she was taking over, and Angela-Marie was the new girl, out of her depth and miserable.

It went on day after day. "Don't they let you have any tea? But how do you manage to eat all that thick bread without a drink?" She commented on Angela's sleepy wailing when she wakened in the night. It made her more nervous of the punishments she had once accepted. She winced and drew back when the strap came down, and got double, and she threw up the castor oil, bubbling and sobbing over the second spoonful.

She didn't blame the night nurse, or the dreaded day nurse with her castor oil bottle. She didn't blame Miss Struthers, who wielded the strap so efficiently. The one she blamed was Barbara Gordon, the friend who encouraged and demoralised her at the same time; the friend she suspected liked to see her suffer and cringe, but who hid it with sympathy and egged her on to rebellion so that she would suffer even more.

And then, one day, Barbara was admitted to the Infirmary as a patient.

The orphans, kept healthy by hardship and the dread of Nurse, were admitted only in cases of severe illness. Once you went into the Infirmary, it was well known, you hardly ever came out, except to go to the mortuary. Barbara had never complained, but the matron had noticed her face growing thinner, and her eyes larger; she had noticed the cough which hacked away morning and night, and the hectic colour of her cheeks in the evening. That, and the dread word "consumption" on her admission papers, ensured her a bed; the nature of her illness guaranteed her a room to herself.

The others envied her. There were rumours of beef tea and switched egg served mid-morning, and luxuries like cream on her porridge, and slices of chicken instead of orphanage mince. The fact that these delicacies, laid on to tempt her appetite, were as often as not refused, would have driven them mad if they had known. But they didn't know. They climbed up to the window sometimes and stared in, but Barbara was too lethargic to bother; and Angela-Marie, who had longed for a friend, felt a little flower of hope grow in her heart. Perhaps Barbara would die.

It seemed, indeed, that she might. Nurse, who was a reasonable enough woman, was so troubled that she sought about for anything at all to revive or interest her patient. Weighing one lot of trouble against another, she decided that it would do no harm to bend the rules and let Angela-Marie visit her now and again; so Angela tiptoed into the ward, her stomach still queasy from her recent dose, and stopped beside what she was sure was her friend's deathbed.

"How are you, Barbara?"

Barbara's hands peeped over the white sheet, and her eyes glittered.

"I'm tired…"

"When will they let you out?"

"I don't know… you've got castor oil on your lips. Why don't you wipe it off?"

Why don't you leave me alone?

"Can't you come in when you don't smell of castor oil? It upsets me. Surely you can come in some other time?"

"I'll see. I'll ask Nurse."

But she didn't ask. She waited till Nurse was at her tea. Quietly she went along the dark corridors, under the gas turned down low, to where Barbara lay alone in the little room with the blinds drawn and the fire nearly out. It hurt to listen to her breathing. Angela didn't speak. She took a pillow from the other bed, and pressed it firmly over her friend's face. She leaned on it long after the feeble roars had quietened, and the struggling stopped. There was not a tremor in the body, not a breath coming from the lips. Calmly, Angela put the pillow back on the bed, under the top one, and went out.

She couldn't sleep that night, but she pretended, so that no-one would notice. Late, very late, the footsteps came shush, shush along the passage, candlelight growing on the wall, and the fat nurse paused at the bed. "Come on now, up. Up like a good girl!" Angela-Marie rubbed her eyes and stumbled out of bed, and the old woman, surprised, felt the dry sheet, and checked it again. "That's a good lass. My, my, that deserves a sweetie." She rummaged in the pocket of her dressing gown, and Angela-Marie accepted it with a great feeling of gratitude, and went to sleep at once with it clutched in her hand.

It went on for three nights. Matron praised her, Miss Struthers asked her personally how she was getting on, and said she was glad not to have seen her for the last few days. On the day of the funeral, she tossed in her lily almost light-heartedly. So much for friendship.

She was lying awake, dry and grateful, when the moment came, the moment she looked forward to all day, the simple accolade of the night nurse's praise. Shush, shush, went the slippers, the candle glow flickered and grew stronger on the wall. She shut her eyes, feigning sleep, as she heard the words, "Come on now, up. Up, like a good girl!" and she opened them dreamily, struggling up in bed...

It was Barbara Gordon!

She opened her mouth to scream. There was Barbara, in her grave clothes, a dripping candle in her hand. Her black mouth smiled, her black eyes were hollow. Angela-Marie found her scream sticking in her throat, her breath trying to force its way past the scream, and then she ran in terrible silence and panic, hand in hand with Barbara, unable to break free, down the dark passages, out to the grounds, to where the mortuary lay on its own in a corner of the gardens with its bier and its cross and its scary-looking candles that were only lit for the dead.

The night nurse got into trouble, of course, though the Governing Body, listening to her tears and explanations, realised that she had meant well. Surely it was unwise to give a sweet to a half-sleeping child, especially a hard sweet on which one could choke? Better to reward her in the morning, when she was wide awake...

The orphanage children, cheered by the drama of two funerals in three months, dropped their single snowdrops into Angela-Marie's grave with varying emotions. (The Governors had decided that the way things were going, the cost of lilies was going to be prohibitive.) Angela had not been a popular child. She had been a figure of scorn, a pee-bed. On the other hand, her death came to them with more impact than Barbara's. Barbara had wasted away with consumption, decently hidden from public gaze; Angela had died by a misadventure, the sort of thing that could happen to anybody. Sweets were scarce at the orphanage, and were often saved to suck and savour in bed.

Barbara, furthermore, had lain quiet in her grave. No grim legends had sprung up after her burial. Angela, on the other hand... already the whispers were going around, the rumours of sounds heard when they filed past with their last tributes; the sound of someone trying to scream, someone screaming without breath...

Sounding far more terrified than if she had only choked on a sweetie.

CHANGELING

he witch had been sitting on the gargoyle all day. Moreen had watched, saying nothing, while mother combed her hair and tied the ribbon and said, "There! Now stand quiet at the window till mummy gets ready." She had kept quite still, crushing flies under the curtain, and sometimes looking at the people in the street; but always she looked again at the gargoyle where the witch sat drowsing, with her hair like nettle blossom, and her shoulders hunched high like wings.

"What are you always looking at?" said her mother, abstract in a haze of face powder and two kinds of perfume.

"That gargoyle," said Moreen, and her voice caught with a sound like a sob. "Isn't it funny?"

Her mother went over. "Oh, that one? Can you see its face from here, darling? Your eyes must be better than mine. I'll borrow daddy's opera glasses and look some time."

Moreen knew that there was something queer about her. Her mother had never mentioned the witch, and yet there it was, a black hump arching out into the sky. And it was nonsense not to be able to see the gargoyle's face. It was grinning, with whiskers parallel to the wide lips. It had a face like a door knocker, and round ears. The witch was even clearer. Moreen knew that the eyes were looking at her, even though they were shut, and that the hands were green as verdigris, and crippled with warts. Moreen did not like the thought of the witch being feminine. You could not think

The witch had been sitting on the gargoyle all day

of it. Undressing a witch, there would be nothing under the black clothes, nothing but a broomstick, and a short stalk for the head to go on.

In the afternoon, at tea in Mrs Black's house, she sometimes forgot. There was a bronze canopy over the fire, and it was nice to see the fire, even though it was too warm. The carpet at Mrs Black's was fawn, and everything else was fawn and new, and not used very much. Mrs Black had only been in her bungalow a little while. The bungalow was different from Moreen's house, new and uncracked, but not nearly so solid.

Biting her chocolate biscuit at tea, or whispering to her mother, and being led to the bathroom, Moreen had quick, sickening memories of what might be waiting on top of the gargoyle when she saw it again, but she put the thought away from her. At five o'clock, Mrs Black said goodbye to them at the gate. After the quiet of the new road, with its villas and rockeries, the High Street was bedlam with red buses and red freestone houses and the sun soon to be red with setting. Moreen looked up at the church clock. "Half past five," she said, but what she wanted to say was, "Oh, mother, the witch is still there!" Her mother could not see the witch. She had shifted a little, but was still asleep, like a lump of carrion festering on a rock.

Moreen wanted her mother to sit with her at bedtime. She looked so feverish that she got her own way. Mother spoke about sending for the doctor. "I don't like it," she kept saying. "Can't you tell mummy what's wrong? Is your head aching? Your eyes are far too bright, dear." At last sleep came, breathing in from the open window in dark sighs. The child looked very young and babyish. The woman put the night-light on the table and stood still, watching the dull orange tongue lapping up the gloom. Ten o'clock. Moreen should have been asleep hours ago. One had to be firm with children. The woman yawned. Ten o'clock.

The moon was a thin rind curled low in the sky. The spire was squint on the church, and all the houses were leaning backwards. The lighted windows were at all angles, like red postage stamps. Smoke went sideways, a dim black flag in the night.

"I'm seeing things as if my eyes were crossed," thought Moreen. The bare cliff of the steeple shot out the gargoyle like a dangerous ledge. There was no witch, nothing but space, and a sky the deep colour of bluebells. But below the window came a scrabbling like knives scratching along a plate, and a green hand like verdigris clutched at the sill. It was a palsied hand, crippled with warts, but it clung with nail and sinew, and raised the witch's head over the sill. Moreen choked into a little whimper, because the witch's eyes were open now, and looking at her.

"I'm old," said the witch, getting her knee over the sill. "I'm nearly done. I had to climb that last bit."

"Yes," said Moreen, but she wanted to scream for her mother.

The wind clutched the candlewick, and tweaked off the waving tongue. "You were watching me," said the witch. "You looked up at me at half past five."

"Yes," said Moreen. Her hands and feet were cold under the covers.

"I've come for you," said the witch. "I don't want to frighten you. It's not me that wants you, it's the little people."

"No. I don't want to go! I'll scream!" The witch was horrible with the many horrors of the old, the shawlies who swear at closes and smell of gin, the cretins who gape and do not understand, and the fusty poor who never wash. "I'll scream for my mother, and she'll push you out into the street, you nasty old pig!"

The witch stepped back and did not fall. Solid pillars of air held her level in space. "You'll have to come," she said. "Your mother can't help. I thought all little girls wanted to go to fairyland!"

"I want my mother!"

"Your mother won't wake till morning."

"I don't want to go!"

"No, dearie, and the changeling they've put in your little bed doesn't want to come here, either. She'll have to, though, like it or not. Your mother won't know the difference, but she won't love her the same. It's not me that says it has to be, it's the little people."

"I want my mother. Go *away*, you dirty witch! I don't like you!"

"It's not my fault. See, the changeling's there already. She doesn't want to come here, but she's taking it better than you."

There was a head on the pillow, a strange, fair head like her own reflection. She hated it. The face smiled from the frills, pale and stupid, the kind of face that always did as it was told. A heavy body was beside her in bed, seeming to sweat, suety. There was no room for her. She edged away, and the cold blue linoleum pressed her bare feet. The window swung towards her; the floor dropped away. The moon, curled low in the sky, dangled over the chequered tiles, and all the dogs in the street seemed to be howling. She screamed, "Mother, mother, I don't want to go! Oh mother!" But the witch was the person who caught her hand. "All right, dearie, I'm rested now. I won't let you fall. You won't need to see me again, unless you want to, after we get to the little people."

She screamed. Nobody listened.

*

She had resisted the witch? "Yes," she said. They did not scold her, but she felt afraid of the way they talked. She hated the little people, sharp as thorns and shrill as treble chanters. She was afraid when they said she would forget. "I don't want to forget!" she screamed. "I want my mother! I want my mother!" She was very brave for seven years old, but she was afraid.

"You will forget your mother!" they said, chirping and dancing round about, and clapping their hands on the soles of their feet. "You will forget your mother! You'll forget yourself, you'll forget your house, you'll forget everything. You'll forget everything. But you'll always try to remember, and never quite find out what you want to remember. Serves you right!"

They were cruel and slight, nipping her on the arms out of curiosity. "Why does it serve me right?" she sobbed. "I want to go home! I haven't done any harm. I didn't want to come here. It was the witch brought me."

"We sent for you, and you struggled with the witch! You struggled! You should have come when you were told!"

"I didn't want to. I didn't want to leave my mother."

"You'll forget your mother! You'll forget everything, but you'll never stop trying to remember. Serves you right!" They were hostile, these dark little red and brown people, hostile and far too old for her. The youngest had age written on their faces; the oldest were spry and dreadful. They resented her, resented her youth and her strangeness, and the way she did not want to stay. They tormented her in little stabs of spite. She wept, and they gathered round in squeaking wonder. None of them understood how much she wanted her mother, none of them liked her.

She forgot. She forgot about everything. She sat beside a lake, thinking of summer, and the work they had made her do. She had had heavy labour among the spiked petals and the drugging scent of flowers, and she had had unpleasant tasks with bees, whose legs were clogged and clarted with pollen. It was a lifeless, hot summer, a season in a sealed sphere of glass. Beyond the glass was something she could not call to mind, and round the sphere mist was quiet and thick. She lived in a land of twilight, of low stars and dim green woods. Everything was low. Sometimes, she felt as if the sky was no higher than a ceiling.

Once the sphere had cracked and the mist had thinned. It had been on the brightest day of summer, when the sky was the colour of stone, and the sun a dull lamp burning in one corner. The sky gradually turned white. She heard a shaking rumble and a pounding regular thud which jarred her body. Shadows sketched lightly on the mist-pall, moving large like ferns magnified to fern trees. Something flickered. She was in a green and yellow landscape, with strong white light glaring on grass. Pink flowers stared at her from a bush, laughing above a collar of green leaves on thorns. She was choking as thoughts rushed over her like water.

The rumbling and pounding passed. A huge animal with a cart had gone by; its shadow inked over the view, and for a moment, very dimly, superimposed on the air and the ground, she could see the lake, and the wee people scurrying along, all unconscious. They were frail and transparent, and vanished again as the sun shone on them. She did not know which world was real.

Dog-roses and vetch bloomed bright among the green, and the road smelt of nettles and cow-dung and honeysuckle. These were strange things to her, but safe and comforting. She wanted to sob.

She was very near to what she wanted to remember. Then a little boy in blue trousers tumbled through the hedge, stared at her, and said "Ooh!" His fat hand, with black-rimmed nails, bulged above her in fleshy pillows, his fingers cut the light into four sections. The light strips grew narrower as the sound of the cart faded into flat air. It seemed as if the sky was closing with his fingers. She was sitting by the lake, with the waves like grey syrup under the mist, and the sun sinking into the crawl of the tide, to sizzle like a black ember.

It was autumn. Yellow leaves soaked sodden into the lake, and rain and frost raced each other over the brilliant berries. She would not work. She felt sick when she moved from the lake, and her head was a hollow iron ball, with words rolling round and knocking into each other. What the words were she did not know. She sat by the lake and poked her fingers between the pebbles, waiting for the mist to break again. The little pixie things were angry with her because she sat and dreamed all day. They grumbled. She watched them frisking and cheeping as they worked, and turned her back on them till they were tired of her sulking, and then they tried to be kind. They had wanted her to come to them, and during the long winter she would have to play with them. She would have to. Sad or dull, she would have to sing and play and be lively.

"The harvest's in!" they screamed, when the wind crisped and freshened over the gathered grain. "The harvest's in, and you never helped us! You never helped! If you were afraid of work, it's all done now, and all we have to do in the winter is to have fun. Oh, we'll have jolly fun, when the snow comes! There won't be any flowers left, and we'll hang icicles on the branches, and sweep the snow away from under the trees, and dance mad on the bare ground. Dance like this, like this, like this!" They stamped about in front of her, clapping their hands on the soles of their feet. She turned away from them. "I don't want to dance. I want—" She had nearly said it that time, the words that were knocking in her head. "What—what do you want?" piped the little people, tweaking their fingers at her, deeving her. "Oh, I hate it here! I *hate* it!" she sobbed, and they all ran away.

She went with them into the forest, the dark forest where they danced. It was blue midnight, but the frost shone white. They swept up the hoar with twigs and bristles, and danced to the snap of dry branches, clapping their hands on the soles of their feet. They danced fast and jerky, and the Northern lights swept fans and floods of mauve and crimson above the pines. Everything outside the dance was silent, except when a fir-cone trembled and dropped, or the lush firs lifted bloomy layers and sighed. They dragged her into the circle and spun her round. She felt cold. Her feet went heavy with desire for rest, and she tripped clumsily. They pushed her on and on; she sank to the ground and screamed at them. "She is no good to us," they muttered among themselves. "She is no good. We'd be better without her." They turned to her and scolded. "You could have been happy here, but you'll never be happy now. It's your own fault; you struggled with the witch. You struggled too much!"

"What witch?" she said. "I don't remember a witch. There's something—I don't know."

"She's no good," said the little people. "She won't play. She won't work, and she won't play. We will send her back again."

So they let her sit by the lake a while longer. One day the witch appeared, older and a little more weary. The nettle blossom of her hair had blight on it, and the warts on her fingers were mildewed. She grinned, lolling her tongue about like lard in a hot pan. "Moreen!" she crooned. "It has been a long, long time, Moreen!"

The child did not know her name. The witch snatched her by the wrist and circled her in the air above the excited fairies. The little red and brown people threw stones after them, and bits of gravel pinging and stinging at their legs. Moreen wept. She hated them.

They flew through grey, choking tunnels of cloud, where the thunderclaps sulked and rested. Moreen was tired, too tired to see where she was going.

Where—what place? There was an emptiness, a shabbiness about it, but the line of the houses was the same. She felt inside as if she ought to know where she was, but she could not remember. The house at the corner had its windows misted over with damp, and there were lace curtains, and geraniums gasping for air against the panes. She did not want to go to that house, but there was a bell pull at the door, and letters on a brass plate, and she knew she would have to put her hands on the bell and tug it a little sideways. She knew how her fingers would grip on the black handle, but she did not understand or wonder what made her know.

She rang the bell, and her eyes went squinting over the curlicues on the stained name plate. A shadow moved behind the curtain of the glass door. When the door opened, there was an old woman standing in a long skirt, a fat, square-looking woman, with her hair piled grey over her head, all knobs and pins and the concealed teeth of combs. Her blouse was frilled, high at the neck so that it should have choked her, but it only made her sweat. The child could smell the dirty scent of her and the shut-in smell of the house. There seemed to be mice there.

"Well," snapped the woman, "what do you want!"

"I—I don't know."

"Come, come; don't be silly. You wouldn't have rung the bell if you hadn't wanted something. Are you a new pupil?"

"Pupil...?"

"Yes. A music pupil. Do you want to learn the piano?"

"No. I don't know."

"Tut-tut! Who sent you? What's your name?"

"I don't remember."

"Oh dear, tiresome child! You'd better come in till I find out what you want. Wipe your feet, now!"

It was a sad, dark house. Somebody in a room was playing a monotonous little jig on a piano. The woman opened the door and leaned in, pressing her weight on the handle, and the child knew without seeing that the piano was black with a musty smell, and a girl in a pink dress sitting at it.

"Clara! You are not yet ready for the jig. Get on with your scales, as I ordered you."

A flat, sunless voice said, "Yes, Miss Moreen."

They went upstairs, on a red and blue carpet. On the landing a she-dog dragged her tired body to a basket. The woman opened a door to a room where there was a big bed and a desk. It was a dirty room, full of furniture. "Now!" she said, sitting down and wiping her moist hands. "I suppose you have come for music lessons. Did your mother send you?"

"No." She began to cry. "I was away. They took me to a place where there was a lake, and woods, and—"

"Oh, you've been on holiday? Well, don't waste all the afternoon. If you don't want lessons, what do you want? What's your name? Where do you come from?"

The piano was faint behind the closed door, doh me soh doh soh me doh, arpeggios crawling like the fat she-dog. The child did not know what to say. She looked at the closed, steamy window. There was a dead fly on the sill, but beyond was the sky, like blue enamel, with a steeple stretching towards it. High in the stonework was a clock, and above that a gargoyle, jutting out as if it wanted to be sick. Astride its back was a witch, loose and insecure as a piece of burnt paper. The child opened her mouth and screamed.

"This is my house! I remember it by the witch sitting on the gargoyle! It's my house."

The woman's face was like dirty suet. "Here, that's enough! You're not well. This isn't your house. I've lived here all my life, and my mother lived here before she died. You sit quiet and I'll get you a drink of water. It's that hot—I thought there was something not quite right about you..."

"But it's my house. I know it by the witch. Don't you see it?"

"No. There's no witch, dearie, it's just in your own mind you're seeing it. You sit quiet and I'll see what I can do for you. Oh dear, such a bother..."

She went out of the room, leaving the door open, and the old dog waddled in. The piano was still tumbling out notes,—doh me soh doh, soh me doh—but it stopped on a black key, and the door banged. The child was watching the witch, but she could see things happening in the street. A little girl in a pink frock ran over to the doctor at the corner. Soon the window was too steamy to see any more.

THOSE LIGHTS
AND VIOLINS

SEPTEMBER 16TH

unt Rachel has just invited me to St Mervyn's for an extended, off-peak holiday. Funny, in all the years she and Mum have written to each other, I've never met her. You'd think, living at the seaside, she'd have asked us down occasionally, but people who keep boarding-houses don't invite relations. They're too busy letting their rooms at a profit.

The reason she's asked me is that I'm at a loose end after finishing university. I haven't got a job yet, and neither have quite a few of my equally well-qualified friends. Aunt Rachel's getting on a bit, and ought to be retiring soon, and Mum thinks, reading between the lines as usual, that she's got some idea of leaving the boarding-house to me. I can't imagine myself running a seaside boarding-house. Still, it would be churlish not to go. A change wouldn't do me any harm.

SEPTEMBER 18TH

Today I went to the travel agent's to get a brochure about St Mervyn's. It looks a wonderful place, built around a little bay, golden sand cupping the water, with high cliffs at one end, and, in the middle of the bay, a romantic-looking rock with what looks like a castle on top. The whole town seems to sparkle, the houses clustered bright round the bay like a tiara on corn-blonde hair.

I've written to Aunt Rachel, accepting her invitation.

SEPTEMBER 25TH

The view from The Haven is the view on the brochure—the curved bay, and the rock with its castle right in front. It is quiet, though, so quiet that footsteps echo on the promenade, and the view is empty most of the time. Only the moving waves and the seagulls give it life.

Aunt Rachel isn't at all like my mother. She wears her hair in an old-fashioned bun, she has the beginnings of a dowager's hump, her hands are mottled with brown, and she stumps about restlessly, at a loose end now that the guests have gone. Actually, there are still two left, Mr Anderson and Mr Haley, but they are not so much guests as regulars, staying on through the winter at a reduced rate.

I met them today at lunch. Mr Anderson is grey-haired, quite distinguished-looking, and wears a Harris tweed jacket. "He's writing a book about St Mervyn's," Aunt Rachel whispered to me. "Used to lecture in history." Mr Haley is tall and bald, with a clever face disfigured by what seem to be acne scars. I feel edgy in his company, as if he's ill at ease, and it rubs off on me, but both of them are very gallant and eager to please. Maybe they're bored, alone with Aunt Rachel. It's on the cards I'm going to be bored too.

However, I'll give it a try. Aunt Rachel's doing her best. She treats her boarders like the family she's never had, scolding them, cossetting them and, now that she's growing old, being cossetted in turn. We all eat together in the kitchen, and Messrs Haley and

Anderson defer to her, and yet humour her. The fact that she doesn't realise this makes her seem older still.

SEPTEMBER 26TH

I went for my first walk this afternoon. The streets were as quiet as Sunday. Far out, the tide winked across the damp sand, so far away that it was nothing but a luminous line. I started to walk across the sand, making long detours to avoid the lanes of water that the tide had left, and, at last, with the sea in my face and a darkness of rain coming over, I found myself almost at the huge rock I could see from The Haven.

Somehow, the nearness terrified me. On top of the rearing rock was this grey building, a bleak and frightening place, its site shared with the seagulls, the windows salt-caked, sea-spattered, buried deep in stone. There was something frightening, too, in the dangerous steps cut in the rock, and the iron handrails guarding deep drops to the sea.

And yet I had to go on. Surely, with the tide so low, it should be possible to walk right up to the rock, to clamber over weed-streaked ledges and stand triumphantly looking over to St Mervyn's, curved like a sickle around the bay.

But the rock was cut off, after all. A moat of water swilled restlessly, sucking and pounding at the steps, and an iron ring plopped and chinked with the lift of the tide. I was afraid of the dwarfing height of the rock, and the water inching higher as I watched. Suddenly I began to run, in a panic between the sand and the sky, because I was too far out, too small, cut off between the running rivers and the tide beginning to turn. My footsteps dented dry and filled up again, and when I reached the promenade the white waves were already thundering nearer.

Tonight, at teatime, I tried to find out something about the castle, or whatever it is. I meant the question for Mr Anderson, but before it registered Aunt Rachel came in with the answer.

"Oh, that's the Mount Hotel. St Mervyn's Mount, you know. You get a lot of Americans going there."

"It's shut though, isn't it? It seemed pretty dead-looking to me."

"Oh yes. They couldn't keep a place like that going all year. It's just a daft notion, anyway. They go because it's almost an island. They lay on a motor boat at high tide to bring the guests over to the town, but—I dunno. They don't mix much. They just come and go, and keep to themselves."

"I tried to walk over," I said, "but there was this deep channel."

"You don't want to go over there." Mr Haley removed a kipper bone, and frowned. "It could be very dangerous."

"You could be cut off, easy as that," butted in Aunt Rachel, snapping her fingers. "The tide... you want to be careful."

Mr Haley looked annoyed at the interruption. For a second I had the feeling that he was going to say, "That's not what I meant," but Aunt Rachel went on rabbiting happily, "... very exclusive. They bring their own staff, and they say that the staff never leave the Mount all summer. Of course, they'll be well paid for it, but... I dunno. It must be like living in a lighthouse."

I was going to say that a lighthouse is always neat and trim, whereas the hotel was neglected, to say the least, but suddenly I noticed that Mr Haley looked anything but well. He pushed back his chair and went striding out of the room, and Mr Anderson cleared his throat and changed the subject. When Haley came back, he didn't join in the conversation.

OCTOBER 1ST

There is absolutely nothing to do in St Mervyn's. I've been to church with Aunt Rachel, but it was a dreigh and dreary experience, a choir of tired landladies and a cold, salty draught making the sermon drier. Tonight I slipped out desperately and tried the pub. I fancied an orange-lit bar with soft music and deep carpets, but all that was open was the Harbour Light, a men's pub; old men, mostly, drinking morosely with their feet in the sawdust. I didn't know you still got sawdust on floors! I slipped out again, guiltily, but not before I had seen Mr Haley knocking back a whisky, and looking as if it wasn't his first. I wonder what Aunt Rachel would say to that?

OCTOBER 2ND

Had a chat with Mr Anderson. Aunt Rachel had gone to bed early, and I promised to make the supper. There were just the two of us. Mr Haley was out, and I remarked that he seemed to like a drink.

Mr Anderson appears to know all about it. I gathered that he tried to cover up for him so that Aunt Rachel wouldn't know. Luckily, Haley was a quiet drunk. He just got moody and depressed, and usually it was quite easy to get him to bed without causing any disturbance.

"What does he do?" I asked.

Mr Anderson puffed at his pipe, and told me through his clenched smoker's teeth, "He's a sort of preacher."

"A preacher?"

"Yes. He's an entertainer as well. He's quite good, actually; that lean, lugubrious type often are. He does a one-man show, with a one-man band—ridiculous, but it needs quite a lot of skill, and it attracts the crowds. He only operates in the summer, of course. He's a great success with the kids, Splitter Haley. He just—slightly—frightens them, and that's an attraction."

"Is that his real name? Splitter?"

"Seems to be. Unless it's a stage name. I gather his father was a conjuror or something. Splitter decided not to follow in his father's footsteps, but to take Holy Orders; or else the father wanted him to 'better himself'... And then something happened—I don't know what—and he more or less cracked up. Now he does this minstrel business, with a bit of seaside mission thrown in."

"Queer mixture. And he doesn't do anything at all in the off season?"

"No. He must have a bit of money. I've never worked out how much he makes in the summer. He does well enough. The kids follow him like the Pied Piper. As I said, they like to be frightened."

"What does he do to them?"

"Nothing. It's just that they sense that *he's* frightened."

"But what's he frightened *of*?"

Mr Anderson just shrugged his shoulders and went on puffing at his pipe.

OCTOBER 10TH

This may be a swinging resort in the summer, but right now it's a dump. The only thing that interests me is St Mervyn's Mount, and that fascinates me. The colour of the rock changes as the sun shifts and shadows the ledges, and sometimes, when the tide is high, and waves break over it, it seems to shiver under a shower of silver needles. One of these days I'll have another go at reaching it.

OCTOBER 16TH

It's all fixed! I'm going over to the Mount! I mentioned at dinner-time, casually, that I was going to walk over at low tide, and Splitter Haley's face went sort of gaunt and guarded. I kept on talking to cover up, and all of a sudden he seemed to pull himself together, and blurted out that he had the use of the hotel rowing boat and would I like him to row me over?

Eyebrows raised. Eating stopped. "How come *you* can use the boat?" asked Mr Anderson, rather enviously.

"I used to work there a while back. A sort of chaplain to the guests."

"You never!" This, obviously, was a revelation to Aunt Rachel. "And you never told me! What was it like? Was it as posh as—?"

I wasn't bothered about that. All I knew was that I didn't want to go; not with him. I don't know what I was afraid of, but I *was* afraid, and I didn't know how to get out of it.

"Isn't it private?" I asked.

"It doesn't matter. It's empty. It's been empty for years."

"Oh, no!" Aunt Rachel stopped gouging bits out of an apple dumpling and looked up, surprised. "It's always well booked. You can see the crowds going backwards and forwards. Will I give you some custard, dear?"

"It *used* to be busy," said Splitter, so vehemently that I wondered if he was drunk already. But he wasn't. He looked sick. His clever, scarred face was whitish, and he shivered. "But no one's been there for years. Not a soul."

"I beg your pardon, Mr Haley." Aunt Rachel put down the custard jug, to give all her attention to the argument. "I may be getting old, and I know I lose my knitting, or my glasses, but I'm not as bad as all that. Everyone knows the Mount Hotel's busy every summer. They must make a packet out of all those rich Americans."

"Well, it's empty now," I said, to keep the argument from going any further, "and if Mr Haley wants to take me over..." I had made up my mind. I was going to go.

"I hope it's safe. I don't know if your mother would like it."

"I'll go along too, if it's all right," said Mr Anderson. "Keep an eye on her." And he winked.

Aunt Rachel relaxed immediately. Haley, evidently, was the one she had reservations about. "What I'd like," she said dreamily, "would be to go over one night, for dinner. It's so lovely, all lit up, and you can hear the music, sometimes, over the water. But there's never time..."

OCTOBER 17TH

It's been foggy all week, just as we've made our plans for going to the Mount. Sometimes the fog shifts, and the wet sands come into view, the sluggish sea, the whole lost curve of the bay, with the Mount looming hazily like an ogre's castle. Colour leeches into the landscape, muted marine colour, all dripping; then the mist comes up again, like steam, and the foghorns go moan, moan, and condensation blooms the walls and trickles down the paint. Aunt Rachel grumbles a lot. The cold gets into her bones.

NOVEMBER 1ST

The wind freshened yesterday, and today we're going over.

NOVEMBER 8TH

I haven't been able to write about the visit until today. I still haven't got it all sorted out in my mind. It was so... unbelievable, so absolutely terrifying!

We went over at high tide, the water choppy, splashing my trousers, and Mr Anderson sitting with his pipe clenched in his mouth and his anorak hood tight round his face. Splitter Haley reeked of whisky. If I'd had to go with him on my own I'd have called the whole thing off.

If he was drunk, he'd rowed himself sober by the time we got to the Mount. The boat bobbed, tethered to its iron ring, and we scrambled on to the zigzag steps of the rock. Water heaved and receded, and there was so much sea, so much noise and turmoil that I felt my stomach turning over. Splitter Haley led the way, hanging on to the iron handrail, and I clambered after him, glad to get away from the waves.

The steps were treacherous, uneven in size, and slimy with lit-tered seaweed. All around the gulls cried, a sad, mewing screech, and I felt that if I watched them I would lose my balance. The Mount was higher than I expected. When I reached the top I turned and looked backwards, over Mr Anderson's ridiculous hooded head, and there was St Mervyn's, clean and snug and compact, with its sickle of sand, and the cliff sweeping up at one end.

"Note the impressive entrance," said Splitter, acting the courier. "The guests were always tickled to death by the entrance."

"Were," he said. I noticed that.

It was certainly impressive. The door was iron-studded, the guns pointed landward with a blunt, black menace, and there was an iron lantern swinging on a bracket. "We'll go round here," he said. "You'll be all right. Just don't look down."

I looked, of course, as soon as he said it, leading me round the side of the rock. We were crossing a bridge over a deep chasm, and through the pattern of the ironwork I could see green water swilling and slapping against black walls. I stood clutching the rail, afraid to move. "Give me your hand," said Splitter, looking back at me. "There you are. I've got you. You're all right now."

But the back of the rock was even worse. Here we were shut off from St Mervyn's, and there was nothing in front of us but waves, thrusting and curling over in angry fringes of white. The sky was grey, the waves were grey, and there was no way of measuring the horizon. Over the grey, tossing water was America—nothing but sea, all the way to America, except perhaps for an odd, lonely rock like this.

The bleakness got hold of me like horror. "Two feet thick," Splitter was saying with dismal pride, pointing to the walls. "And the glass is thick, too. It has to be. The spray hits the windows like bullets."

And then he produced a key.

"You're not going *in*?" I yelled at him, over the noise of the waves.

He didn't answer. He turned the huge key in the lock. Surely when he gave up his job he should have given up the key as well?

"I'll show you the kitchens first," he said, leading the way downstairs. "The place used to be a fort, and these were the dungeons. It dates back to Cromwell's time."

I was beginning to feel stifled. There were shafts and pipes, and a smell of stale fat, and too much glossy green paint all streaked with condensation. No windows at all. Fancy being shut up here all summer, no windows, and the boom and thud of the waves...

"I don't think much of it," I said candidly. "I thought it would be more modern than this."

Haley didn't answer. I turned for confirmation to Mr Anderson, and caught my breath at the look on his face. He was a sickly yellow colour, and he was swallowing hard. "Are you all right?" I asked, thinking he was suffering from the journey over, and remembering that we had the return trip in front of us; but he said nothing, and I didn't want to embarrass him, so I left it at that for the moment.

"The place stinks," I said. "It would turn your stomach."

"Well, what do you expect? It's been a long time..." Haley sounded aggressive now. He hurried us out, over the thick grey linoleum, blotched with grease and spillage; but at the door Anderson put a hand on his arm, and Haley jumped. It was like touching a nervous cat.

"Wasn't there a bottle dungeon? I remember reading—"

"No. Not that I know of. This is deep into the rock already." He held the door open, pointedly, and we filed out.

I was glad to go upstairs again, to the daylight. The light was grey and muted, like the light that comes through frosted glass; but it wasn't frosting that dimmed the windows, it was salt. It was better here, though, warmer, richer. Money can insulate stone passages, dank walls, and a lot of money had been spent here. I was beginning to feel more comfortable. The air was growing warmer every minute, as if the sleek gold radiators in the passage were turned on. They *were* turned on! I laid my hand on one, and drew it away quickly. So the hotel *was* still in use, then? But how could it be, with no cooking facilities? Unless, of course, they had installed new, modern kitchens. Of course.

But why had Splitter Haley insisted that it was empty? He was forging along now, with the pride of one who knows his way about. He opened a door, and stood aside.

Music. Soft music, soft deep carpets, warm lamps on the wall. There was wine on the tables, and people talking, rich people, dressed for the evening. In one corner a couple danced slowly, holding each other up, and I could smell cigar smoke...

It was all just as Aunt Rachel had pictured it, except that, surely, Splitter Haley had no right to usher us in, in our damp and scruffy clothes, to stare and envy. But no one paid any attention. They went on with what they were doing, smiling and dancing and drinking; but slowly, more and more drearily, dragged out like a record running down, the smiles stretched and dreadful, the dancers turning in a dream, the drinks poised above the black parted mouths... in a moment they would all be frozen forever. I screamed and screamed, and they were gone—flick!—like that. It was cold, and there was damp everywhere, mould and cobwebs, and all the furniture stained and damp... and then we were in the boat, rowing away, and I don't remember crossing the dreadful bridge, or going down the steep steps, or anything except us rowing away as quickly as possible.

We went to the pub. I couldn't have gone to Aunt Rachel's just then. We all had a stiff dram, and then we sat around the smoky little fire while they tried to talk me out of my terror.

"It was the way they *did* everything," I sobbed. "Slower and slower, and that music running down, and the dreamy way they turned their heads—"

"Who?" asked Mr Anderson.

"The guests!" I snapped at him. I couldn't understand why he was asking. "I thought the place was shut up, but they were all there, all those posh people—"

"There wasn't anybody," said Splitter Haley. "I thought it was the way the place looks, all those spiders' webs... some girls don't like spiders. I thought that's what it was."

"It was like that afterwards." I blew my nose, and tried to explain. "At first, it was all bright and lovely, but the people... began running down, and moving like ghosts... and then, when I screamed, they vanished. And *then* it was like you said, as if it had stood empty for years."

"It has," said Haley suddenly, and, very slowly, Mr Anderson nodded.

"And *you* didn't see the people?" I asked.

"No. Not... what you said."

"Nor me," said Haley. "But you're right. That's how it was, all dying one by one..."

I was more frightened than ever. If there's one thing worse than seeing a ghost, it's knowing that you're the only one who's seen it. Splitter Haley filled his glass again, but he was sober, dead sober. I was sure of it.

"There's been nobody at that hotel since I was there, and that was, oh—eight years ago. Something happened—I may as well tell you now. It was plague. Bubonic plague. One of the new guests had been in North Africa, and by the time we discovered what was wrong, it was too late. It was beginning to spread among the others."

He paused for a while, and we waited.

"The staff walked out; fair enough, they weren't engaged to nurse that sort of thing. We didn't tell them exactly what was wrong, but they sensed it was something serious, something they didn't want to catch. We let them go; we even paid them for the rest of their term on condition they kept their mouths shut, and I suppose it worked out all right. There was no comeback, and we never heard of any other cases being reported. Thank heaven for that."

After another long silence, he went on again.

"You maybe wonder why we didn't inform the authorities. They could have helped us. But think of the owner's point of view, the talk and the scandal. It wouldn't bring back the dead, would it, and we were sealing off the infection. There was a resident doctor, and he stayed, and made it as easy as he could; but it was hard work, just the owner, the doctor and me, looking after the patients, trying to bathe their sores and keep their beds clean—it was too much. And then the owner took ill and died, and I got a touch of it myself..." He fingered his scarred face, and I tried not to look at him.

"I did what I had to do. I prayed with them, I administered the last rites..."

"I've never heard of a hotel chaplain," I said dubiously.

"No, but this wasn't an ordinary hotel. It—"

"How many died?" interrupted Mr Anderson brusquely.

"Well… it was near the end of the season, you see, and we were tailing off. There weren't many left, though. Only one or two." He looked at us pathetically, willing us to understand.

"How do you mean? What happened to them?"

"Well, we decided, the doctor and I—we saw that the others didn't—didn't live. They might have said something, you see, if we'd let them go. But it was done kindly. We were always kind to them. We had hoped, you see, to keep the hotel going. After all, once this lot were gone, there would be others who would need—"

"You mean you let people die, you killed them, just because—"

"All *I* did," pleaded Haley, "was to give them a Christian burial. A funeral service. None of them went without a blessing."

"But where…?"

"There *was* a bottle dungeon!" Mr Anderson struck the table with his hand. "Under that ship's linoleum…"

I closed my eyes as horror piled upon already unbearable horror. Once, at St Andrew's, I had seen a bottle dungeon; deep, pitch-black, no ventilation, no way of getting in or out except by a rope ladder. The guide lowered a light down the neck of the bottle to show smooth walls, curved and cold, and then put out the light for a moment of dead silence and blackness. A woman screamed…

"It's sealed off now," said Splitter. "There would be nothing to see. It was all done according to the prayer book. 'We commit their bodies to the deep… in sure and certain hope…'"

"The deep?"

"The sea comes in, at high tide. The crabs would eat them. It's part of God's plan; like vultures. People condemn vultures, but—"

"If that's true," said Mr Anderson—and I could see that he believed it; he had seen his own ghosts, the rotting dead being swilled about by the waves—"if that's true, how did you get away with it? People can't disappear like that. What about their families, their relations?"

"What you don't realise," said Splitter, dragging himself back from the nightmare, "what nobody realises is that these people were not quite... acceptable. They were all a bit... queer, one way or another. Nothing outrageous, but just enough to be an embarrassment to their families. That's what the hotel was *for*. They were all rich, see, nearly all American. It was worth a good deal of money to their relations to have daft Aunt Rebecca or eccentric Uncle Silas out of the way for a while, some place where they would be looked after and supervised—why else do you think they always came across by boat? It looked like a gimmick; it was really because you couldn't have them wandering about on their own.

"So no questions were asked; and we were quite honest about it. We wrote to the next of kin, and broke the news of their death, and said we'd attended to the burial, and it was a load off their minds. There wouldn't even be a question of legacies. It was the relations who had the money. So, up till now, no questions have been asked; and who's going to say it ought to be stirred up again?"

Neither of us felt ready to answer; but another idea had struck me.

"Aunt Rachel insists the hotel's full every summer. She just takes it for granted. I mean, she lives just opposite, and she *sees*—"

"Well, that's the funny thing." Haley took another gulp, and thought for a moment. "Nobody has ever realised that the hotel was closed. All sorts of people saw the hotel car calling at the station, and the guests being ferried backwards and forwards, but—how many of our lot actually spoke to them? Ask any shopkeeper if they ever bought anything on their shopping expeditions. They'll all say no, they went next door, or round the corner—never to them."

("They don't mix much," Aunt Rachel had said. And no wonder.)

We sat gloomily, staring at the fire. How could I tell her—how could I tell anyone—that for years they had been seeing ghosts in broad daylight?

Mr Anderson got out his pipe and began the preliminaries to a comforting smoke.

"If this is true," he said again, as his match flame was sucked into the bowl, "and I'm inclined to believe what you say"—he blew out a rich, grey cloud—"what made you stay on? Obviously the place won't open again. I would have thought you'd have gone as far away as possible."

Haley's ruined face was intolerably sad as he lifted his glass again.

"I couldn't leave. I daren't forget. Children come here, innocent children, and the least I can do... you see, there's something evil about that place. Not a temporary thing, not an isolated incident like the one we've been discussing, but away back, right through the centuries. You, sir, you noticed it—"

"I know." Anderson's colour drained again, and he laid down his pipe. "I went rather further back than you. Some dreadful things went on in those dungeons—"

"Don't tell me," I said quickly.

*

That is where the matter stands. At the moment, none of us want to say any more about it. All I can think of is getting away from St Mervyn's as soon as possible.

There's Aunt Rachel to think about, of course, I couldn't possibly give her my real reasons for leaving. She was talking tonight about retiring, and saying she'd celebrate by having dinner at the Mount, "with all those lights and violins."

"It's over-rated," we told her. "Far too bleak and blustery. We're far more comfortable here."

Pray God she never goes to find out for herself.

SUSPENDED SENTENCE

went as far as the library today. My head still aches if I try too hard, or talk too much, but I'm feeling a lot better. It's just that I haven't got things sorted out properly yet. Maybe if I tell you, you'll be able to make some sense out of it.

Yes, the accident. On the motorway. It wasn't quite the way you think. What you don't know, what you don't understand, is that I'd seen it all before. The motorway, I mean. I'd seen it long before it was built.

No, I'm fine. Quite comfortable.

I think I'd better start at the beginning. You knew I'd been born and brought up where the motorway is now, down in the Kingsgate. It was the old part of town, low houses, white pavements, and wee shops; quite a respectable place, but fairly poor; only nobody told us we were poor in those days.

When I look back, it always seems to be summer, the roads dry and dusty, the pavements white, and the doorsteps edged with rubbing stone. People brought chairs out to the pavement, hard kitchen chairs, and sat at their doors, watching us as we played. There were always crowds of us playing in the street, at whatever game happened to be in season.

It must have been about twenty years ago that this thing happened that I want to tell you about. We were playing at skipping ropes. They'd just tarred the road and covered it with fawn grush, and it made the Kingsgate look like a room with a new carpet. Mrs

Mackie's shop door was open, and we knew that Mrs Mackie was behind the counter, in the dark, with flies crawling over the sweeties, and the cheese sweating. We were all afraid of Mrs Mackie. We would have braved her den if someone had given us a ha'penny to spend, but having nothing, it was almost a relief not to have to go in, up to the counter, scoring the ha'penny along the white wood, knowing she grudged the time she had to spend on bairns.

The rope went beat, beat, flinging up an odd sprinkle of gravel, and my arm ached with turning. Nancy Lockhart was in the middle, out to play and had gym dress and scarlet jumper—far better clothes than we had to wear to school! Her father had a draper's shop, and didn't she know it! She skipped slowly, showing off, and we all chanted as she jumped,

> "Lady, lady, drop your hankie,
> Lady, lady, pick it up.
> Lady, lady, show your shoe.
> Lady, lady, that will do!"

On the last line she tripped, and I threw down the rope and yelled, "Out!" I was desperate for somebody to take my end. But Nancy didn't take it. Knees back, chin forward, she pushed her face at me, and screwed it up.

"I am *not* out! It was your fault. You pulled the rope!"

That was Nancy, all over. She always had to be boss, she always had to win. I braced my own legs and shouted back at her, and next minute we were at each other like cats. I got tight hold of her hair; and then somehow she got her feet twisted round mine so that we both fell, me underneath, with my head cracked on the sharp gravel.

No, I'm not talking too much, honest. This is all quite relevant. Missus Mackie came out in her curlers and her black apron, and asked Nancy what I'd been doing to her; but... I don't remember that. There was a roar in my ears, and... cars running past; not the square black cars like the Doctor and Mr Lockhart had, but different kinds and different shapes, bright shiny colours going past in a blur. It wasn't a road you could walk on, or cross, or enjoy in any way. There were no houses, no pavements, only the cars, two or three abreast, never stopping. I was so bewildered, so lost, that I started to cry, and then I heard my mother say, "She's coming out of it now. You're all right, love," and I was sitting at the table, with her bathing my head, and the two girls who had brought me home staring at me, with their mouths open.

My mother looked worried when I told her about the cars, and she put me to bed, and said if I was still talking gibberish in the morning she would get the Doctor in. I didn't mention it again, but sometimes, on and off, the thought of it comes back to me again, like a picture interposed between me and what I was looking at, the cars sliding along like beads on a string, incredibly fast, with a low continuous roaring.

And now, of course, it's all come true. There *is* a motorway there. I was prepared for changes, having been away so long, but somehow it shocked me, seeing it so exactly as it had been that day. I stood at the side of the road, with the cars going past, endlessly, and took my bearings from the chimneys and steeples in the distance. Yes, this was it, this had been the Kingsgate. If I shut my eyes, I could see it, summer, the roads dry, the pavements, white, and Mrs Mackie's door open. I could smell the shop, the cheese, and firelighters, and the stale smell of Mrs Mackie herself. My home was only a few doors away. There was an ache of love, a great sob aching and bursting in me...

No, no, let me go on. I want to try to explain fully. I told you I could see it all in my mind. The picture behind my closed eyelids was still there, clear and solid, when I opened them. There was nothing there, nothing else, I tell you, but the Kingsgate; and so I crossed the road to go home.

I don't remember being knocked down. The bump, the dirling crash I felt, came after, and had nothing to do with the cars. It was... Wait till I get this straight. I'll just lie back and think for a minute, and work out how to explain it.

You see, when I got over—when I got there, it was different again; the Kingsgate, the same street, same houses, but—different. Shabbier, somehow. It was a wee while before I puzzled out what was wrong with it. It was the road. You'll remember I told you how I remembered it, tarred with a crisp layer of grush? Well, this road was all holes, and loose stones, and full of dirt and horse dung. It was hot, and dry, so luckily there was no mud, but eugh! the smell was enough to knock you over! And though it was dry, the gutters were wet where people had emptied things. A woman came out of Mrs Mackie's shop—it *was* Mrs Mackie—and she threw a pail of something out at the door.

There was something disturbing about all this. It was like looking at an old photograph. The more I looked, the more changes I saw. Here and there, where a house should have been, there was a wooden gate, leading to fields. Some of the houses I knew had thatched roofs, and the women standing at their doors were years out of fashion. Life seemed to have gone backward; and though my own clothes felt familiar, they were different too, long and fancy and—and *sleazy*. They hadn't been washed for a long time. Nobody fastidious would have worn clothes like that.

I didn't know what to do. I looked round at the poor houses, and nobody looked back at me. It was as if they didn't want to know. I began to walk, picking my way among the horse dung and worse that pocked the road, and there, coming towards me was a man, a handsome man, kind and open looking. I went up to him, and put my hand on his arm to attract his attention, but he didn't look too pleased. He shook me off impatiently, and when I saw that he wasn't going to speak to me, I started to cry, and hung on to him.

And it was then that Nancy Lockhart came up and started to scream at me; Nancy dressed to kill, as usual, her lips tinted, and her hair piled high. She told me to take myself off. "Accosting a man in broad daylight!"—the man too came in for her tongue for not being firm enough with me. I couldn't get a word in edgeways. How was I to know that this was *her* man? She shrilled and yelled at me, with everybody at their doors looking on; and then she called me—she actually called me "Street Pest!" That's what she said. "Street Pest! We could do without the likes of you!" and it's then that I went for her, spitting and pulling her hair, and we went down into the dirt, both of us, rolling and fighting like animals.

It was a vicious fight. Oh, there were some folk who enjoyed it! They all crowded round shouting and jeering, but the ones who cheered me on had something derisive in their voices. There was no respect for me. And then—then Mrs Mackie came out with a pail of water, and threw it over me! Nancy got some of it, but it was meant for me. She spoke to me as if we were dogs to be separated. "Get out, you slut! There's filth enough in the street without you!"

They took me in front of the magistrate for "assault on the person of Miss Nancy Jane Lockhart, daughter of James Lockhart, Merchant." As if I hadn't had provocation! But there was worse than that, to do with—with that name she called me, Street Pest. The judge said that if I went on like this I would end up on the gallows; and standing there, with my face painted, and my body in need of a wash, I heard myself say, yes, I knew that, that was where I would end.

No, it wasn't a dream. I know better. I went to the library today, to look up the files to see if there were any old photographs of the Kingsgate, to see if they tallied with what I saw, and I found... *this*. I copied it out... "Janet Martin, street pest, attacked Miss Nancy Lockhart, after being admonished... On being asked if she did not think her way of life fitted her only for the gallows, she said boldly, yes, she realised that was her destination..."

I swear I never saw that cutting in my life. I've never looked up the files before—never had any reason to. I don't like it. It frightens me. Suppose... isn't there a theory that time goes both ways, backwards and forwards? We can't see into the future; but I did. I saw that the street would be wiped out to make a motorway long before motorways existed; and then... memory only goes so far back, but I saw backwards, over a hundred years, and that was true too. This cutting proves it. It looks as if something that binds me to time has slipped, and I'm swinging loose.

I used to think that if people came back after death, they returned as something better, but I don't know how I stand. If that was me, importuning men and fighting in the gutter, I've left that sort of thing behind me, thank God. But—have I? Didn't I go back to it, years later? Could I go back instead of forward, still further, to Heaven knows what kind of life? And how long would it take me to retrace my steps to what I am—to what I think I am now?

I don't even know if Janet Martin did die on the gallows. Could it be that this has still to come? Because if Nancy Lockhart is still around, and I meet that little bitch again, before God I won't be able to hold myself...

THE CURATOR

rosbie walked along, his eyes turned to the shop windows, a suitcase in his hand. He went at the pace of the crowd, and the crowd was in no hurry; foreigners, half of them, all of them able to afford a holiday in Britain, and a quick tour of Scotland; all of them able, then, to walk into any of these shops and order the sealskin brooches, the mink, the tartan, the Shetland jumpers, the shortbread and bottles of whisky.

Everything was for the tourist. The restaurants were packed to the door, the pubs let out light and heat and great whiffs of malt and tobacco, and in the bookshops stood brown and yellow men with their faces to the wall and their noses deep in paperbacks. There were too many tourists, too many *young* people. He shifted his suitcase to the other hand, and stared at the strollers to see if there were any of his own generation; but prosperity rejuvenates, on the surface, anyway, and the gentlemen with cameras and casual shirts forged along with an air of youth. White beards showed off the affluent tan, tinted glasses suggested brighter suns and broader horizons; and yet, alien as they were, these were the people he knew, his bread and butter; in a way, the only people he met.

He was curator of the Memorial, a great thrusting edifice which tossed a whirl of turrets to the sky, and commemorated a man who had done some service to the city. Nobody was sure what exactly J. Crawford Melvin had done. A library or two, a park, an art gallery, a lot of civic amenities and architectural horrors were laid to Mr Melvin's credit—but everyone knew his name and memorial.

On duty, George Crosbie wore a uniform which made him look something between a policeman and a bus inspector. He crept about, hunch-shouldered, suspicious, while his assistant beamed and touched his hat as he pocketed tips. Crosbie was never offered so much as a penny.

The two men changed duties on alternate weeks. One week Crosbie was at the entrance, taking the money and pushing pink tickets through the little window. Next week, he would be on one of the platforms, urging the crowds to keep moving. Drooping, long-nosed, he watched the legs shuffle past him, slim hips in jeans, fat Americans, big crimplene-clad bottoms, and lovely young legs in tights and sandals; every back turned, everyone going away from him, up and up the ever narrowing spiral.

A more gregarious man would have enjoyed the constant coming and going, but Crosbie liked his own company. That, and the pigeons. The Memorial harboured whole colonies of them, nesting in carved cornices and dizzy niches where the dust swirled and grey droppings streaked the walls and crusted the stone curlicues.

For some unaccountable reason, Crosbie loved the pigeons— perhaps because his partner disliked them. The genial Mackenzie was not above making capital out of them. He pointed them out to visitors, holding on to nervous, protesting girls who wanted to look but daren't in case they turned dizzy; he encouraged the men with the cameras to snap them from perilous positions; but then, when he had roused his audience to maudlin ecstasies over the glimpse of smooth eggs or little bald heads and gaping beaks, he would dash their enthusiasms with disgust. "Tchah! Dirty brutes! They smear everything, they foul all the gutters. Stand here on a hot day, and the smell would make you sick!"

But Crosbie, friendless, lacking the gift of easy chat, was somehow drawn to the despised birds. At quiet moments he would peer over the balustrades, checking up on the nests, watching the parents come and go. He didn't want to share the sight with the visitors. He even resented Mackenzie knowing about them. Sometimes, at night, he would imagine he heard them cooing softly, talking as husband and wife talk in bed together, and in the early mornings he heard the first rustle as they stirred themselves to fly into space in search of food. It hurt him a little that when he laid out crusts for them they gobbled the bread so dispassionately. To them, it was no different from the scraps they picked up on the ground.

Every day, Crosbie swept the 303 steps of the Memorial, from the bottom up. It was his responsibility to keep the place clean, to look after the photographs and documents in the museum room, and to make returns of the tickets issued to visitors. He had an "office", a bleak little cupboard at the bottom of the stairs where he hung his coat and stored his cleaning materials and sometimes made a cup of tea. Mackenzie was never allowed into this office. All *he* had to do could be done in the cubby-hole where he sold the tickets.

Crosbie had his reasons for not allowing anyone into his office. He was actually living in the Memorial, and had been doing so for some months. Before that, he had had a room, a bleak and grudging room where he slept and kept his clothes. In all the time he had been there, neither he nor the landlady had added one homely touch. He accepted the cheap yellowish linoleum, the draggled pink candlewick, the bits and pieces of carpet. There was never the glow of a fire, but in the worst of winter a paraffin heater oozed fumes from a thin blue flame.

And then, suddenly, the room was wanted for a nephew returning from abroad. He protested. There was nowhere for him to live, nowhere at all—not, at least, until the summer crowds had gone, and then the lodgings they vacated would cost much more than he had been paying up till now. He begged his landlady for more time, and finally he quarrelled with her, so that she ordered him out on the spot. He packed the little he had, took it to work with him, and that night, when he locked up the Memorial, he stayed inside.

Ever since, he had been making it his home. At night he slept on two chairs, covered with his coat and an old travelling rug. He washed and shaved in the "office", and kept a secret cache of bread and butter and tea. Sometimes he fancied a slice of bacon for breakfast, but he was afraid to cook it in case the smell gave him away; and in the evenings he had to see Mackenzie off the premises, and make a pretence of getting ready to follow him. He could have left with him, and spent an hour or two in a tearoom or pub; but that meant re-entering the Memorial, and perhaps being seen; and anyway, he was best to keep away from pubs. The Memorial had no lavatory. After one nerve-wracking night of nipping in and out to the Gents', he had decided that abstinence had its virtues.

He looked forward to his assistant's day off. It meant that he could rise at leisure, maybe boil an egg for breakfast, and leave the washing-up till later. His own day off, on the other hand, was a burden to him. There was nothing to do but wander the streets like a tramp, always carrying the suitcase which held his uniform. "Off for the weekend?" Mackenzie asked regularly, nodding at it, and Crosbie, surly, told him to mind his own business.

It was enough to make anyone surly. The night before, Mackenzie was given the key. It was a huge heavy key, so large and obsolete that if he had tried to have a duplicate made it would have been news. This meant that there was no chance of nipping back in for a sleep. It meant, too, that Crosbie had to leave in his uniform, and change at the railway station. Somehow it would have seemed all wrong to wear uniform off-duty. He had a need to appear anonymous, undistinguished by any official marks, just as, at the Memorial, he had no identity beyond that of curator.

He did the thing in comfort, to make it something of an occasion. He paid for a changing room, had a bath and a shave, repacked his case, and made the ritual last as long as possible. This done, he took his dirty clothes to a launderette, and sat gloomily, watching them whirl away through the sudsy window. Next he went to a pub, had a drink or two, bought himself a fish supper, and then went to a Working Men's Hotel. Few of the men there had ever worked, and the word "hotel" was a euphemism. It was, in fact, a model lodging house, and every time Crosbie went there he vowed never to do it again.

The entrance was reasonable enough, broad stone stairs well scrubbed, going up to the sleeping quarters and down to the kitchen. There was always a smell of soup coming from the kitchen, but after beer and fish and chips it lost some of its appeal. Beyond the entrance, the rest of the hostel was depressing, the common room with sawdust on the floor, and the television set flickering dimly through the smoke; the derelict men in caps and overcoats which they never seemed to take off; and upstairs, the beds, adequate and clean, in cubicles, but meagre in space, and surrounded all night with a racket of groans and coughing. It was more comfortable than stretching across two chairs in the museum room, but Crosbie always fell asleep feeling shamed and humiliated and desperately homesick for the Memorial.

He was always there early, too early, waiting for Mackenzie to let him in; and Mackenzie seemed, almost spitefully, to wait till the last possible moment. Shivering, Crosbie would wait on one of the seats in the gardens, watching his breath cloud the cold morning. His feet left dark marks on the grey dew, and the wood of the seat felt damp. A few of his pigeons fluttered down, and sparrows gathered round his feet, cheeping loudly, tilting their cheeky brown heads. The great clock, overlooking the gardens, jerked on, a half-minute at a time, and the top pinnacles of the Memorial seemed to recede into a faint mist. Two floors below, one of the gargoyles was missing. Probably Crosbie was the only person who noticed it.

Once inside, surly as ever, he would grunt to Mackenzie, go into his office, and bang the door. Thank God, that was it over for another week; and in two days' time, it would be Mackenzie's turn. He would have the place to himself. It was as if the Memorial belonged to him, and him alone.

He always went on a tour of inspection after his day off. The museum room was unlit, and he pressed the switch, peering round suspiciously. Everything all right, so far.

Outside, on the first landing, he looked down experimentally. In some ways, this seemed the worst balcony of all. One climbed quickly, fresh on the first shallow flight, and the height came as a shock, people staring up, foreshortened, and the flowerbeds like scraps stuck on to green paper. Higher up, it wasn't so bad. The horizon beckoned over roofs and towers to the sea, and the eye was level, or higher than, the frieze of spires which graced the tilted streets. What lay below was irrelevant, masked by the diminishing pinnacles which, from this height, seemed to angle out and expose the core of the Memorial, the centre stalk, at the tip of which Crosbie stood like a captain on the bridge of his ship.

Like a good captain, he knew every inch of his command. With a batter of wings, a pigeon flapped past him, and this reminded him of the nests below. Cautiously, he leaned over.

Tucked away behind a whirl of stone, the nest lay bare and empty, a bit of broken shell sticking to one corner, and a few smoky feathers fluttering at the bottom. Furious, rushing down the stairs with practised speed, he confronted Mackenzie in his cubby-hole.

"Have you been at thae pigeons?"

"Been at them? What do you mean, *at* them?"

"Interfering wi' them. One of the nest's been herried."

"Well, I never touched it. Heavens, I could never reach it! Have some sense, Mr Crosbie!"

"Oh, I've sense enough! I know you've never liked them! But just you wait. I'll watch you! You let me see you interfering wi' thae birds, and you'll hear about it. Now, I'm warnin' you!"

"Ach!" Mackenzie gave a quick, half-humorous wave of his hand, and dismissed the whole subject. The old man was getting more crabbit every day. Better to take no heed, and just let him rave.

Muttering, Crosbie went into the museum room. After a night in the model, the Memorial was like home to him, but he did not relish a day of patrolling the winding stairs and balconies. It was tiring work keeping the people moving, harrying them up, and then coaxing them down. They all wanted to cluster at the top and pick out landmarks, and this caused jams on the stairs.

Today, the public were more annoying than usual. One woman, in the dark bit where there was hardly room to squeeze past, suddenly announced that she had claustrophobia, and began to scream, so that her husband had to help her down, hysterical and protesting, upsetting all the other people who also felt that the stairs were too dark and too narrow, but who were bravely trying to hide their fear. He caught a youth chalking a small arrow and the word UP at one of the concealed entrances, and gave him a lecture about defacing public property. "Well, it's true, innit?" argued the youth. "People get lost. You should have signs up," and he tossed the chalk over the side. That was a particularly dangerous thing to do. In cases like this, the drill was to order the offender down; but how, thought Crosbie, do you get a person off the Memorial in a crush like this? The public seemed to be siding with the wrongdoer. Mackenzie would have handled it better, no doubt; but when Mackenzie was on duty up here, he, Crosbie, would be bent double, pushing tickets through a small window...

You couldn't win.

And then he saw the child, leaning recklessly over the balustrade.

She was a thin child, in a long, rather old-fashioned pink frock, with her hair strained back in a sort of Alice in Wonderland style. At that moment, nobody was with her. As he looked, he saw that she was trying to get a leg over the balustrade. He noticed all this in the few petrified seconds before he sprinted silently towards her, hands out, and then—there was nobody there. Half afraid—surely she couldn't have toppled, in the instant of his eyes shutting in terror?—he forced himself to look over, but he could see nothing, no body lying, all blood and broken joints, no crowds hiding their eyes from horror. All he saw was a pigeon on a pinnacle, with empty space behind it; and all at once he felt a white weakness sweep over him, a sudden realisation of the height, and the danger of his own position. He felt himself fall, slow, slow, the breathless dunt as he struck projecting stone, the long drift down, the streaked galleries flashing past as if he were rushing down in a lift, floor after floor, and yet taking a long, long time... Sick, he recovered himself, pushed himself away from the balustrade, and tottered to meet the batch who were coming up.

"Which of youse has got a wee girl with you? A wee girl in a pink frock?"

Nobody seemed to have an answer.

"Well, watch her," he grumbled. "Do you want to get me into trouble? Weans is not allowed up unaccompanied."

Two days later he saw her again—but at night.

He often prowled about at night, taking a last look over the city before he settled to his somewhat uncomfortable rest. On a clear night, lights traced the blackness like lurex thread, lights twinkling for miles and miles, right over to the sea where, even there, an odd flash lit the water. He liked the scene, but it humbled him. The lights meant nothing to him. He was lonely, apart from them, shut up in a tower because there was nowhere for him to go. Even the pigeons were asleep.

And then the child came up to him, not near, but near enough to be seen in the reflected shine of the city lights.

"Hello," she said.

Crosbie glowered at her, mindful first of all of the rule book.

"What are you doing here? The Memorial closes at six o'clock."

"I live here," she said.

"No, you don't. Nobody lives here." He almost said, "except me", but he stopped himself in time.

"I've lived here for years. Longer than you."

So she knew, then? Warily, in case he gave himself away, he decided not to press the point.

"Come on, now. You'll need to get down. I'll let you out."

"I don't want out. I can't *get* out. I'm going to stay here for ever and ever."

"Oh no, you're not. You're going down that stair—"

"You can't make me." She moved to the balustrade, and, hastily, he changed his tone.

"Come on down to the museum room. It's nice there. I'll put on the electric fire, and we'll have a cup of tea."

For a minute, she considered, and then she was past him, teasingly, spiralling down in the dark, sure-footed, and into the room before him. He looked at her, droll, old-fashioned, and hesitated with the kettle in his hand.

"Will your mother not be looking for you?"

The face clouded. "No." She sounded more childish now, less sure of herself. "She's—I don't know where she is. She's dead."

Something about the way she said it, the way she phrased it, sounded strange. Once more he hesitated, puzzled.

"Well, who looks after you, then?"

"Nobody." A little inconsequential shrug. "I'm on my own here. Ever since I got killed."

"Killed?"

"I fell over, into the gardens. Years ago. Long before you were here."

"Any more of that daft talk and out you go. You shouldn't be here in the first place."

"But it's true! See yon broken gargoyle? That was me. I struck it coming down."

"Away and don't be daft. You—"

"But I did! Long ago. They never mended it. The edge isn't so sharp now. If you weren't such a stupid old man you'd have seen me before this."

"You mean you're a...?"

"Aye, I'm a ghost. You cannie catch me, for a wee bawbee...!"

And he couldn't. It was not that she was intangible, only that she seemed always to elude him. Slowly, he came to terms with the facts; one, that the Memorial was haunted, and two, that Mackenzie must never know.

It was the beginning of a new life for him. Lonely, inarticulate and homeless, he found himself looking forward to seeing the child, lying awake, waiting for her to come, exasperated when she kept him waiting.

Jean, she was called. Just Jean. That was all he could find out. She was a sorry, neglected little creature, only half-clad, her dress not nearly warm enough for the nippy autumn days, and he worried about her, sharp and wan with the cold. She was vulnerable, too. A word could send her lips quivering, and more than once he had reduced her to tears.

She was such a little brat! Her fingers were into everything, she poked and fiddled and answered back when he checked her. Many a time he felt that she would be the better of a good smacked bottom—she had fallen to her death, he discovered, by sheer showing off and disobedience—but how can you smack a ghost? She gloried in it, tantalising him, at the same time as she seemed to yearn, sometimes, wistfully, for a little petting, a little human contact.

"What was it like," he asked her once, "when you...?"

She seemed to concentrate. "All dark and fast, and bright lights... and... I knew it was past, and couldn't happen again, ever..."

He had a feeling she was sorry it had happened.

She grudged him his days off. For some reason or other, she refused to show herself to Mackenzie. "Don't go," she said. "If you liked me, you'd stay." He felt that it would be a relief to get away from her clinging demands, but all through his long days of freedom he found himself thinking of her, trying to placate her. Sheepishly, he went into stores and bought clothes for her, clothes that he selected himself from the counters, judging her size, and guessing what she should wear. He brought them back in his suit-case, white cotton pants, coloured bobby-sox, warm slippers with bunny faces on them, and he laid them out, hoping she might take them, and put them on...

But she didn't, or couldn't, he never knew which. Nor did she taste the lollipops or sherbet dabs he bought to tempt her. She wasn't like a real child at all, except in her almost malicious teasing. "You cannie catch me, for a wee bawbee..." She eluded him, shrill and swift and tempting.

And then, one day, Mackenzie found the clothes lying in the office.

Crosbie was growing careless—or was it Jean who had left the door open? He didn't know. Mackenzie's excuse was that he wanted more tickets. He came in and saw the child's knickers, the bunny slippers, and a pile of coloured comics and cheap necklaces. So *that* was how the dirty old devil spent his time…?

"… for a niece of mine," mumbled Crosbie, but he knew Mackenzie didn't believe him. And what else could he say? "Knock next time you come in!" he shouted. "You've no bloody business in here!"

Things were going to pieces. There was less trust than ever between him and Mackenzie, and Jean was beginning to tire him out. He couldn't stand the long, exhausting days and the nights when she kept him from sleeping. Desperate, he was driven to make one more attempt to find lodgings, somewhere he could have a little peace; anywhere, no matter how expensive, so long as he could make ends meet at the end of the week, and call the place his own.

So here he was, wandering along again at the pace of the crowd, staring at the shop windows all decked for the tourist. Bright maps concertinaed together to direct him, picture postcards revolved on stands, floral dotted parks, pillared ruins under a blue sky. The Memorial was a great favourite, its lacy spires snapped in sunshine, always in sunshine, its vital statistics in a wedge of print at the back. George Crosbie knew these statistics off by heart.

Forced to the inside of the pavement, he could not take his eyes from the shops. Idly, he read down the list of tartans, picturing himself, ludicrously, in a kilt. He stared at honey jars and boxes of rock, antique chairs and clerical gowns. No, it wouldn't do. He cut across the park, on the side farthest from the Memorial, and climbed the steep streets to the old town. Things would be cheaper here. Maybe there would be lodgings to spare.

But the old town, historical, picturesque, had also been tarted up and made trendy for tourism. The shops were cluttered with skean-dubhs and cameos, cairngorms and old Masonic medals, and they served exotic meals in expensively converted tenements. Down a close he saw the Memorial, its topmost balcony crawling with people. It was as if he was tied to it, circling as a dog circles a tree on the end of his chain. His loose lip drooping, he turned away and watched a one-man band clash and gyrate along the gutter, a man making himself ridiculous for the sake of a few coppers. "I could be worse," he thought. "I could be like that."

He turned away, walking further and further, till the sun went in, and it grew grey towards teatime. Here, the streets were shabby, the shops small and cluttered, bargains painted on the windows with white paint. He began to knock on doors. Landings smelled of bacon and kippers and sliced sausage, and, greasy lips, still chewing, said *no*. It was a bad time to ask. He tramped up and down so many stairs, saw grey yards from dusty landing windows, and stroked thin cats ingratiatingly. No one would take him in.

When at last he found someone who had a room, and was willing to let it, he was too tired to be particular about the price. He paid a week in advance, and sat stiffly on the bed, taking his boots off. It was what he called a posh bed, with a gold-quilted cover with a nylon frill, and the landlady told him he was expected to take it off. He agreed, agreed to everything. There was a bedside lamp, a cheap chest of drawers, and a cupboard for his clothes. Somewhere to come home to at nights... his landlady had hinted, too, that for a small extra charge she might see to his washing.

Lying on two pillows, with the blankets tucked in, he couldn't sleep for sheer comfort. He lay awake, too, worrying about Jean.

Maybe she would cry tonight, left on her own. It was a lonely life for her. She was just a bairn, after all, and surely a bairn shouldn't have to suffer so long...? Maybe, at Sunday School, they had told her that she would go to Hell if she didn't behave, and she hadn't believed it.

Hell was leaving a child alone in the Memorial, year after weary year. Mercy tempered it a little by the companionship of an old grouch like Crosbie...

"I'll see her in the morning," he consoled himself, as he fell asleep with the clock ticking on for three.

She was angry at being left; tearful at first, huddled away in misery, and then spiteful, like the little brat that she was. In the half-hour before the Memorial opened to the public, she riled him till his hand itched to slap her, but something, pity, or guilt, he didn't know what, made him try to conciliate her. She wasn't used to his mildness, and it maddened her more. Desperately, she drew on powers that frightened even herself. Watching him wickedly, with her red tongue going lick, lick round her mouth, she let herself over the balustrade, and... walked, floated, she couldn't quite explain it, down to where the pigeons snuggled in a cave of sooty stone. Crosbie, his mouth loose with shock, saw her lift the birds from their nest, and slowly, one by one, thraw their necks, rummle the nest to rubbish, and chuck the lot down to the grass beneath.

He went for her then, straight down to where she stood on nothing, laughing at him, straight down as he had seen it happen before, the streaked galleries flashing past, gargoyle and turret and pinnacle, the sooty carvings and the weathered stone, down and down...

"I'll be like her," he thought. "For ever and ever—" and then, in a rueful flash, "and I've paid my room, a week in advance..."

He didn't die. They kept him in the Infirmary, and did all they could for him, and then they sent him out, legless, on a little wooden platform on wheels. He became quite adept at propelling it along among the tourists, and the tourists found him almost an attraction. "Ah well," they sighed, comfortably, dropping the odd coin into his hat, and thinking of their own niggling afflictions, "you always see somebody worse off than yourself!"

Crosbie lives now in the Working Men's Hotel; permanently. It is cheap and handy, and there are people there who are willing to carry him up the stairs and give him hints on how to capitalise on his disabilities. This is where he learned to carry with him a small melodeon. He doesn't play, but from time to time he moves it open and shut, tunelessly. It's better than begging. It looks as if he's making an effort, and the tourists like that; and it makes up for the surliness of his attitude. If he were less surly, more of an extrovert, he could make a good thing out of publicising the fact that he got his injuries falling off the top of the Memorial; but probably they wouldn't believe him.

He has a lot to put up with. Frustration is the worst of his troubles. Once the one-man band went by, banging and blasting away splendidly, knees going, elbows going, drums and cymbals and mouth organ all in a crashing medley of noise. Crosbie envied him. You have to be fit to be a one-man band.

Then there are the pigeons. They waddle past him, fat lilac birds, on their way to where another man feeds them, and makes a grand display of it. Children feed them too, buying packets of stuff from a vendor in the gardens. None of them are *his* pigeons; none of them care. His own birds stick to the Memorial, and never come near him.

Perhaps worst of all is the torment of watching the Memorial. With a genius for self-punishment, he has stationed himself where he can see all that goes on. All day the visitors inch and crawl along the balconies; all day Mackenzie jollies them along; but at night (and he sits at his pitch long after the Memorial has emptied) he sees the child flitting about, the pink frock pitifully worn, the long hair floating. Sometimes she cries for him, sobbing for him to come back, promising to be a good girl if he'll only come up and speak to her. At other times, he will hear her teasing him, taunting him, with an artless invitation to play.

"You cannie catch me
For a wee bawbee..."

THOU SHALT NOT
SUFFER A WITCH...

he child sat alone in her bedroom, wearing the fringe of the counterpane in and out of her fingers. It was a horrible room, the most neglected one of the house. The grate was narrow and rusty, cluttered up with dust and hair combings, and the floorboards creaked at every step. When the wind blew, the door rattled and banged, but the window was sealed tight, webbed, fly-spotted, a haven for everything black and creeping.

In and out went her fingers, the fringe pulled tight between nail and knuckle. Outside, the larches tossed and flurried, brilliant green under a blue sky. Sometimes the sun would go in, and rain would hit the window like a handful of nails thrown at the glass; then the world would lighten suddenly, the clouds would drift past in silver and white, and the larches would once more toss in sunshine.

"Jinnot! Jinnot!" called a voice from the yard. "Where've you got to, Jinnot?"

She did not answer. The voice went farther away, still calling. Jinnot sat on the bed, hearing nothing but the voice which had tormented her all week.

"You'll do it, Jinnot, eh? Eh, Jinnot? An' I'll give you a sixpence to spend. We've always got on well, Jinnot. You like me better than her. She never gave you ribbons for your hair, did she? She never bought you sweeties in the village? It's not much to ask of you, Jinnot, just to say she looked at you, an' it happened.

It's not as if it was telling lies. It has happened before; it has, eh, Jinnot?"

She dragged herself over to the mirror, the cracked sheet of glass with the fawn fly-spots. The door on her left hand, the window on her right, neither a way of escape. Her face looked back at her, yellow in the reflected sunlight. Her hair was the colour of hay, her heavy eyes had no shine in them. Large teeth, wide mouth, the whole face was square and dull. She went back to the bed, and her fingers picked again at the fringe.

Had it happened before? Why could she not remember properly? Perhaps it was because they were all so kind to her after it happened, trying to wipe it out of her memory. "You just came over faint, lassie. Just a wee sickness, like. Och, you don't need to cry, you'll be fine in a minute. Here's Minty to see to you..."

But Minty would not see to her this time.

The voice went on and on in her head, wheedling, in one ear and out of the other.

"Me and Jack will get married, see, Jinnot? And when we're married, you can come to our house whenever you like. You can come in, and I'll bake scones for you, Jinnot, and sometimes we'll let you sleep in our wee upstairs room. You'll do it, Jinnot, will you not? For Jack as well as for me. You like Jack. Mind he mended your Dolly for you? And you'd like to see us married thegither, would you not?

"He'd never be happy married to her, Jinnot. You're a big girl now, you'll soon see that for yourself. She's good enough in her way, see, but she's not the right kind for him. She sits and sews and works all day, but she's never a bit of fun with him, never a word to say. But he's never been used to anyone better, see, Jinnot, and he'll not look at anybody else while she's there. It's for his own good, Jinnot, and for her sake as well. They'd never be happy married.

"And Jinnot, you're not going to do her any harm. Someday you'll get married yourself, Jinnot, and you'll know. So it's just kindness... and she *is* like that, like what I said. Mebbe she's been the cause of the trouble you had before, you never know. So you'll do it, Jinnot, eh? You'll do it?"

She did not want to. The door rattled in the wind, and the sun shone through the dirt and the raindrops on the window. Why did she want to stay here, with the narrow bed, the choked grate, the mirror reflecting the flaked plaster of the opposite wall? The dust blew along the floor, and the chimney and the keyhole howled together. "Jinnot! Jinnot!" went the voice again. She paid no attention. Pulling back the blankets, she climbed fully dressed into the bed, her square, suety face like a mask laid on the pillows. "Jinnot! Jinnot!" went the voice, calling, coaxing through the height of the wind. She whimpered, and curled herself under the bedclothes, hiding from the daylight and the question that dinned at her even in the dark. "You'll do it, Jinnot, eh? Will you? Eh, Jinnot?"

Next day, the weather had settled. A quiet, spent sun shone on the farm, the tumbledown dykes and the shabby thatch. Everything was still as a painting, the smoke suspended blue in the air, the ducks so quiet on the pond that the larches doubled themselves in the water. Jinnot stood at the door of the byre, watching Jack Hyslop at work. His brush went swish swish, swirling the muck along to the door. He was a handsome lad. No matter how dirty his work, he always looked clean. His boots were bright every morning, and his black hair glistened as he turned his head. He whistled as his broom spattered dung and dirty water, and Jinnot turned her face away. The strong, hot smell from the byre made something grip her stomach with a strong, relentless fist.

Now Minty came out of the kitchen, across the yard with a basin of pig-swill. With her arm raised, pouring out the slops, she looked at the byre door for a long minute. To the child, the world seemed to stop in space. The byreman's broom was poised in motion, his arms flexed for a forward push; his whistle went on on the same note, high and shrill; and Minty was a statue of mute condemnation, with the dish spilling its contents in a halted stream.

A moment later, Jinnot found that Jack Hyslop was holding her head on his knee. Minty had run up, her apron clutched in both hands. Beatrice, the dairymaid, was watching too, bending over her. There was a smell of the dairy on her clothes, a slight smell of sourness, of milk just on the turn, and her hair waved dark under her cap. "There now," she said. "All right, dearie, all right! What made you go off like that, now?"

The child's face sweated all over, her lips shivered as the air blew cold on her skin. All she wanted now was to run away, but she could not get up to her feet. "What was it, Jinnot?" said the voice, going on and on, cruel, kind, which was it? "Tell me, Jinnot. Tell me."

She could not answer. Her tongue seemed to swell and press back on her throat, so that she vomited. Afterwards, lying in bed, she remembered it all, the sense of relief when she had thrown up all she had eaten, and the empty languor of the sleep which followed. Beatrice had put her to bed, and petted her and told her she was a good girl. "It was easy done, eh, Jinnot? You'd have thought it was real." She gave a high, uneasy laugh. "Aye, you're a good wee thing, Jinnot. All the same, you fair frichted me at the beginning!"

She was glad to be left alone. After her sleep, strangely cold, she huddled her knees to her shoulders, and tried to understand. Sometime, in a few months or a few years, it did not seem to matter, Minty and Jack Hyslop were to be married. Minty was kind. Since Jinnot's mother had died, she had been nurse and foster mother, attending to clothes and food and evening prayers. She had no time to do more. Her scoldings were frequent, but never unjust. Jinnot had loved her till Beatrice came to the dairy, handsome, gay, and always ready with bribes.

"You're a nice wee girl, Jinnot. Look—will you do something for Jack and me—just a wee thing? You've done it before; I know you have. Some time, when Minty's there..."

And so she had done it, for the sake of sixpence, and the desire to be rid of the persistent pleading; but where she had meant to pretend to fall in a fit at Minty's glance, just to pretend, she had really lost her senses, merely thinking about it. She was afraid now of what she had done... was it true then, about Minty, that the way she looked at you was enough to bring down a curse?

It could not be true. Minty was kind, and would make a good wife. Beatrice was the bad one, with her frightening whispers—and yet, it wasn't really badness; it was wisdom. She knew all the terrible things that children would not understand.

Jinnot got up and put on her clothes. Down in the kitchen, there was firelight, and the steam of the evening meal. Her father was eating heartily, his broad shoulders stooped over his plate. "All right again, lassie?" he asked, snuggling her to him with one arm. She nodded, her face still a little peaked with weakness. At the other side of the room, Minty was busy at the fireside, but she did not turn her head. Jinnot clung closer to her father.

*

All the air seemed to be filled with whispers.

From nowhere at all, the news spread that Jinnot was bewitched. She knew it herself. She was fascinated by the romance of her own affliction, but she was frightened as well. Sometimes she would have days with large blanks which memory could not fill. Where had she been? What had she done? And the times when the world seemed to shrivel to the size of a pinhead, with people moving like grains of sand, tiny, but much, much clearer, the farther away they seemed—who was behind it all? When had it all started?

In time, however, the trouble seemed to right itself. But now, Jack Hyslop courted Beatrice instead of Minty. Once, following them, Jinnot saw them kiss behind a hayrick. They embraced passionately, arms clutching, bodies pressed together. It had never been like that with Minty, no laughter, no sighs. Their kisses had been mere respectful tokens, the concession to their betrothal.

Minty said nothing, but her sleek hair straggled, her once serene eyes glared under their straight brows. She began to be abrupt with the child. "Out the road!" she would snap. "How is it a bairn's aye at your elbow?" Jinnot longed for the friendliness of the young dairymaid. But Beatrice wanted no third party to share her leisure, and Jinnot was more lonely than ever before.

Why had she no friends? She had never had young company, never played games with someone of her own age. Her pastimes were lonely imaginings, the dark pretence of a brain burdened with a dull body. She made a desperate bid to recover her audience. Eyes shut, her breathing hoarse and ragged, she let herself fall to the ground, and lay there until footsteps came running, and kind hands worked to revive her.

So now she was reinstated, her father once more mindful of her, and the household aware of her importance, a sick person in the house. The voices went on whispering around her, "Sshh! It's wee Jinnot again. Fell away in a dead faint. Poor lassie, she'll need to be seen to... Jinnot—Jinnot... wee Jinnot..."

But this time, there was a difference. They waited till she waked, and then questioned her. Her father was there, blocking out the light from the window, and the doctor sat by the bedside, obviously displeased with his task. Who was to blame? Who was there when it happened? She knew what they wanted her to say; she knew herself what to tell them. "Who was it?" pressed her father. "This has been going on too long." "Who was it?" said the doctor. "There's queer tales going around, you know, Jinnot!" "You know who it was," said the voice in her mind. "You'll do it, Jinnot, eh?"

"I—I don't know," she sighed, her eyes drooping, her mouth hot and dry. "I... only..." she put her hand to her head, and sighed. She could almost believe she was really ill, she felt so tired and strange.

After that, the rumours started again. The voice came back to Jinnot, the urgent and convincing warning—"She *is* like that, like what I said..." For her own piece of mind, she wanted to *know*, but there was no-one she could ask. She could not trust her own judgement.

It was months before she found out, and the days had lengthened to a queer tarnished summer, full of stale yellow heat. The larches had burned out long ago, and their branches drooped in dull fringes over the pond. The fields were tangled with buttercups and tall moon daisies, but the flowers dried and shrivelled as soon as they blossomed. All the brooks were silent; and the nettles by the hedges had a curled, thirsty look. Jinnot kept away from the duckpond these days. With the water so low, the floating weeds and mud gave off a bad, stagnant smell.

Over the flowers, the bees hovered, coming and going endlessly, to and from the hives. One day, a large bumble, blundering home, tangled itself in the girl's collar, and stung her neck. She screamed out, running into the house, squealing that she had swallowed the insect, and that something with a sting was flying round in her stomach, torturing her most cruelly. They sent for the doctor, and grouped round her with advice. Later, they found the bee, dead, in the lace which had trapped it; but before that, she had vomited up half her inside, with what was unmistakably yellow bees' bodies, and a quantity of waxy stuff all mixed up with wings and frail, crooked legs.

She looked at the watchers, and knew that the time had come. "It was Minty Fraser!" she wailed. "It was her! She *looked* at me!" She screamed, and hid her face as the sickness once more attacked her in heaving waves.

They went to the house, and found Minty on her knees, washing over the hearthstone. One of the farm-men hauled her to her feet, and held her wrists together. "Witch! Witch! Witch!" shouted the crowd at the door.

"What—What—"

"Come on, witch! Out to the crowd!"

"No! No, I never—"

"Leave her a minute," roared Jack Hyslop. "Mebbe she—give her a chance to speak!" His mouth twitched a little. At one time, he was thinking, he had been betrothed to Minty, before Beatrice told him... he faltered at the thought of Beatrice. "Well, don't be rough till you're sure," he finished lamely, turning away and leaving the business to the others. Those who sympathised with witches, he remembered, were apt to share their fate.

The women were not so blate. "Witch! Witch!" they shrilled. "Burn the witch! Our bairns are no' safe when folks like her is let to live!"

She was on the doorstep now, her cap torn off, her eye bleeding, her dress ripped away at the shoulder. Jinnot's father, pushing through the mob, raised his hand for the sake of order. "Look, men! Listen, there! This is my house; there'll be no violence done on the threshold."

"Hang her! Burn her! A rope, there!"

"No hanging till you make sure. Swim her first. If the devil floats—"

"Jinnot! Here's Jinnot!"

The girl came through a lane in the throng, Beatrice holding her hand, clasping her round the waist. She did not want to see Minty, but her legs forced her on. Then she looked up. A witch... she saw the blood on the face, the torn clothes, the look of horror and terrible hurt. That was Minty, who cooked her meals and looked after her and did the work of a mother. She opened her mouth and screamed, till the foam dripped over her chin.

Her father's face was as white as her own spittle. "Take the beast away," he said, "and if she floats, for God's sake get rid of her as quick as you can!"

It was horrible. They all louped at her, clutching and tearing and howling as they plucked at her and trussed her for ducking. She was down on the ground, her clothes flung indecently over her head, her legs kicking as she tried to escape. "It wasna me!" she skirled. "It wasna me! I'm no' a witch! Aa-ah!" The long scream cut the air like a blade. Someone had wrenched her leg and snapped the bone at the ankle, but her body still went flailing about in the dust, like a kitten held under a blanket.

They had her trussed now, wrists crossed, legs crossed, her body arched between them. She was dragged to the pond, blood from her cuts and grazes smearing the clothes of those who handled her. Her hair hung over her face and her broken foot scraped the ground. "No! No!" she screamed. "Ah, God...!" and once, "Jinnot! Tell them it wasna me—"

A blow over the mouth silenced her, and she spat a tooth out with a mouthful of blood. She shrieked as they swung and hurtled her through the air. There was a heavy splash, and drops of green, slimy water spattered the watching faces. If Minty was a witch, she would float; and then they would haul her out and hang her, or burn her away, limb by limb.

She sank; the pond was shallow, but below the surface, green weed and clinging mud drew her down in a deadly clutch. The crowd on the bank watched her, fascinated. It was only when her yammering mouth was filled and silenced that they realised what had happened, and took slow steps to help her. By that time, it was too late.

What must it be like to be a witch? The idea seeped into her mind like ink, and all her thoughts were tinged with the black poison. She knew the dreadful aftermath; long after, her mind would be haunted by the sight she had seen. In her own nostrils, she felt the choke and snuffle of pond slime; but what must it feel like, the knowledge of strange power, the difference from other people, the danger? Her imagination played with the thrilling pain of it, right down to the last agony.

She asked Beatrice about it. Beatrice was married now, with a baby coming, and Jinnot sat with her in the waning afternoons, talking with her, woman to woman.

"I didn't like to see them set on her like yon. She never done me any harm. If it hadn't been for me—"

"Are you sure, Jinnot? Are you sure? Mind the bees, Jinnot, an' yon time at the barn door? What about them?"

"I—I don't know."

"Well, I'm telling you. She was a witch, that one, if anybody was."

"Well, mebbe she couldn't help it."

"No, they can't help the power. It just comes on them. Sometimes they don't want it, but it comes, just the same. It's hard, but you know what the Bible says: 'Thou shalt not suffer a witch...'"

She had a vision of Minty, quiet, busy, struggling with a force she did not want to house in her body. Beside this, her own fits and vomitings seemed small things. She could forgive knowing that. "How... how do they first know they're witches?" she asked.

"Mercy, I don't know! What questions you ask, Jinnot! How would I know, eh? I daresay they find out soon enough."

So that was it; they knew themselves. Her mind dabbled and meddled uncomfortably with signs and hints. She wanted to curse Beatrice for putting the idea into her head; she would not believe it; but once there, the thought would not be removed. What if she was a witch? "I'm not," she said to herself. "I'm too young," she said; but there was no conviction in it. Long before she had been bewitched, she had known there was something different about her. Now it all fell into place. No wonder the village children would not call and play with her. No wonder her father was just rather than affectionate, shielding her only because she was his daughter. And no wonder Beatrice was so eager to keep in with her, with the incessant "Eh, Jinnot?" always on her lips.

Well, then, she was a witch. As well to know it sooner as later, to accept the bothers with the benefits, the troubles and trances with the new-found sense of power. She had never wanted to kill or curse, never in her most unhappy moments, but now, given the means, would it not be as well to try? Did her power strengthen by being kept, or did it spring up fresh from some infernal reservoir? She did not know. She was a very new witch, uncertain of what was demanded of her. Week after week passed, and she was still no farther forward.

She continued her visits to Beatrice, though the thought of it all made her grue. It angered her to see the girl sitting stout and placid at the fireside, unhaunted, unafraid. "You'll come and see the baby when it's born, eh, Jinnot?" she would say. "Do you like babies? Do you?" Nothing mattered to her now, it seemed, but the baby. In the dark winter nights, Jinnot made a resolve to kill her. But for Beatrice, she might never have discovered this terrible fact about herself. Beatrice was to blame for everything, but a witch has means of revenge, and one witch may avenge another.

She had no idea how to cast a spell, and there was no-one to help her. What had Minty done? She remembered the moment at the byre door, the upraised arm, and the long, long look. It would be easy. Bide her time, and Beatrice would die when the spring came.

She sat up in the attic, twining her fingers in the fringe of the bed-cover, in and out, under and over. Beatrice was in labour. It had been whispered in the kitchen, spreading from mouth to mouth. Now, Jinnot sat on the bed, watching the larches grow black in the dusk. She was not aware of cold, or dirt, or darkness. All her senses were fastened on the window of Beatrice's cottage, where a light burned, and women gathered round the bed. She fixed her will, sometimes almost praying in her effort to influence fate. "Kill her! Kill her! Let her die!" Was she talking to God, or to the devil? The thoughts stared and screamed in her mind. She wanted Beatrice to suffer every agony, every pain, and wrench, to bear Minty's pain, and her own into the bargain. All night she sat, willing pain and death, and suffering it all in her own body. Her face was grey as the ceiling, her flesh sweated with a sour smell. Outside, an owl shrieked, and she wondered for a moment if it was Beatrice.

Suddenly, she knew that it was all over. The strain passed out of her body, the lids relaxed over her eyes, her body seemed to melt and sprawl over the bed. When she woke, it was morning, and the maids were beaming with good news. "Did you hear?" they said. "Beatrice has a lovely wee boy! She's fair away wi' herself!"

Jinnot said nothing. She stopped her mouth and her disappointment with porridge. It did not cross her mind that perhaps, after all, she was no witch. All she thought was that the spell had not worked, and Beatrice was still alive. She left the table, and hurried over to the cottage. The door was ajar, the fire bright in the hearth, and Beatrice was awake in bed, smiling, the colour already flushing back into her cheeks.

"He's a bonny baby, Jinnot. He's lovely, eh? Eh, Jinnot?"

She crept reluctantly to the cradle. Why, he was no size at all, so crumpled, so new, a wee sliver of flesh in a bundle of white wool. She stared for a long time, half sorry for what she had to do.

The baby was snuffling a little, its hands and feet twitching under the wrappings. He was so young, he would not have his mother's power to resist a witch.

She glared at him for a long minute, her eyes fixed, her lips firm over her big teeth. His face, no bigger than a lemon, turned black, and a drool of foam slavered from the mouth. When the twitching stopped, and the eyes finally uncrossed themselves, she walked out, and left the door again on the latch. She had not spoken one word.

It seemed a long time before they came for her, a long time of fuss and running about while she sat on the bed, shivering in the draught from the door. When she crossed to the window, her fingers probing the webs and pressing the guts from the plumpest insects, she saw them arguing and gesticulating in a black knot. Jack Hyslop was there, his polished hair ruffled, his face red. The women were shaking their heads, and Hyslop's voice rose clear in the pale air.

"Well, that's what she said. The wee thing had been dead for an hour. An' it was that bitch Jinnot came in an' glowered at it."

"Och, man, it's a sick woman's fancy! A wee mite that age can easy take convulsions."

"It wasna convulsions. My wife said Jinnot was in and out with a face like thunder. She was aye askin' about witches too, you can ask Beatrice if you like."

"Well, she was in yon business o' Minty Fraser. Ye cannie blame her, a young lassie like that... mind, we sympathise about the bairn, Jacky, but—"

They went on placating him, mindful of the fact that Jinnot was the farmer's daughter. It would not do to accuse *her*, but one of the women went into the cottage, and came out wiping her eyes. "My, it would make anybody greet. The wee lamb's lying there like a flower, that quiet! It's been a fair shock to the mother, poor soul. She's gey faur through..."

They muttered, then, and drifted towards the house. Jinnot left the window, and sat again on the bed. She was not afraid, only resigned, and horribly tired of it all.

When they burst into her room, clumping over the bare boards, her father was with them. They allowed him to ask the questions. Was he angry with them, or with her? She could not guess.

"Jinnot," he said sternly, "what's this? What's all this?"

She stared at him.

"What's all this? Do you know what they're saying about you? They say you killed Beatrice Hyslop's bairn. Is that true, Jinnot?"

She did not answer. Her father held up his hand as the men began to growl.

"Come now, Jinnot, enough of this sulking! It's for your own good to answer, and clear yourself. Mind of what happened to Minty Fraser! Did you do anything to the baby?"

"I never touched it. I just looked at it."

"Just looked?"

"Yes."

A rough cry burst from Jack Hyslop. "Is that not what Minty Fraser said? Was that not enough from her?"

"Hyslop, hold your tongue, or you lose your job."

"Well, by God, I lose it then! There's been more trouble on this bloody farm—"

"Aye! Leave this to us!"

"We'll question the wench. If she's no witch, she's nothing to fear."

The women had come in now, crowding up in angry curiosity. The farmer was pushed back against the wall. "One word, and you'll swim along with her," he was warned, and he knew them well enough to believe them. They gathered round Jinnot, barking questions at her, and snatching at the answers. Every time she paused to fidget with the fringe, they lammed her across the knuckles till her hands were swollen and blue.

"Tell the truth now; are you a witch?"

"No. No, I'm not!"

"Why did you kill the baby this morning?"

"I—I never. I can't kill folk. I—"

"You hear that? She can't kill folk! Have you ever tried?"

She cowered back from them, the faces leering at her like ugly pictures. She would tell the truth, as her father said, and be done with all this dream-like horror. "Leave me alone!" she said. "Leave me, and I'll tell!"

"Hurry then. Out with it! Have you ever tried to kill anybody?"

"Yes. I tried, and—and I couldn't. It was her, she started telling me I was bewitched—"

"Who?"

"Beatrice—Mistress Hyslop."

"My God!" said Jack and her father, starting forward together. "Hold on, there! Let her speak."

"She said I was bewitched, an' I thought I was. I don't know if it was right... it was all queer, and I didn't know... and then, when she said about witches, she put it in my head, and it came over me I might be one. I *had* to find out—"

"There you are. She's admitting it!"

"No!" She began to shout as they laid hold of her, screaming in fright and temper till her throat bled. "No! *Leave* me alone! I never; I tried, and I couldn't do it! I couldn't, I tell you! She *wouldn't* die. She'd have died if I'd been a witch, wouldn't she? She's a witch herself; I don't care, Jack Hyslop, she is! It was her fault Minty Fraser—oh God, no! NO!"

She could not resist the rope round her, the crossing of her limbs, the tight pull of cord on wrists and ankles. When she knew it was hopeless, she dared not resist remembering Minty's broken leg, her cuts and blood and bruises, the tooth spinning out in red spittle. She was not afraid of death, but she was mortally afraid of pain. Now, if she went quietly, there would only be the drag to the pond, the muckle splash, and the slow silt and suffocation in slime...

She had no voice left to cry out when they threw her. Her throat filled with water, her nose filled, and her ears. She was tied too tightly to struggle. Down, down she went, till her head sang, and her brain nearly burst; but the pond was full with the spring rains, and her body was full-fleshed and buoyant. Suddenly, the cries of the crowd burst upon her again, and she realised that she was floating. Someone jabbed at her, and pushed her under again with a long pole, but she bobbed up again a foot away, her mouth gulping, her eyes bulging under her dripping hair. The mob on the bank howled louder.

"See, see! She's floating!"

"Witch! Burn her! Fish her out and hang her!"

"There's proof now. What are you waiting for? Out with her. See, the besom'll *no'* sink!"

So now they fished her out, untied her, and bound her again in a different fashion, hands by her side, feet together. She was too done to protest, or to wonder what they would do. She kept her eyes shut as they tied her to a stake, and she ignored the tickle of dead brushwood being piled round feet and body. She could hardly realise that she was still alive, and she was neither glad nor sorry.

They were gentle with her now, sparing her senses for the last pain. At first, she hardly bothered when the smoke nipped her eyes and her nostrils; she hardly heard the first snap of the thin twigs. It was only when the flames lapped her feet and legs that she raised her head and tried to break free. As the wood became red hot, and the flames mounted to bite her body, she screamed and writhed and bit her tongue to mincemeat. When they could not see her body through the fire, the screams still went on.

The crowd drifted away when she lost consciousness. There was no more fun to be had; or perhaps, it wasn't such fun after all. The men went back to the fields, but they could not settle to work. Jinnot's father was gnawing his knuckles in the attic, and they did not know what would happen when he came down. Beatrice tossed in a muttering, feverish sleep; and beside the pond, a few veins and bones still sizzled and popped in the embers.

A HORIZON OF OBELISKS

hey opened the grave in the evening, digging deep, beyond the grass roots, and the roots of small things tangled in the mould like hairs.

The man in the grave felt the chill just before dawn. Soil pattered, rotten wood cracked, and he shrank as the air pressed on him. "Cold," he thought, "right through to my bones," and he moved the bones, disconnected now, under the flesh he thought was there. "Cold," he thought. His arms folded, hugging himself, and there was a wetness of dew, and a weakness over him. He remembered the weakness, and the light going down low, and a queer pinpoint of it lingering on after they had washed and bound him and knelt by his side. Now the light was growing again, and he scrabbled up and lay on the ground like a newly hatched bird, waiting for the day to dry him out.

The sun came up like polished copper, and the angel on the mortuary dome preened its wings and curved them like pincers. Weakly, the man went down the paths, left and right, looking for the way out. It seemed to take a long time. What he remembered about the graveyard went back to his childhood, hot days among the tombstones and daisies, and his mother watching him, smiling on the grass beside a cypress tree. He had always enjoyed going to the graveyard. Heaven, he had thought, would be just like this, smooth grass, bright beds of flowers, and a horizon of obelisks and angels. Perhaps this *was* Heaven...?

He accepted the fact that he had died, remembering how life had narrowed to a needlepoint and gone. But what, then, of the Resurrection? He had always pictured it as a great flapping of wings and an uprush of souls, all crying together and vanishing into the sun, but there had been no trumpets splitting the air, nothing ascending from the green mounds. The angel on the mortuary was rigid against the sailing sky, and he himself had nothing about him that was celestial. In his mind he was as he had once been, a raw, red man in working clothes with a fuzz of ginger over his baldness. He passed his hand over his eyes, and looked about him distractedly. All through the chill of his waking he had heard a bleating and lowing and the flustered clucking of hens, and he remembered how it had once been a comfort to him to know that, when he died, he would lie within sound of the cattle market. That was where he had worked; but how long ago, he could not remember.

Here now was the way out, a little arch let into the grey wall. He looked over his shoulder, as if to ask permission, but no-one stopped him as he laid his hand on the latch, and there was no fiery sword to bleed and burn through him. He stepped out on to the pink grush, and weakly, meekly, made his way past the grave-digger's lodge to the blue tar of the roadway.

It was early yet, the sun level along the streets, and he went with the determined plod of a child making for home. The school playground was a wash of sunlight, and all the pointed windows stood open. By ten o'clock the place would echo like a church with the plainsong of the multiplication tables, but now there was only the janitor, whistling in his peaked cap and boiler suit.

Downhill, where the road narrowed, the butcher was dressing his floor. He walked backwards, blue and white, like a sailor on

274

the golden sawdust, and the man paused, idle and interested; but there was an uneasiness, too, in the death around him, the great bull swinging in chains, the sheep's heads, the bones pink on their ashets—he did not know whether it was kinship or pity. Quickly, he backed out of the shadowed street to where the sunlight sliced the pavement.

What was the time? The clock blazed gold, and the weather vane was as small as a golden bee. It was so high that he had to lean back, his eyes screwing up and up the weathered stone, pasts the frets of the belfry and the white scuds of bird lime. Half past seven. The clouds raced and dizzied him, and his eyes darkened and dropped to the ground. The street was bare, the whole proud sweep of it smiling and empty, but the birds were busy, brown sparrows and slate-coloured doves feeding and fluttering together.

The man went down among the shabby houses behind the church. He was holding himself in as a hurt child holds itself till it reaches home. Down here the pavements were scrabbled with yesterday's games, and the doorsteps dipped in the middle. He paused in a close, and listened in brown shadow. Away up the stairs he heard his own door slam, and he knew that a white flake had fallen from the gas mantle. Every crack in the plaster was familiar, the dusty windows on the landings, the gas pipes branching from the wall. When his mother came to the door he would cling to her and let himself go, put his head on her lap and clutch her skirt and sob and sob and stay with her for ever...

The knocker was a grinning brass cat with a bow on its neck, but he poked, two-fingered, at the letterbox. Nobody answered. He knocked harder, listening for a footstep inside, and then he turned away. He did not want to disturb the neighbours, to have them coming out in their dustcaps and aprons, rubbing at the doorknobs as they spied. Down the stairs again, he searched in the yard, in the wash house, among the house-proud scorings of pipe-clay. She might be filling the coal bucket, or emptying the ashes, or shaking the rugs. She was so clear in his mind that he could almost touch her; but she was not there, and he went away with the love in him taut and swollen.

He hung about, hoping to meet her in the streets. The shops put their shades out, and he wandered up and down, remembering this kind of day, the bright joy of it, long ago. No-one spoke to him, and he did not look at faces. The things he added to the turmoil of his mind were little pleasures his mother had shown him, secret things, the amber glass of a door handle, a fluted light in a fruit shop, an alley where the cobbles were sea-rounded and smooth; but he was at a loose end, like a child playing truant...

Playing truant... from what? He would not think about it. The school emptied, the streets filled with yells and running feet. Every cafe in the town was bursting full, steaming with beef and broth and custard; and then it was afternoon. The clock on the station kept at its eternal semaphore, the signals shifted, the trains fussed and sighed; and past the station wall and the horse trough went the orphan children, four deep, with a Sister of Mercy behind them. Her boots kicked up the hem of her long blue skirt, and her white flyaway hat was like an arum lily. The man wanted to speak to her, because nuns were good women who would help anyone who asked, but he could not explain what troubled him. Time eluded him, like the memory of what had come after this repeated present. He could not think beyond this day, with the dust blowing, and the farmers jostling in the streets, and the brown droves of cattle going by with lowered horns and a yapping at their heels. He did not know what was going to happen next, but when it did happen, it was as if someone had jogged his memory. On a day like this, his mother had taken him into an icecream shop, and in the cool dark they had supped from little glass dishes. Outside, a beggar had squeezed his accordion, with a dirty capful of pennies in the gutter—and there was the beggar, his grey head frowsy, his hands grained with dirt. "*No,*" his mother had said, as he tugged at her sleeve, "*No, he'll just drink it,*" and she had dragged him away from the sighing music and the man's turned up eyes.

The orphan children had gone now, through the chapel gates, and the man stood, lost for a moment, by the dusty horse trough. The roadway filled with a carpet of fawn fleeces, and a car crawled behind them, another and another car, all black. Rigidly, the man stood, watching the funeral. This had happened too, a long time ago. He and his mother would stand on the edge of the pavement, not staring, but taking it all in, the long coffin in the glass hearse, the rainbow wreaths, and the stuffed-looking mourners, not looking out of the window in case they should enjoy the ride. He had had to take off his cap... stiffly, he put his hand up, but the cars had passed, round the corner by the market.

He could not follow them. His mother had never intruded when a funeral was on, but later, when it was all over, they would tiptoe in, and look at the wreaths, and read the black-edged cards among the petals. Vaguely, with a sense of filling in time, he made his way to the market. Soon the selling would be over, the rings silent, the pens empty, and children would run round in the empty space gathering feathers and handfuls of white down.

The afternoon was ebbing away in lessening enchantment. A lone cow filled the barns with its bellowing, and men with stiff brooms were sweeping the cobbles. These were none of the men he knew, and they did not pass the time of day. The day was nearly over for them, and all they wanted was to finish and go home for tea.

Timidly, he rubbed a hand over his face. The day, this peculiar day, was ending for him as well. The workers would go to their separate homes, wash at the running tap, and sit down at the table with a woman to wait on them; but he could not go back to that. He was still living out his childhood, the past condensed into a few bright hours, and the hours' slow saddening towards evening. The house would grow dark, the teaplates sour with beetroot and vinegar, the kettle whining as the fire died. And after he had washed, and climbed into the recess bed, listening to his father clearing his throat and knocking out his pipe, the curfew bell would ring, knell, knell, knell, and he would want to sob, thinking of all the evening hymns.

"Change and decay in all around I see..." But he would hold back his weeping because his mother would be tired by that time, and she might not have patience with him...

Weary, a little bewildered, he turned away from the dunged cobbles and the mournful lowing. Opposite were the main gates of the cemetery, wrought-iron gold-embossed, with a humble little door at the side for those who entered on foot; and through this door went the man, shutting it after him as his mother had taught him when he was a child.

This, he had thought, must be like entering Heaven; but surely Heaven was never meant to be so lonely? There had been no joy in his day, nothing but a yearning and an ache in the heart. If this was Heaven, his mother would come now, surely, in the cool of the evening, walking reverently past the grave, poking among the flowers with stiff gloved fingers...

He knelt to look at the cards, but his eyes were blurred, and it was a long time before he realised that she was buried there, and that hers was the funeral he had seen in the wake of the jogging sheep. There was no sorrow in knowing that she was dead. She would sleep as he had done, under the roots and the small pebbles, but if God was willing she would not wake till the Resurrection. He prayed that she would not waken. He himself had been meant to sleep on, but the early cold had roused him.

He sat on an iron bench marked FOR THE USE OF THE PUBLIC, and his arms folded, hugging himself. The ache inside him had eased a little with understanding. At least there would be no more searching; and maybe tomorrow, or one of the grey or golden tomorrows in store, the trumpet would sound, the graves would open, and eternity would begin,—or end.

He sat for a long time, telling himself that there was nothing to be afraid of. The lone cow mourned in the market, and far away, a train trailed its own scream after it. The angel on the mortuary dome flapped its wings against the green sky, and then huddled down to sleep, but the man on the bench could not sleep for the chill. "Cold," he thought. "Right through to my bones..."

APPENDIX I

The Letter from Mervyn Peake

On the following page is a reproduction of a letter sent by Mervyn Peake to Dorothy K. Haynes following the publication of the first edition of *Thou Shalt Not Suffer a Witch* (1949). Peake had initially declined his publisher, Methuen's, request to illustrate the book in order to concentrate on *Gormenghast*, but on receiving the stories from Haynes he was inspired to contribute eight line drawings, two of which have been included in this current anthology.

This illustration in the letter would later inspire Haynes's story "The Peculiar Case of Miss Grimond", published in Mary Danby's *The 8th Fontana Book of Great Horror Stories* (Fontana, 1973) and collected in *Thou Shalt Not Suffer a Witch* (1996).

The letter reads:

Dear Miss Haynes,

How long I've been in answering your letter which I was so happy to get. I am most glad that you liked the drawings which I made for your book & I wish I could have done the cover for your novel Robin Richie—if its anything like your other stories in the intensity of its atmosphere. Is it published yet?

I wish I could come & see you in Scotland, but how can I get up there? What excuse can I make? We're no longer in Sark—as you can see. But do you ever come to London because DO let us know & come and see us.

I'm having a sequel (horrid word) of Titus Groan published in June called "Gormenghast"—I would love you to read it & to know if you liked it.

[below the illustration]

Illustration to an unwritten story by Miss Haynes
                                    With best wishes
                                                Mervyn Peake.

Dear Miss Haynes

How long I've been in answering your letter which I was so happy to get. I am most glad that you liked the drawings which I made for your cover & I wish I could have done the cover for your novel Robin Ritchie — if its anything like your other stories in the intensity of its atmosphere — Is it published yet?

I wish I could come & see you in Scotland, but how can I get up there? what excuse can I make? We're so large in Sark — as you can see — But do you ever come to London because DO let us know & phone and see us.

I'm having a sequel (horrid word) of Titus Groan published in June called "Gormenghast" — I would

love you to read it & to know if
you liked it.

Illustration to an unwritten story by Alan Hanson
With best wishes
Mervyn Peake.

APPENDIX II

The Text of "Suspended Sentence"

"Suspended Sentence" was broadcast on BBC Radio 4 on 17 October 1974. It begins "I went as far as the library today" and tells the story of a timeslip incident. The narrator is evidently trying to convince the reader that her memory was no mere dream. After researching the incident in the library she discovers that one Janet Martin is accused of assault and likely sent to the gallows. The narrator is not sure if Janet Martin was hanged in the end, or if these events – seemingly from the past – will come around again. What is great about this story from an editor's point of view is the material in the archive. There are three typescripts plus the transmission script which gives us the date. One typescript begins "They let me out of bed today", but Haynes has scribbled this out and wrote "I was outside for a while today." In another typescript Haynes has decided on "I went as far as the library today", which plants the seed for the visit to the library later in the story. This typescript matches the transmission script well, and is the text chosen for this volume.

There is another typescript, however, which reveals a different track for the story. It begins "For years, I'd waited for Rosie to come home." This is a different narrative voice than the other versions of the story. In this version, Rosie's testimony is a "report", given to a Dr. Heriot. The report begins "I went as far as the library today." This means that Haynes at one point considered a frame narrative for the story. Not only this, but the typescript has the "report" under its own title: "Swinging Loose". As mentioned in the Introduction, this phrase connects to a line from the story. What is more, this script is also marked up to an unusual degree by Haynes, who was clearly experimenting with some revisions. For example, she changes the name "Janet Martin" to "Rose/Rosie Davidson" to match up with the beginning of the story and the named narrator who gives the report. She also edits out the phrase "swinging loose". Instead of "It looks as if something that binds me to time has slipped, and I'm swinging loose" Haynes writes "It looks as though I've slipped loose in time, & can swing both backwards & forwards."

memory only goes so far back, but I saw backwards, over a hundred
years, and that was true too. This cutting proves it. It looks as
~~though I've slipped loose in time , & can swing both backwards &~~
~~if I've something that binds me to time has slipped, and I'm~~
~~swinging loose.~~ forwards.

Both convey the same meaning, but to see her editorial work is rather interesting. The bottom of the script is signed by the author and a note is placed beneath. Haynes here ruminates on another skipping song, saying:

> There was another song we sang when we were skipping, a song that always frightened me a little. It ended
>
> > In comes May
> > In comes Rosie
>
> For evermore, it was so sad. But now I think it would be a comfort just to go out once and for all, for ever.

THE OPENING OF THE NESTED-NARRATIVE VERSION OF
"SUSPENDED SENTENCE"

SUSPENDED SENTENCE.

For years, I'd waited for Rosie to come home. There
were nieces and nephews I'd never seen, and I was beginning to
forget what Rosie herself looked like. Photogrpahs are all
very well, but I wasn't prepared to see her so plump andbrown
and....matronly. I/ don't suppose she'd like me to say that,
but that's how she struck me, at first; a pleasant, motherly
type, with white teeth flashing in that marveelous deep tan.

She deosn't look so well now. The very day she got
home she had to go and get herself knocked down. It's a
wonder she wasn't killed. She had shock and bruises and
concussion, but no bones broken, and I suppose that's a lot to
be thankful for. But....I don't know. She's not doing as well
as she should. She's home now, staying with me, but there's
something holding her back, and I'm so worried, because I can't
get her mind off the accident. I want to know all about her
life in Johannesburg, and that wonderful house she's got, and
I'm sure it would do her good to talk about it, for a change;
but no. Sometimes I think she needs a good shake to jerk her
out of it, and one of these days I'll do it. After all, she <u>is</u>
my young sister.

But no. Not now. I've just had a talk with the
doctor. He rang me up, very discreetly, and asked to see me,
and when I got to the hospital I discovered that this Dr.
Heriot was a psychiatrist. I said, a bit uppitty, that I
didn't think my sister needed a psychiatrist, and surely concussion had nothing to do with the mind; but he told me it

was she who had begged to be allowed to speak to him, before
she was discharged, and he found what she had to say very
disturbing, so disturbing that he wanted my opinion on it.
It seems that she — well, never mind. He showed me the report
of what she'd said, taken from a tape recording, and he asked
if this was in character, and could I vouch for the background
to the story. It sounds authentic enough to me. There's a
conviction about it that makes _me_ see things I've forgotten.
But — oh God, what can I do to help? What can anybody do?
Certainly Dr. Heriot is puzzled.

I'll go over the report again, calmly this time, and
try to puzzle out what it means.

"I went as far as the library today. My head still
aches if I try to think too hard, or talk too much, but I'm
feeling a bit better. It's just that I haven't got things
sorted out properly yet. Maybe if I tell you, you'll be able
to make some sense out of it.

Yes, the accident. On the motorway. It wasn't
quite the way you think. What you don't know, what you don't
understand, is that I'd seen it all before. The motorway, I
mean. I'd seen it long before it was built.

No, I'm fine. Quite comfortable.

I think I'd better start at the beginning. You knew,
or maybe you didn't, that I'd been born and brought up where
the motorway is now. Down in the Kingsgate. It was the old

For more Tales of the Weird titles
visit the British Library Shop (shop.bl.uk)

We welcome any suggestions, corrections or feedback you may have, and will
aim to respond to all items addressed to the following:

The Editor (Tales of the Weird), British Library Publishing,
The British Library, 96 Euston Road, London NW1 2DB

We also welcome enquiries through our X (Twitter) account, @BL_Publishing.